T0065716

# A Life for a Life

A NOVEL

## ERNEST HILL

Simon & Schuster

SIMON & SCHUSTER
Rockefeller Center
1230 Avenue of the Americas
New York, NY 10020

SIMON & SCHUSTER and colophon are registered trademarks
of Simon & Schuster, Inc.

Designed by Ruth Lee

Manufactured in the United States of America

10  9  8  7  6  5  4  3  2  1

Library of Congress Cataloging-in-Publication Data

Hill, Ernest
    A life for a life : a novel / Ernest Hill
        p.   cm.
    1. Afro-Americans—Fiction. 1. Title.
PS3558.I3875L54     1998
813'.54—dc21                          98-17554
                                       CIP

ISBN 0-7432-8160-8
ISBN 978-0-743-28160-7

For information regarding special discounts for bulk purchases, please contact Simon & Schuster Special Sales at 1-800-456-6798 or business@simonandschuster.com

*To Ma Bessie,*

*one of the most compassionate people I have ever known.*

*Rest in Peace*

# ACKNOWLEDGMENTS

Thanks to

Frank Weimann, for being a terrific agent
Leslie Kallen, for introducing me to Frank
Richard Walter, for introducing me to Leslie
Dominick Anfuso, for giving me the space to be creative
Ana DeBevoise, for answering my questions
My family and friends, for being my family and friends
My readers, for buying my books
My characters, for telling me their stories
And everyone else, for not being upset because I forgot to
acknowledge them.

# CHAPTER ONE

He sat IN A SMALL WOODEN CHAIR WITH HIS HANDS TIED BE-HIND HIS BACK. YES, HE WAS GUILTY AS CHARGED, BUT it had all been a mistake, a misunderstanding. The day had begun innocently enough. He had met Beggar Man, Crust, and Pepper on the corner under the big oak tree. It was hot, one of the hottest days that any of them could remember. It was too hot to be outside, and sitting in the pool hall under that old window fan wouldn't be much better. They needed air-conditioning, and the only place in the projects that was air-conditioned was Kojak's Place.

They all knew what went on at Kojak's Place, but they were hot and they agreed that they would stay just long enough to cool off, or just long enough for the sun to move from the center of the sky, or just long enough for a few clouds to rise. None of them knew how long that would be, but it couldn't be that long. So like a pack of wild animals drawn to a communal watering hole in spite of the dangers lurking nearby, they marched forward.

Even after they started walking, they searched for possible alternatives. A movie would do the trick, but they didn't have a dime between the four of them. They could mill about downtown in one of the department stores, but they knew they wouldn't be inside long enough to stop sweating before someone asked them what they were looking for. A dip in the town pool would be ideal, but even though it was 1987, in Brownsville, Louisiana, for all intents and purposes, that much-desired treat was still for whites only. So it was Kojak's Place or no place.

When they went inside, all he wanted was relief from the heat.

He only wanted to sit in the back and wait for the sun to go down. It was the others who wanted to have a little fun once they were inside, not him. It was Crust and Pepper who followed the two skimpily clad prostitutes through the room and up the back stairs, not him. They were working girls, and he knew as well as Pepper and Crust that their empty pockets meant none of them had what it took to gain the women's attention or garner their affection. It was Beggar Man, not him, who took a seat at the bar and tried to talk Walter into giving him a free drink. He didn't bother. It was too hot outside and there were too many people inside for Walter to be giving away drinks.

When he sat beside her, it was purely coincidental. He saw the empty seat before he saw her. She was beautiful, and he couldn't help but notice her too short cutoff jeans, or her snug-fitting crop top that drew attention to her voluptuous breasts and exposed her flat, taut stomach. Even after he noticed her he said nothing. He sat silently, staring out the window, enjoying the cool air, wondering how long before the sun went down or a few clouds rose. She spoke first. "What brings you to Death Row?" He was sure that he had never seen her before, but as soon as she spoke, he knew she was from the area. She had said, "Death Row." Everybody knew that the Brownsville Projects were a bad place, but only the locals knew about Chatman Avenue. People died on Chatman Avenue. So many people, so often, that the locals began calling it Death Row.

After a brief silence, he answered her question. "Relief from the heat," he said dryly.

"Is that all?" she wanted to know.

"What else is there?" he asked.

"Whatever you want," she responded. "This is Kojak's Place."

"And what do you know about Kojak's Place?" he asked.

"More than most," she said boastfully.

"Is that right?" he responded sarcastically.

"That's right," she told him. "I'm his sister."

He had been running with the fellows for only a couple of weeks. They were all older than him. He had just turned ten, but he looked older. In fact, most of the people around town affectionately called him Little Man. As a group they called themselves the Posse, and his brother was their leader. On his birthday his brother had told him it was time. And then he was one of them. Each day they had taught him something new. But today they had carried him further than ever before. They had taken him to Kojak's Place. Now he was on his own, and she was his first big test.

After she told him who she was, she asked him to accompany her to one of the back rooms. When they arrived, she offered him Kojak's glass pipe. When he told her that he only smoked weed, she just laughed. When he told her he was broke, she told him that he didn't need any money. When he asked her if she was sure that it was OK, she assured him that it was. So, for an hour and a half, they smoked. Inside, under the cool, dry air, away from the heat and humidity, in a private room, they smoked. It was her party, and he was her invited guest. That's what he told Kojak when he demanded payment for his drugs. That's what he told Kojak just before Kojak hit him on the side of the head with that empty whiskey bottle. That's what he told Kojak before Kojak dragged him out behind the club and into the small storage shed. That's what he kept trying to tell Kojak as Kojak was tying him to that chair. That's what he screamed as Kojak placed the gun barrel next to his temple, mumbling, "You gone pay me or die."

He had closed his eyes never expecting to open them again. He had anticipated hearing the gunshot. He had anticipated feeling the excruciating pain of a bullet boring through his skull. He had imagined his lifeless body slumped over in the chair, a pool of blood collecting at his bound feet. He had heard the deafening wail of his brokenhearted mother, the angry moan of his dejected brother, the pitying words of his friends, and that question that white folks always ask, "Why do these people do this to each other?"

There was no point in pleading. This was Kojak, a ruthless dope dealer who killed with impunity. He and the cops had an understanding. He gave them a cut of his profits, and they gave him free reign to peddle his drugs and his women, as long as he confined his business to places like Death Row. Kojak was a businessman. Little Man had smoked that for which he could not pay. Therefore he had to die.

He didn't know how he knew to come. Someone must have called him. Maybe Crust, maybe Pepper, maybe Beggar Man; he didn't know who, but someone. When he heard him yell, "Kojak!" he flinched. When he felt the gun barrel fall from his head, he opened his eyes. When he saw him standing there, he sighed. It was D'Ray, his brother.

For a moment D'Ray and Kojak stood staring at each other. They were two different versions of the same thing. At thirty-five, Kojak was a seasoned criminal. At fifteen, D'Ray was just beginning. D'Ray spoke first.

"What's the deal, Kojak?" he asked loudly.

"Who wants to know?" Kojak responded, looking him over carefully.

"D'Ray," his brother answered.

Kojak frowned. He didn't recognize the name. Perhaps if D'Ray had said, "Outlaw," that would have made a difference. After all, that's what most people called him.

"D'Ray who?" Kojak asked.

"D'Ray Reid," he told him.

Kojak smiled wryly. The last name was familiar.

"You Papa World's boy?" he asked.

"That's right," D'Ray told him.

Kojak looked at D'Ray and then at Little Man.

"Him too?" he asked.

"Him too," D'Ray told him. "He's my little brother."

"I'm sorry to hear that," Kojak said coldly. "World always been good to me."

"He been good to a lot of people," D'Ray added.

For a brief moment Kojak's eyes softened.

"How World making out these days?" he asked.

Papa World was in South Louisiana serving a life sentence in Angola State Penitentiary for killing a white man.

"He's making the best of a bad situation," D'Ray told him.

"That's what we got here, young blood," Kojak said. "A bad situation."

"It don't have to be," D'Ray countered. "What's the problem?"

Kojak raised the gun and rubbed the barrel against his cheek.

"He's a thief," Kojak said.

D'Ray shook his head in disagreement. "He's a little hardheaded, but he ain't no thief."

"Well, what would you call a person who takes what he can't pay for?" Kojak asked.

"What he take?"

"Crack."

"Crack!" D'Ray shouted.

"Yeah, crack," Kojak said. "He must be a fool stealing from me. Little nigguh just don't know, I'll take 'im out."

Little Man started to speak. Kojak wheeled and pointed the gun at his head.

"Wait," D'Ray yelled. "I'll pay you."

Kojak lowered the gun.

"You got money?"

D'Ray patted his front pockets, then extended both hands in front of his body with both palms up.

"Not on me," he said. "Let me owe you. I'm good for it."

"You must be tripping."

"Come on, Kojak," D'Ray pleaded. "Cut us some slack. He's just a kid."

"Kid!" Kojak barked. "Ain't no kids in the projects. Papa World's boys ought to know that as good as anybody."

"I need a little time," D'Ray told him.

"Ain't no time," Kojak responded.

"Give me till tomorrow," D'Ray said. "I swear on my daddy's honor you'll get your money."

There was silence.

"What you say, Kojak?" D'Ray asked. "How about first thing in the morning?"

"Papa World always been good to me." Kojak spoke as though he was thinking out loud. "You got one hour."

"One hour!" D'Ray yelled.

"One hour," Kojak responded coldly. "Papa World or no Papa World, you ain't back with my money in a hour, you can tell your mama she got one less mouth to feed."

D'Ray turned to leave, then stopped.

"How much he owe you?"

"One hundred dollars," Kojak told him.

"One hundred dollars!" D'Ray shouted.

"Homeboy, the clock's ticking."

# CHAPTER TWO

D'Ray HURRIED OUTSIDE. HE DIDN'T HAVE MUCH TIME. HE WANTED TO RUN, BUT HE DIDN'T KNOW WHERE TO GO. Where would he get $100? He couldn't think. He began to panic. "Calm down. Calm down," he whispered to himself. "Think."

He heard a familiar noise coming from inside the club. He crossed the yard, climbed the four concrete steps, and pushed the door open. Inside, people were crammed together, laughing and dancing and making the sounds that men make when they are drinking. As he stood gazing at the crowd, he thought of something. It was Friday. Payday. Maybe he could borrow the money. He entered the room, pushed his way to the bar, and began scanning the crowd, looking for familiar faces. He didn't see anyone. Who was he kidding? This was the projects. It would take all night to find someone who could spare $100. He looked at the old clock hanging on the wall. Five minutes had passed since Kojak's warning. Behind him, the cash register rang. He turned and watched Walter remove several crumpled bills and hand them to a customer.

That's it, he thought. The cash register. There wasn't enough time to borrow the money, but there was more than enough time to take it. He pushed away from the counter, then paused. "Not here," he mumbled to himself. "There are too many people." He rushed to the door, pushed it open, and leapt to the ground. He stumbled, regained his balance, and began to run. Slowly at first, then faster. He needed a weapon. He would go home and take his mother's pistol. She kept it in her bedroom under the mattress. As he ran, he began to formulate a plan. He would rob a convenience store. But not in Brownsville. It was still too light out. Someone who knew him might see him, and he would be captured before he had a chance to pay Kojak. He would go to Lake Providence. He could make it there and back in twenty-five minutes, easy. He began to breathe in short, quick gasps. His legs began to throb, and his lungs began to burn. His mother's house was on the adjacent street. He jumped a drainage ditch, crossed through someone's yard, passed behind the house, and turned north on the next street.

The houses along the street were bustling with activity. But he neither looked at anyone nor spoke to anyone. Not the old folks sitting on the porch, not the young men playing cards on the hood of an old broken-down car, not the small children shooting marbles in the grassless yard. Even when his neighbor yelled, "Is anything the matter?" he didn't speak, partly because he hadn't heard her and partly because he didn't have the time.

When he reached his mother's house, he raced up the steps, pulled open the screen door, and twisted the doorknob. The door was locked. Frustrated, he drew back his fist and began beating the door with the flat part of his hand.

"Who that, banging on that door?" his mother yelled from inside.

"Hurry up and open this door," he shouted in response, drawing back his fist and striking the door again.

"If you hit that door again, I swear 'fo Gawd I'm gone knock the fool out of you."

His mother opened the door and he pushed past her.

"Why you huffing and puffing?" she asked.

He didn't answer her.

"Who you running from? What you done got into now?"

D'Ray turned to walk away. She grabbed his arm and spun him around.

"Boy, don't you hear me talking to you?"

He pulled away from her.

"Mama, I ain't got time for this," he snapped.

"You better make time," she warned him.

"Everything fine," he told her. "Just leave me alone."

"Where Little Man?" she asked.

"How am I supposed to know?" he asked.

She went out onto the porch to look. He raced into her room, reached under the mattress, and removed the gun. He heard her coming. He raised his shirt, stuck the gun in the waist of his pants, and rushed from the room.

"What you doing in my room?" his mother asked as he raced past her.

"Nothing," he lied. "I got to go."

"Where you going?" she yelled.

He didn't answer. He leapt from the porch and raced down the street.

"You tell Little Man he better not let night catch him away from this house," she yelled from the porch.

His mind began to race. What time is it? How was he going to get to Lake Providence? What if he was late getting back?

He needed a car. He ran to the main highway and thumbed a ride. He rode to the white section of town near the park and got out. Across from the park was the parish baseball field. Behind the field was a parking lot. Next to the parking lot was a cluster of oak trees. Cautiously he crossed the street, eased into the woods, and hid behind a tree. From where he stood, he had a clear view. A game was in progress and the parking lot was filled with several long rows of neatly aligned automobiles. He took a deep breath, grabbed the tree with both hands, and slid down into a crouch. Then, holding on to the tree with his right hand, he took a small step to the left and paused. He looked to his left, then to his right, and back to his left. Satisfied that all was clear, he lowered himself to his hands and knees and crawled to the closest vehicle. He raised his head, looked through the window on the driver's side, then moved to the next vehicle. It was a small pickup truck. The keys were in the ignition. He opened the door, slid under the wheel, and started the engine. A nervous charge swept through his body. Had the sound of the engine drawn attention to him? He surveyed the parking lot again. All was quiet. He pulled the truck in gear and backed out, mumbling, "Please, don't let nobody see me."

When he made it to the highway leading out of the parking lot, he stopped. To go left would mean driving past the ballpark. But to go right he would have to pass a small group of whites walking toward him on the right shoulder of the highway. He couldn't chance driving past the ballpark. The owner would surely see him. He slumped in the seat until he could barely see over the dashboard. He pulled the truck into gear and slowly depressed the accelerator. The truck crept forward. He turned right and drove toward the pedestrians. As he passed, he glanced at them out of the corner of his eye. He guessed they were a family—two parents, three children. The woman grabbed the two smaller ones and the man grabbed the largest one. All of them moved off the road and into the ditch. None of them looked at him. When he had passed them, D'Ray checked the rearview mirror. They had moved back onto the shoulder and resumed their journey.

D'Ray decided to take a secondary road to the main highway leading out of town. At the next intersection he turned right, drove a quarter of a mile, and came to a second intersection. Now he was in the sparsely populated area that was owned by several of the town's wealthiest white farmers. He turned right at the stop sign and drove past what had been the old rodeo grounds. Three miles later he reached the point at which the road intersected with the main highway just outside the city limits. He turned left and sighed. He had made it out of town. He had driven only a few minutes when he saw the sign. *Lake Providence 8 miles.*

He wondered about the time. He began searching the console for a clock. He didn't see it. He reached down and turned on the radio. Several bright yellow numbers appeared on the panel. He pushed the select knob. It clicked and the time appeared. "Six-twenty-five." He read the time out loud. He had thirty-five minutes to rob the store and get back. He could feel his heart pounding. A single bead of sweat rolled from his armpit and wound its way down to his wrist. He felt his foot depress the accelerator. He watched the speedometer climb to sixty. Easy, he told himself. Don't get stopped by the cops. You got time. You got time.

A country-and-western song was playing on the radio. He turned the dial to an R&B station. "That's better," he mumbled. The music calmed him. He gripped the steering wheel with both hands and stared ahead. He was on a straight two-lane highway. Both sides of the road were lined with a dense stand of moss-covered trees. Some of them were standing on dry land, but many were sitting in shallow swamp water. His mind raced forward to Lake Providence. Time dictated the plan. He would hit Clem's Grocery Store. It was a small family-owned store south of town near the black community. It was off the main highway, and Mr. Clem usually ran the store alone. The hit should be quick and easy, and nobody should get hurt.

He saw the traffic light ahead. Lake Providence was just around the bend. He stepped off the accelerator and gently depressed the brake. As the truck slowed to a stop, he pressed the select knob to check the time. It was 6:33. He didn't have much time. He parked the truck on a side street one block from the store. When he walked into the store, he glanced at the clock on the wall. It was 6:38. He quickly surveyed the store. There was one customer at the counter and two middle-aged women milling about in one of the center aisles. He glanced back at the counter. Mr. Clem wasn't there. A young-looking black boy was operating the cash register. Was Mr. Clem in the store? He didn't see him. He walked to the back of the store, carefully avoiding the two women. He looked at them a second time. They never looked up. They were engrossed in their shopping. He went to the glass-fronted refrigerator, opened the door, and took out a soft drink. The customer at the counter was leaving, and the two women had moved to an aisle closer to the back. One of them was looking at a list, while the other was examining the shelf. He couldn't wait any longer. He hurried to the front, set the drink on the counter, and looked toward the front door. No one was coming. He looked up at the boy. He was about sixteen, slender and well dressed. He even wore a tie with his store apron.

"Will that be all for you?" the boy asked.

"Yeah," D'Ray heard himself say.

Suddenly he felt a surge of nervous energy. He had to remain calm. He glanced over his shoulder. Now the women were at the back of the store. The boy picked up the soft drink and began fingering the cash register keys.

"Where Mr. Clem?" D'Ray asked.

"We ran out of ice," the boy said without looking up. "He went to get some more. He'll be back in a minute."

D'Ray wondered how much money was in the cash register.

"Business must be good," he remarked.

"Been heavy off and on all day. Had a big rush 'round five. Done slack off now, though." He paused and looked up. "That'll be thirty-five cents."

D'Ray reached his hand into his pocket, then stopped.

"Look here, little brother," he said softly. "I got myself a major problem. Somebody I love is gone get killed in a few minutes if I don't make it back with a hundred dollars. I got a gun. I don't want to use it, but I will. Just give me the money out the cash register and won't nobody get hurt."

Terrified, the boy extended his unsteady hand, pushed a button, and the drawer to the register flew open. He hesitated.

"Come on," D'Ray whispered through clenched teeth. "Hurry up."

D'Ray looked around. The women were still preoccupied with their shopping. He looked toward the door. No one was coming. The boy stood paralyzed.

"Hurry up," D'Ray commanded a second time.

The boy didn't move. Impatient, D'Ray reached his hand across the counter and into the register. Suddenly, the boy slammed the register closed. It caught D'Ray's hand and he jerked it back. He was bleeding. The boy reached underneath the counter. D'Ray saw him. He pulled the gun from his waist and fired twice. The boy fell back against the wall. Behind him, D'Ray heard the sound of glass breaking. He turned and looked. One of the women had dropped a jar. Both of them were staring in his direction, screaming and yelling frantically.

D'Ray leaned across the counter and opened the register. He reached in, grabbed all of the bills, and ran out of the store. He darted behind the building, sprinted to the truck, and climbed inside. His mind was racing. Was the boy dead? Was somebody chasing him? Had they called the police yet? He fumbled in his pocket, looking for the keys. He had stuffed the money in the same pocket. As he pulled his hand from his pocket, money spilled onto the seat. He had a burning desire to count it, but there was no time. He was sure they were chasing him. He drove north toward town, turned left, and doubled back south. If someone had seen him leave, he wanted them to think he had headed north. At the signal light he turned left. He stared at the sign. *Brownsville 8 miles.* He reached over and pushed the select knob. It was 6:43. In the distance he heard the sharp, piercing sound of a siren. He checked his rearview mirror. He saw the vague image of an ambulance streak past the intersection. He watched the dull glow of the traffic light become smaller and smaller until it was no longer visible. He felt momentary relief. They were all rushing to the crime scene. He thought of the two women in the store. They were hysterical. It would be a while before they were able to tell what had happened. By that time he would be in Brownsville.

What was going on there at this very moment? Was the game over? Had the owner discovered that his truck was missing? Were the Brownsville police looking for him? It was still light out. He had to be careful.

Suddenly he became aware of the blood running down the back of his hand. In the excitement he had forgotten about the cut. He removed his injured hand from the steering wheel, turned it over, and wiped the back of his hand across the leg of his pants. Then he raised his hand to his mouth and began sucking the injury. He removed his hand and inspected it. He had a moderate cut on his middle finger above the knuckle. He placed the cut back in his mouth. He had to stop the bleeding.

He thought back to the store. Why hadn't the boy just given him the money? "Stupid nigguh," he mumbled angrily. He began to tremble. A chill raced the length of his body and exploded inside his head. He had broken into houses before. He had snatched purses. He had even stabbed someone with a knife, but he had never killed. He hadn't checked, but he knew the boy was dead. He knew by the way he had fallen against the wall. He knew by the way his head had hit the floor. He knew by the way he had lain, motionless . . . soundless. And why was he dead? Protecting money that didn't even belong to him.

D'Ray took his hand from his mouth and removed the rest of the money from his pocket. He hadn't counted it, but now he knew. On the seat, buried underneath the mound of various denominations of currency, he saw the corner of a $100 bill. He placed the injured finger back in his mouth and focused on the highway. "Hold on, Little Man," he mumbled. "I'm coming."

When he reached Brownsville he drove to the salvage yard and parked the truck. He was less than five minutes from Kojak's Place. He checked the clock one last time. It was 6:52. He grabbed the money, stuffed it into his pocket, and sprinted to Kojak's Place. When he entered the shed, Kojak was standing in the corner. He held a cigarette in one hand and the pistol in the other. Little Man was still sitting in the chair with his hands bound behind his back, only now he wore a blindfold and his mouth was gagged. Kojak had prepared him for execution.

A small single-bulb lamp sitting on a tiny table was the only source of light for the moderate-size room. D'Ray moved next to the lamp, reached into his pocket, and removed several bills. He separated one and put the others back in his pocket.

"Your money," he said, extending the $100 bill toward Kojak.

Kojak raised the cigarette to his mouth and inhaled. The end lit to a bright red glow, then dimmed. He removed the cigarette from his lips, tilted his head back, and blew a cloud of white smoke into the air. He lowered his eyes, looked at the money, and then at D'Ray.

"That all of it?" he asked.

"Yep," D'Ray told him. "One hundred dollars."

Kojak dropped the cigarette and slowly ground it into the floor with his foot.

"Bring it here," he ordered after a moment of silence.

D'Ray crossed the room and extended the money toward Kojak. Their eyes met. Neither man blinked or spoke. Kojak took the money, folded it in half, and put it in his front pocket. Then he reached down, raised his pants leg, and removed a large knife from a carrying case that was strapped to his ankle. He took the knife by the blade and extended the handle to D'Ray.

"You boys tell Walter that old Kojak said to give you a drink on the house."

D'Ray's finger had begun to bleed again. Kojak walked over to the small table that the lamp was sitting on. He pulled open the drawer, removed a small container of Band-Aids, and tossed them to D'Ray.

"Nothing personal," he mumbled. "Just business. Give my best to Papa World."

# CHAPTER THREE

After KOJAK LEFT THE SHED, D'RAY HURRIED ACROSS THE ROOM, KNELT, AND CUT THE ROPE BINDING FROM LITTLE MAN'S feet. Then he moved behind the chair, cut the binding from his hands, and removed the gag from his mouth. Little Man rose from his seat, removed the blindfold, and began massaging his left wrist with his right hand. For a brief moment D'Ray looked Little Man over carefully. Physically he appeared to be OK, but the frightened look in his eyes and the strange expression on his face revealed the truth. He was a scared little boy who had just learned a most important lesson about the world that he inhabited—there is a fine line between living and dying.

D'Ray had a strong desire to throw his arms around him, hold him tight, and tell him that it was OK to be scared. But he knew better. If Little Man was to survive the cruel world into which he had been born, he not only had to come to terms with the fear that he was feeling; he also had to learn to use that fear to terrorize others as he had been terrorized.

"You alright?" D'Ray asked, breaking the silence.

"Yeah," Little Man answered. He spoke so softly that his voice was barely audible.

"Little brother, you got to learn the rules," D'Ray told him.

"I know," Little Man mumbled. "But she said it would be alright."

"She who?" D'Ray asked.

"Kojak's sister," Little Man told him.

"That don't matter," D'Ray said after a brief silence. "Rule number one. Ain't no trouble like woman trouble. Always remember that."

"I will," Little Man said sheepishly.

"Rule number two. It's for other folks to do what you say and not for you to do what they say. You understand?"

"Yeah," Little Man answered, forcing a faint smile.

There was a brief silence.

"Come on. Let's go home," D'Ray said, gently placing his arms about Little Man's neck and playfully pulling him close. "Mama looking for you."

D'Ray left the shed first and Little Man followed. As they walked, neither of them spoke. D'Ray looked at Little Man out of the corner of his eye. Little Man had moved up next to him on his right side. His every movement and every step was in perfect synchronization with D'Ray's—the occasional movement of his head from side to side, the slight dip of his shoulders, the rhythmic swagger that was characteristic of D'Ray's slow-gaited strut.

D'Ray focused his eyes ahead. He wouldn't regret murdering the boy. He had done what he had to do. He had killed so that Little Man could live. He hadn't created the situation, he had simply responded to it. What living thing would not have done the same, killed to protect its own? No, he wouldn't regret what happened. He had only played the hand that fate had dealt him. Besides, the boy had a choice. He had given him a way out. He had given him a way to live, but he chose death. It was as much his fault as D'Ray's. He broke the rules and he paid with his life. D'Ray looked up into the sky. The sun had completely disappeared.

By now they were looking for him. More than likely they had figured out that he was from out of town. He knew that it was only a matter of time before they notified the Brownsville police to be on the lookout for a murder suspect. But what did they know? The women had only glimpsed his face, of that he was sure. But they had seen his clothes. He wore a loose-fitting, gray tank top that hung well below the waist of the baggy blue stonewashed jeans that he had intentionally purchased two sizes too big. His feet were adorned with a pair of expensive multicolored high-top sneakers, which were strung with two different colored laces.

They would know that he was about six feet tall, 180 pounds. They would know that he was dark complexioned. They would know that his hair was cut in a very popular style, short on top and virtually nonexistent on the back and sides, with the distinctive wave pattern peculiar to those who choose the brush over the comb as their primary grooming instrument. They would know that his face was void of any facial hair, save for the neatly groomed mustache that covered his full, shapely lips. And they would know that he was a teenager between the ages of fifteen and eighteen. But with all they knew, they didn't know much. They would be looking for clothes more than a person. He would go home, change, and get rid of the clothes.

He knew that the police would come. Maybe today or maybe tomorrow, exactly when he could not say. But they would come. And he would be a suspect, not because they knew anything, but because they knew him. He had a record, and there was trouble nearby. They would come because he was his daddy's son. They would come because they didn't know where else to go. They would keep coming until they caught someone else, or until he proved that he didn't do it.

As the two of them approached the house, D'Ray saw a car parked out front, on the street. He paused for a minute and examined it. It was a late-model Ford with an Illinois license tag. Someone was inside with their mother, but neither he nor Little Man knew who it was. He was glad they had company. Now his mother wouldn't be able to ask a lot of questions that neither he nor Little Man wanted to answer. They climbed onto the porch and D'Ray knocked. Within seconds his mother opened the door, smiled, and stepped aside. D'Ray walked in first and Little Man followed closely behind. D'Ray's eyes fell on the short, robust lady sitting on their living room sofa.

"Honey, this is your aunt Peggy from Chicago," his mother said as she closed the door and walked back into the living room.

"Mira," D'Ray heard the lady say, "you trying to tell me that these great big old handsome chillen is your two boys?"

"Yeah," his mother said, smiling proudly. "Them's my two crumb snatchers."

"Lawd Jesus," Peggy exclaimed, rising from the sofa and walking toward D'Ray. "Look at these fine boys. Turn around, honey, and let your aunt Peggy look at you," she told D'Ray.

D'Ray turned slowly in a complete circle and stopped. Embarrassed, he lowered his eyes and began nervously cracking his knuckles.

"Sugar, do you remember your aunt Peggy?" she asked.

"No ma'am," D'Ray said, looking up at her, then quickly lowering his eyes again. "I know you Mama's sister, but I don't remember you."

"Well, how could you?" she responded. "You was just a little old something when I married and left here." She paused and stared at him. "But just look at you now. Growing like a weed. I mean, I left, you was a child; I come back, and you is a man. You better come here and hug your auntie's neck."

D'Ray gingerly stepped toward her. She reached up, put her arms around him, pulled him close, and began swaying from side to side. D'Ray tried to keep their bodies from touching. He didn't want her to feel the gun stuffed in the waist of his pants.

"It sho' is good to hold you," Peggy said. She loosened her grip, clutched both of his hands in hers, and stared into his eyes. "You sho' is a handsome devil." She released his hands and turned her attention to Little Man. "Now, who might you be?" she asked playfully.

"My name is Curtis, but everybody call me Little Man," he told her.

"Well, come here, Little Man, and hug my neck." She pulled him close and hugged him tight. As she hugged him, she rubbed her hand up and down the middle of his back. "Now, I know you don't remember me," she laughed. "You wasn't nothing but a itch in your daddy's britches when I left here."

"Peggy!" Mira exclaimed. "Don't talk like that 'round them boys."

"Aw, hush now, Mira. You know young folks these days done heard worst talk than that."

"Well, they might hear it out on them streets, but they ain't gone hear it in here."

"Girl, you always was a prude."

"Just 'cause you live in the projects don't mean the projects got to live in you."

"Mama, anything in there to eat?" D'Ray interrupted. He wanted to leave the room and change clothes just in case the police came.

"It's some chicken and dumplings on the stove."

D'Ray and Little Man started toward the kitchen.

"Wait," their mother stopped them. "I need y'all to do something 'fo you eat."

"Do what?" D'Ray asked angrily.

"Boy, I done told you 'bout talking to me like that."

"Mama, what you want us to do?" D'Ray fought to soften the tone of his voice.

"Little Man," she began, "go in there and get that old spray gun and spray in here befo' them mosquitoes eat us alive. D'Ray, see if you can't make that old fan work and brang it in here."

"Where it's at?" D'Ray asked.

"In my room," she told him.

"Mira, why don't you let 'em eat first?" Peggy asked.

"They can eat when they get through. Ain't no sense in us setting up here sweating and fighting mosquitoes when we don't have to. Y'all go'n now and do like I told you."

D'Ray went into his mother's bedroom, closed the door, and moved next to the bed. He raised his shirt, removed the gun, and placed it underneath the mattress. Then he unplugged the fan and took it to his bedroom. He had to change clothes. Even if the police didn't come tonight, they would come. And when they did, they would ask questions. They would want to know what time he came home. They would want to know how he was acting. They would want to know what he was wearing. His mother and his aunt would be his alibi. They would swear that he was wearing dark-colored jeans and a light-colored T-shirt. They would swear that he was talking and laughing and not acting like a person who had just killed somebody. They would not be sure of the time, but they would be almost certain that he was home at the time of the murder. His mother would know that she had seen him earlier. So, even if he wasn't home, she knew he was in town. She knew he wasn't in Lake Providence.

D'Ray changed clothes, plugged in the fan, and turned on the switch. The motor hummed but the blades didn't move. D'Ray went to the door and stuck his head out.

"Mama, this old fan needs oiling," he shouted.

"It's a can of oil under the sink in the bathroom," she yelled back.

D'Ray went into the bathroom, removed the small can of oil from the cabinet underneath the sink, found a screwdriver, and returned to his bedroom. He laid the fan on the floor facedown and methodically removed the four small screws. Then he removed the plastic covering and oiled both the blades and the motor. He stood the fan upright and clicked on the switch. The motor hummed and the blades began to move slowly. He took the screwdriver, shoved it between the blades, and gave them a spin. The blades picked up speed. He turned the switch from slow to medium, from medium to high, off, and then back on. Satisfied that the fan was operating properly, he unplugged it, replaced the cover, and proceeded toward the living room. The room was empty and there was a heavy scent of fly spray lingering in the air. D'Ray covered his nose and mouth with his hand, crossed the room, and pulled back the curtain draped over the screen-covered window. He placed the fan in the window, plugged it in, and clicked on the switch. The motor hummed and the blades began to turn. He clicked the switch to high and crouched in front of the fan, allowing the cool fresh air to blow directly into his face.

"Well, give thanks and praises," he heard his mother's voice behind him.

He turned and looked. His mother and aunt were standing in the doorway. Both of them were holding a bowl of ice cream. They entered the room and sat on the sofa facing the fan.

"Fly spray, ice cream, and cool air," Peggy exclaimed jovially. "As the young folks say, we living large."

As both women shook with laughter, D'Ray looked at his aunt's stubby fat legs, then at the heaping bowl of ice cream resting on her lap, and mumbled softly to himself, "And getting larger by the minute."

"D'Ray." His mother interrupted his thought. "Go'n in the kitchen and eat. Little Man already in there."

As D'Ray rose to leave, his eyes met his aunt's.

"Boy, if you ain't Papa World all over," she said, smiling.

"And keep up the devil just like 'im," his mother interjected.

"What you say!" Peggy exclaimed.

"Girl, guess what name he go by?"

"What?"

"Outlaw."

"Child, hush yo' mouth."

"Aw, he thank that's something big."

"Mama, I don't appreciate you talking 'bout me like that," D'Ray spouted angrily.

"Boy, I done told you 'bout buttin' in when grown folks talkin'. Now, go'n in there and eat like I told you."

"Mira, don't talk to him so hard," D'Ray heard his aunt say as he was leaving.

"I wouldn't have to if he wasn't so hardheaded," his mother said angrily. "I mean, he got all of World's old hateful ways. If he ain't careful, he gone end up just like him. In somebody's penitentiary."

The kitchen sat directly adjacent to the living room. The two rooms were separated by a thin, cheaply paneled wall that, from the living room, opened into a short hallway. A couple of steps down the hallway and immediately to the left was the small cluttered kitchen. There was no door, but an opening too large for a single door and too small for a double door. In the center of the floor was a small wooden table. Directly across from the doorway and behind the table was the stove. Next to the stove, on the left side, was a double sink with a single faucet. To the right of the stove, crammed in the corner next to the short adjacent wall, was an old single-door refrigerator. Little Man was sitting at the far end of the table. In front of him was a large plate of chicken and dumplings, on top of which sat a huge square of homemade corn bread. To the right of his plate was an old mayonnaise jar filled with Kool-Aid.

D'Ray walked into the kitchen without speaking. He took a plate from the cupboard, moved to the stove, and dished up a large serving of dumplings. He set the plate on the table, in front of the seat directly across from the stove. He returned to the cupboard, removed a jar, went to the refrigerator, and filled it with Kool-Aid. On the way to his seat he stopped at the stove and took a slice of corn bread. He laid it on his plate and sat down. He could hear his mother and aunt in the adjacent room clearly.

"I shouldn't never got tied up with World," he heard his mother say. "He ain't never gave me nothin' but heartache and misery."

"Well," he heard Peggy say, "Mama and Papa tried to tell you. I mean, they talked against him until the day y'all married."

"Yeah, but I was young and foolish," Mira admitted. "I thought I knew everything."

"Girl, ain't it the truth?" Peggy agreed.

"But, child, World was handsome, though," Mira said. "And fine as frog hair."

"You so crazy." Peggy laughed.

"And the nigguh could talk," Mira continued. "I mean, no matter what Mama and Papa said, World had a answer. That nigguh could lie like a rug."

"Most black men can," Peggy told her.

"You know, World was my first," Mira said. She lowered her voice, but the wall was so thin that D'Ray and Little Man still heard her.

"Is that right?" Peggy asked, surprised.

"Yeah, maybe that's why I was so crazy 'bout him," Mira said. Her tone was more questioning than affirming.

"You know what they say," Peggy began. "Ain't no love like your first love."

"It's some truth to that," Mira said. "That's where us womenfolk make our mistake. We put too much stock in love."

"Yeah," Peggy agreed. "We feels with our heart, instead of thinking with our minds. We emotional where we ought to be practical."

"That's me and World in a nutshell. I knew he wasn't no good, but I couldn't get past thinking that I loved him."

"Girl, you had it bad too." Peggy laughed. "Remember that day Papa told you that you could do bad all by yourself? You needed to find somebody who could help you do better. Remember what you told him?"

"Naw," Mira said. "What?"

"You put yo' hands on yo' sassy little hips, cocked yo' head back, and told Papa, 'I'd rather live in the projects with World than live in a mansion with anybody else.' "

For minutes, both women howled with laughter. They would stop momentarily, then they would start again. Each time they laughed louder, longer, and harder than the time before. When they finally collected themselves, Mira exclaimed in a very loud voice, "Sister girl, I loved that nigguh." Then the laughter started all over again.

"Well, what happened to all that love?" Peggy asked.

"I stood by World through all his trifling ways," Mira said, her voice becoming serious. "When he wouldn't work, I stood by him. I went out and got a job to make ends meet. When he ran Blue and his family out of town at gunpoint 'cause he thought me and him was foolin' around behind his back, I stood by him. When he took to drinking and acting a fool with that bunch of hoodlums he called his friends, I stood by him. But when he killed that white man over nothing, look like all my love dried up."

"What happened?" Peggy asked. "I mean, what did the man do for World to kill 'im?"

"Nothing," Mira said. "He ain't done nothing."

"Must of done something," Peggy insisted. I can't say I know World that good. I left here soon after y'all married. But don't nobody kill a man for no reason."

"You really don't know what happened, do you?" Mira said.

"All I know is World killed a white man. I ain't never knowed how and I ain't never knowed why."

"Foolishness, that's why," Mira said angrily. "White man stepped on World's foot and wouldn't apologize."

"So he killed him!" Peggy exclaimed disbelievingly.

"He killed him," Mira said.

"No!" Peggy said.

"Broke his neck," Mira told her.

"Broke his neck!" Peggy repeated.

"With his bare hands," Mira said. "Hauled off and hit him upside the head with his fist. Tell me he didn't hit him but one time. And killed him dead."

"Lawd have mercy," Peggy exclaimed.

"But that ain't what made white folks mad," Mira said.

"It ain't?"

"Naw, it ain't."

"What did?"

"They got mad 'cause of what World did when he found out the man was dead," Mira said.

"What he do?" Peggy asked.

"He hauled off and kicked that man in the butt and then spit in his face."

"My Gawd, no!"

"Yes, he did. Downtown. With all them white folks looking. He hauled off and kicked a dead white man in the butt and then spit in his face."

"Wonder what possessed him to do that?" Peggy asked.

"Just mean that away," Mira said. "Just hateful and mean. That's why he in the penitentiary. And that's why he ain't gone never get out. I knew World was hateful and mean the first day I laid eyes on 'im, so that ain't what bothered me about what he did. You know what bothered me?"

"Naw, what?"

"His selfishness."

"Is that right?"

"I know it might sound crazy, but it bothers me that he just did what he felt like doing. He didn't think about me. He didn't think about that boy that we had to feed. He didn't think about the child in my belly. He just did what he felt like doing. And that's the thing that killed the last feeling that I had for him."

"So Little Man don't know his daddy?" Peggy questioned.

"Ain't never laid eyes on him," Mira said. "And if I have my way, he never will."

"Mira, I can't go along with that," Peggy said. "You might not want to hear it, but World got a right to see his boy and Little Man got a right to know his daddy."

"World gave up that right when he left us to fend for ourselves," Mira spouted.

"Well, what about Little Man?" Peggy asked.

"He better off without World. We all are."

"I hope you know what you doing."

"I do. World didn't just ruin his life; he ruined ours too. I mean, our name is mud in this town because of what he did. When he killed that white man, I lost my job and ain't a soul in this town will give me another one. And the boys, Lawd knows that white folks 'round here hate them because they hate their daddy."

"Well, Mira, how y'all making it?" Peggy asked.

"Welfare, food stamps, and Sonny." She paused. "And sometimes D'Ray. I don't know where he get his money from and I don't want to know. He quit school and he won't work, but he keep coming up with money. I used to worry about it, but I don't no more. It's just a matter of time before he end up like World. He mean just like him. If I can just save Little Man, I'll be happy."

"Mira, you ought not to make no difference between them boys. It ain't right to love one more than the other."

"It might not be right, but it's the way it is. D'Ray set in his ways and I'm tired of trying to change him."

"Who supposed to raise Little Man? You won't let him see his daddy and you talk against his brother. Who supposed to teach him how to be a man?"

"Sonny, that's who."

"Who this Sonny you keep talking about?"

"My man." Mira laughed.

"Girl, listen at you."

"Peggy, he everything that World ain't. I got me a good man now," she bragged.

"Do I know him?" Peggy asked.

"Not hardly," Mira said.

"He from 'round here?" Peggy asked.

"Moved here not too long ago."

"What he do?" Peggy asked.

"Girl, he a cop," Mira said proudly.

"A cop!" Peggy exclaimed.

"Yeah, a cop," Mira said a second time.

"Honey, I know I been gone a long time, but you trying to tell me that Brownsville got a black cop?"

"Yeah, my man is the first one. He a college man too," Mira bragged.

"Girl, hush yo' mouth."

"He went to junior college over in Mississippi. Studied criminal justice."

"Girl, I'm happy for you."

"We been talking for almost a year now."

"So it's serious."

"Getting that way."

"The boys like him?"

"Little Man ain't never said, but D'Ray don't. He say he a mark that white folks planted in the community to spy on black folks. D'Ray think like that. I'm telling you he just like his no-good daddy," Mira said angrily.

"Mira, you ought not to talk about World and that child like that. What if them boys hear you?" she asked.

"I don't care if they do," Mira said defiantly.

"Well I care," Peggy responded. "I'm uncomfortable with it."

Suddenly all was quiet in the living room. D'Ray could tell by his mother's tone that she was getting angry. And he could tell by his aunt's response that she didn't know what to do or say.

"Why you think Mama always dissing Daddy?" Little Man asked. The two of them were almost finished eating.

"I don't know why she trip like that," D'Ray said. He paused to chew his food. "But sometimes she works my last nerve."

"You really think she don't love Daddy no more?"

"Naw, not now."

"Then I don't guess he'll ever come home."

"Don't look like it."

"So, I'll never have a daddy."

"Don't worry about it," D'Ray said compassionately. "I'm all the daddy you'll ever need."

# CHAPTER FOUR

D'Ray HAD SPENT MOST OF THE NIGHT LYING ACROSS THE FOOT OF HIS BED, WAITING ON MORNING. HE HAD closed his eyes a hundred times, but sleep would not come. He was haunted by a recurring thought. What if someone other than the women had seen him running from the store? It could have been someone passing by in a car or someone looking out the window of a house. Anybody could have seen him. Was there a surveillance camera in the store? He didn't think so, but he couldn't be sure. He hadn't checked. Kojak had pushed him too hard. He had been too careless. Had he worn a mask or pulled a stocking over his face or donned a pair of shades, he would feel better. But he had worn nothing.

The clothes were worrying him. The women had seen his clothes. He had to get rid of them. He knew that getting rid of them wouldn't matter if someone had seen his face, but he needed to do something. He needed to feel that he was covering his tracks. He rolled on his side and looked at the clock. It was 6:30 A.M. He lay back, clasped his hands behind his head, and stared at the ceiling. Suddenly he thought of something. While everyone was still sleeping, he could take the clothes to the garbage barrel behind the house and burn them.

He got dressed, retrieved the clothes, and went to his bedroom door. He eased the door open and peeped out. Everything was quiet. He rolled the clothes into a tight ball, placed them under his arm, and tiptoed to the kitchen. He pulled open one of the small cluttered cabinet drawers and removed a tiny box of matches. He stuffed the box in his pants pocket, removed the wastepaper basket from the corner, and exited the kitchen through the rear door. He crossed the porch, descended the steps, and walked toward the garbage barrel.

The long, unmowed lawn was covered with dew. He moved through the grass carefully, doing his best to keep his sneakers as dry as possible. When he reached the barrel, he removed the lid and dropped the clothes inside. Then he lifted the trash can and dumped the contents into the barrel. Moving quickly, he removed a single piece of paper, twisted it, lit the end, and used it to ignite the contents of the barrel in several different places. Then he found a wide, stiff piece of cardboard and fanned the flames until they grew into a roaring blaze. As he stood gazing at the fire, he thought of something that he had not thought of before. The police would be looking for the murder weapon. He had to get rid of the gun. He turned toward the house and stopped. If he moved the gun, his mother was sure to miss it. But if he left it underneath the mattress and the police found it, they would have him. He had no choice; he had to take it. But where could he hide it? He scanned the yard, searching for a possible hiding place.

He walked to the porch, dropped to his knees, stuck his head underneath the house, and looked behind the concrete steps. He contemplated hiding it there but thought better of it. If the police came they would tear the place apart. He had to take it somewhere else.

When he went inside he discovered that his mother was still asleep. He returned to his room and sat on the bed, thinking. He lay back and closed his eyes. He had no choice but to wait for her to wake up and leave the room.

At seven-thirty he heard a loud knock on the door. He looked out of his window and saw a police car parked on the street in front of their house. Startled, he moved to his bedroom door, cracked it open, and looked out. He didn't see anyone. He started to run, but he heard his mother's voice calling from the other room, "Hold on, I'm coming."

He narrowed the door and looked toward her bedroom. He watched her shuffle from her room and walk toward the door. She was wearing an old housecoat and a pair of dingy white sneakers that looked more like slippers than shoes. The heels of her feet rested on the back portion of her shoes, which now lay flat as a result of being worn in a similar fashion over an extended period of time.

"I'm coming," he heard her call a second time.

D'Ray felt trapped. His heart began to pound. He looked around for a place to hide, but there was nowhere. He walked over to the window and peeped out. He saw the police car and immediately knew he had to leave. He crossed to the old, worn dresser pushed against the wall. He tilted it back, reached underneath, and removed a long white envelope. He opened the envelope and removed the contents. It was the money from the robbery. He stuffed the money in his pocket and moved next to the door. It wasn't much, only $250, but that would be enough to help get him out of town.

"Did I wake you up?" The voice sounded familiar.

"Aw, naw," his mother lied. "Come on in."

D'Ray heard the door creak open, then slam shut.

"I should've been up," she said. "My sister from Chicago in town, and we stayed up half the night running our mouth."

"You sho' it's alright?" he heard the man say. "I don't want to wake up your company."

D'Ray recognized the voice. It was Sonny. He relaxed and listened intently.

"Aw, ain't nobody here but me and them boys," he heard his mother say. "Peggy staying up to Mama's."

"How long she gone be in town?" he asked.

"Oh, 'bout two or three weeks. She on vacation."

"Did she come by herself?" he asked.

"Naw, her husband with her. I ain't seen him yet, though. She dropped him off by his folks before she came by here."

"I'm sho' it was good to see her," he said.

"It sho' was," she said. "Lawd knows it's been a long time."

"Well, I worked the graveyard shift last night," he told her. "I just thought I'd come by and have a cup of coffee with you before I go in."

"Well, I'm sho' glad you did," Mira said. "Come on in the kitchen while I put on a pot."

"I don't want to put you through too much trouble, now."

"Aw, it ain't no trouble at all."

They went into the kitchen, but D'Ray could still hear them talking.

"Last night all hell broke loose 'round here," he heard Sonny say.

"Is that right?" Mira responded.

"Sometime yesterday evening, a white fellow's truck got stole."

"My Lawd," Mira said. "I been livin' here all my life and I ain't never hear tell of nobody stealing no truck."

"Far as I know this here is the first time," Sonny said.

"What's this world coming to?" Mira asked.

"I don't thank the good Lawd hisself can answer that one," Sonny replied.

"You reckon some of that man's folks borrowed it without asking?" Mira said, not wanting to believe that the truck had been stolen.

"Naw, this here fellow was at the ball game and somebody just took it off the lot," Sonny told her.

"Can you beat that!" Mira exclaimed. "Just took it in broad daylight."

"Well, it was probably dark when they took it," he said.

"They got any idea who done it?" she asked.

"Naw, ain't got a clue," Sonny said.

"Well, whoever took it probably long gone by now."

D'Ray pushed the door open wider. His mother was running water into the coffeepot and he was having a difficult time hearing them.

"I guess pretty soon we gone have to start living like city folks," he heard his mother say. "Fastened up in the house with bars on the windows and doors."

"We just might have to," Sonny agreed.

"My Lawd, I hope not," she said.

"There was some trouble over in Lake Providence, too," Sonny said.

"What kind of trouble?" she asked.

"A black boy got killed," he said.

"What happened?" she asked.

"He got murdered," he told her.

"My Gawd, no!" she blurted. "That's too close to home."

"He wasn't nothing but a baby," Sonny said. "Seventeen years old. Somebody shot 'im down and robbed the place."

"Lawd, when will it end?" she asked.

"Only Gawd hisself know that," Sonny replied.

"Did they catch the killer?" she asked, sighing loudly.

"Naw, he got away," Sonny told her. "Two old women saw the whole thang, but they was so scared that by the time the police got there, they didn't hardly know their own name. 'Bout all they could say was the killer was black."

"We could've figured that," she said.

"Ain't that the truth?" Sonny said. "It's a shame, but true."

"Well, since he killed another black person I don't reckon they gone try too hard to find him."

"I don't know 'bout that," Sonny said. "They say Mr. Clem, the white man who the boy worked for, done already put up a thousand dollars reward."

"A thousand dollars!"

"That's what they say."

"Wonder why he do that?"

"I don't know. I guess he took it real hard. But I tell you what, I wouldn't want to be that fellow. For that kind of money you can bet everybody hunting for him."

"Reckon they gone find him?"

"Well, it ain't gone be easy. All they got to go on is the kind of gun he used. But we've tracked down people with a lot less."

D'Ray stepped into the hallway and stopped. While they were in the kitchen talking, he would go into his mother's room and remove the gun. He tiptoed to the door leading into the living room and looked inside. He could still hear them but he couldn't see them. He eased into his mother's room, removed the gun from beneath the mattress, and put it in the waist of his pants. Then he raised the window, stepped through, and slid to the ground. Once outside, he quietly closed the window. At the far end of the street, behind the last house and across a small slough, was a stand of wild trees. He would go there, travel deep within the woods, and hide the gun.

He walked along the back of the house until he came to the porch. He paused and listened. They were still talking inside. He dropped to the ground, crawled underneath the porch, and headed toward the neighbor's backyard. As he crossed through the yard he could smell the heavy scent of bacon frying and coffee brewing. He thought of Sonny. It was nearing eight o'clock. He would be passing by at any minute. D'Ray decided to stay behind the houses and avoid the street until he reached the slough. He passed through one yard, then another, when he heard someone yell from a rear window.

"What you doing back there?"

D'Ray stopped and looked. He didn't see anyone.

"Trying to find Mr. Ben's hog," D'Ray lied. "He got out and we trying to catch 'im 'fo he root up everybody's yard."

"Well, I ain't seed 'im," the burly voice yelled back. "He liable to be down yonder in that slough."

"Yessir." D'Ray spoke in the direction of the voice. "That's just where I'm headed."

"Tell Ben he better keep that nasty thang out of my yard. He root up my turnips, I'm gone kill 'im and eat 'im for breakfast."

"Yessir, I'll sho' tell him."

To cross the slough, D'Ray had to walk across a log that stretched from one side to the other. As he walked, he spread his arms for balance, then slowly and carefully made his way to the other side. He thought of throwing the gun in the slough, but quickly reconsidered. That would be one of the first places they would look. He walked along the edge of the surprisingly thick woods until he found an opening. Then he entered and headed toward the center. As he walked over the dry, brittle leaves, he carefully avoided brushing against the sharp, thorny briars, and he diligently watched for snakes lying on the forest floor.

He came to a large walnut tree and stopped. He decided to bury the gun at the base of the tree and retrieve it later. He knelt down and started to dig with a stick that he had found lying nearby. As he dug, he thought of something. What if they searched the area with a metal detector? He rose to his feet and leaned back against the tree, thinking. He reached up and pulled a leaf from one of the lower branches. He looked at the leaf, then at the tree. The low-hanging branches gave him an idea. He climbed up the tree, hid the gun in a fork near the top, and climbed down.

Beggar Man lived in the house closest to the slough. D'Ray decided to stop by and wait until he was sure that Sonny was gone. When he stepped onto the porch, he noticed that the front door was opened. He walked through the door and stopped. Beggar Man's little sister was sitting in the middle of the floor eating a raw Irish potato.

"Where Beggar Man?" he asked.

"Gone," she said, still gnawing on the potato.

"Where yo' mama?"

"She gone too."

"You here by yo'self?"

"Uh-huh."

D'Ray looked around the room. The floor was covered with dirt and trash. Clothes were scattered over the dirty, worn-out sofa, and a cheap wooden rocker lay face down in the corner. One of the legs was missing. A foul scent lingered in the stale pungent air of the fly-infested room. The lights were out, but he could tell that the little girl had not taken a bath in a few days. Her hair was grimy and matted. Her dress was badly soiled, and tiny white globs of dried mucus were visible in the corners of her eyes and mouth.

"What you doing?" D'Ray asked her.

"Watching TV," she answered nonchalantly.

A thirteen-inch black-and-white television was sitting on top of an older, larger set. A wire clothes hanger had been jammed in the slot where the antenna should have been. The picture was fuzzy, but D'Ray could tell that a cartoon was on.

"How old are you?" he asked.

"Ten," she said.

D'Ray walked over and took the potato from her. Several tiny smudges were visible where she had held it.

"What grade you in?" D'Ray asked.

"Fourth," she said, "but I don't like school."

"Why not?" D'Ray asked.

"Because everybody be pickin' on me," she told him.

"Why they pick on you?" he asked.

"'Cause I'm po' and they rich and I ain't got thangs they got," she said.

Rich, D'Ray thought to himself. Ain't nobody 'round here rich.

"What kind of thangs?" he asked.

"You know, paper and pencils and tablets and thangs like that," she explained. "You can't go to school without no paper and pencil. And I get tired of folks always pickin' on me, then I got to turn around and ask them fo' some paper. I get tired of that."

D'Ray looked at her tenderly, then looked around the room again. He felt sorry for her. Everybody in the projects was poor, but some folks were poorer than poor. He looked at the dirty potato that he held in his hand.

"Don't you know you ain't supposed to eat no raw potato?" he asked coldly.

"Yessir, but I'm hungry and ain't nothin' else to eat," she replied.

"Stop calling me sir." D'Ray spoke sternly.

He went into the kitchen and looked. The cupboards were bare and the only thing in the refrigerator was a plastic milk jug filled with water. Roaches were crawling on the stove and in the sink. When he opened the refrigerator door, a large rat scurried from behind it and disappeared in the far corner.

"Don't y'all get no food stamps?" he asked when he returned to the living room.

"Most times Mama sell 'em."

"What she do with the money?"

"I don't know."

"Is she a crackhead?"

"I don't know."

There was silence.

"Do you know how to cook?" he asked, disgusted.

"Yessir."

"I told you don't call me that."

"I mean, yeah."

"What time yo' mama coming home?"

"I don't know."

"When Beggar Man coming back?"

"I don't know."

"Well, stay here till I come back. And don't be eating no mo' raw potatoes."

"OK, mister."

"And stop calling me mister."

As he left, he wondered how a mother could go off and leave a child that young in a nasty, rat-infested house with nothing to eat but a few raw potatoes. And when he saw Beggar Man he was going to kick his butt.

When he made it to the street, he looked toward his house. The police car was no longer parked out front. He looked around to see if anyone was watching him. Satisfied they were not, he took the money from his pocket, counted out $50, and put the rest back. Then he walked three blocks to the nearest store and purchased two bags of groceries and some school supplies. When he returned, Beggar Man's sister was still sitting on the floor watching television.

"Your mama back yet?"

"No sir. I mean, naw."

"Beggar Man?"

She shook her head.

"You like baloney?"

"I like it a lot," she said enthusiastically, then jumped to her feet.

"You like potato chips and cookies?"

"I like them a lot, too."

"You know how to make Kool-Aid?"

"Yessir. I mean, yeah."

"Here," he said, handing her the groceries. "Take these bags in the kitchen and put 'em up. You can eat the potato chips and cookies and make you a sandwich. Or you can eat some cereal. But don't try to cook none of that meat or make no hot dogs till yo' mama come. 'Cause if you burn down this house, you gone be in trouble."

She took the bags and started toward the kitchen.

"Ain't you gone say nothing?"

"Aw, thank you."

"You welcome."

She turned to leave.

"Hey," he yelled at her. "Wash yo' hands befo' you eat."

"I am."

"And don't tell nobody who brought you that stuff," D'Ray said forcefully. "And when you get through eating, clean up this nasty house."

# CHAPTER FIVE

He left THE HOUSE AND WENT DIRECTLY TO THE BARBER-SHOP. BY NOW HIS MOTHER PROBABLY HAD DISCOV-ered his absence, and when he returned she would surely want to know where he had been. The barbershop was a ruse. He would explain that he needed a haircut and he had not told her where he was going because he did not want to be bothered with Sonny Boy. She wouldn't like it, but she would accept it. Sonny was a subject they had agreed never to discuss.

When he arrived at the barbershop, he stuck his head in the door and looked. There was already a crowd.

"How many you got, Fred?" he asked the barber.

Fred scanned the room and made a quick count.

"Aw, 'bout five ahead of you," he told him. "You can wait or come back. It's up to you."

"I'll wait," D'Ray told him.

"Suit yo'self," Fred said.

D'Ray entered the shop, crossed the room, and slumped down on the only empty chair. He folded his arms over his chest, stretched his legs out onto the floor, and crossed his feet at the ankles. He thought about Sonny. By now he had made it back to the station. He wondered if there was any news about the truck. He hadn't damaged it, so maybe they would find it, return it to the owner, and that would be the end of it. If no one linked him to the stolen truck, then no one would be able to connect him to the murder.

The man sitting next to him accidentally brushed against him with his elbow. Startled, D'Ray snapped his head around. "Sorry," the man belted in a deep baritone voice. "Ain't much elbow room in here, is it?"

"Not much," D'Ray said, shifting his body to create more space between himself and the man.

D'Ray recognized the man. He was an unemployed ex-con that everyone called Professor. He was in his late forties and he spent most of his time in the barbershop, talking to Fred or anyone else who would hold a conversation. D'Ray's entrance had obviously interrupted something. He could tell by the way Professor was sitting on the edge of his seat with his eyes focused on the stranger sitting across from him.

"Well, given your opinion of the white man," the stranger said in a distinct south Louisiana accent, "I don't guess you believe in Martin Luther King's dream?

"Now, Pichon, you done hit the nail square on the head," Professor said calmly. "To be blunt, naw, I don't."

D'Ray looked from the stranger to the Professor, then back to the stranger. He was a thinly built, fair-skinned man with fine curly black hair. He was probably Professor's age, but he could have been a year or two younger.

"Why not?" Mr. Pichon asked, his hazel eyes fixated on the ex-con's face with a cold stare of disbelief.

"'Cause white folks don't believe in it," Professor responded.

"Is that a fact?" Mr. Pichon asked rhetorically.

"Aw, they'll say they do," Professor said. "And they'll play his speech during Black History Month because they know it makes black folk want to forgive and forget all the bad things that white folks done done to 'em. But don't you fool yourself, now. White folks don't care 'bout no nigguh's dream. It don't matter how smart he is. The cold, hard fact is that a black man's dream is a white man's nightmare."

"The truth will set you free," someone yelled.

"I'm a living witness," someone else shouted.

When D'Ray had entered the room, he had been tense and worried about discovery. But now, in the sanctuary of the barbershop, he was beginning to relax. This all-too-familiar bantering annulled his anxiety; it amused him. Life was a game. People like these were insignificant players who made interesting conversation, but in the overall scheme of things their words and ideas were meaningless to people like him, who lived in places like Death Row.

"You see," Professor continued, "for black folks to gain something in this country, white folks got to lose something, or so they think. That's why they kicking so hard against affirmative action."

"I'm not sure about the veracity of that statement," Mr. Pichon said.

"Not sure about what?" Professor asked sarcastically.

"About your reasoning," Pichon clarified himself.

"What's wrong with my reasoning?" Professor asked.

"Have you considered the fact that whites may be opposed to affirmative action simply because affirmative action is wrong?" Mr. Pichon asked.

"Wrong!" Professor exclaimed in a voice louder than intended.

"Yes, wrong," Mr. Pichon said calmly.

"So they're upset because they're being wronged?"

"It's a distinct probability."

"I don't think so," Professor said bluntly.

"Sir . . . ," Mr. Pichon said, choosing his words carefully, "I've followed the debate closely, and as of yet no one has sufficiently explained away the discriminatory aspects of affirmative action."

"Discriminatory aspects!" Professor chuckled.

"Yessir," Mr. Pichon said in a steady voice.

"The myth of the wronged white man," Professor said dryly.

"Sir, it's no myth," Mr. Pichon said with conviction. "I have personal knowledge of a white colleague down in Saint John Parish whose son was denied admission into a very prestigious university with a three-point-four grade point average while a number of blacks were admitted with less."

"And that disturbs you?" Professor asked.

"Of course it disturbs me," Mr. Pichon said. "It should disturb all black folks."

"Why is that?" Professor wanted to know.

"Excuse me?" Mr. Pichon asked.

"Why is that?" Professor repeated the question.

"Sir," Mr. Pichon said in a voice that was calm but forceful, "if we make progress in this country, that progress should be based on merit and qualifications, not reverse discrimination."

"Did all of the other white folks admitted to that school have higher than a three-point-four grade point average?" Professor asked.

"To be honest, I can't answer that question," Mr. Pichon admitted.

"You a schoolteacher, right?"

"That's right."

"Well, then, Mr. Schoolteacher, don't you think you ought to know the answer to that question before you start talking about merit and qualifications?"

Mr. Pichon didn't answer.

"You ever heard of Franklin Roosevelt?" Professor asked.

"Of course," Mr. Pichon said.

"You know where he went to school?"

Mr. Pichon paused and looked at the ceiling.

"No, I can't say that I do," he admitted reluctantly.

"Harvard," Professor told him.

"Excellent school," Mr. Pichon said.

"You know what his high school GPA was?" Professor asked.

"No I don't," Mr. Pichon responded.

"Two-point-zero," Professor told him. "Now tell me how he got into Harvard."

"I don't know," Mr. Pichon said.

"Uncle Theodore! That's how," Professor said loudly. "Now, where is the merit in that?"

Mr. Pichon didn't respond.

"Look at him now," someone said. "Cat got his tongue."

"You ever heard the old saying 'It ain't *what* you know but *who* you know'?" Professor asked.

"Yes, I have," Mr. Pichon said.

"Who came up with it?" Professor asked.

"I can't say with any certainty," Mr. Pichon said.

"I can," Professor said. "White folks."

"They sho' said it," someone interjected.

"Now, does that sound like a people interested in merit and qualification?"

"Hell, no," someone else answered.

"You ever heard of the old-boy network?"

"Of course I have."

"Please tell me who the old boys were."

"White folks," someone yelled.

"Please tell me their purpose."

There was brief silence.

"Go'n and tell him, Professor," someone said. "He ain't gone say nothing."

"To take care of their own," Professor said. "Where is the merit in that, Mr. Schoolteacher?"

"There isn't any," Mr. Pichon said.

"Who do you think is more likely to get an unfair break in this country—black folks, or privileged, rich white folks?"

"Yeah," someone echoed, "who?"

"Sir, none of this alters the fact that affirmative action is reverse discrimination," Mr. Pichon said.

"So you don't have a problem with discrimination, just reverse discrimination?" Professor asked.

"Just because white folks discriminated in the past does not make it right for black folks to discriminate now."

"Well, like Sistah Souljah said, it might not make it right, but it sho' make it even."

"Excuse my French," Mr. Pichon said, "but Sister Souljah is crazy as hell. Besides, this is no time to get even; it's time to get ahead."

"And how do you propose that we do that?"

"By promoting racial harmony," Mr. Pichon said. "Unlike you, I do believe in Martin Luther King's dream."

"Well that's too bad," Professor said.

"Why do you say that?" Mr. Pichon asked.

"Because the problem with dreaming is that when you wake up, you don't see nothing but reality," Professor told him.

"And what is reality?" Mr. Pichon asked.

"Malcolm X," Professor said without hesitation.

"And how do you figure that?" Mr. Pichon asked.

"Malcolm told it like it was," Professor said.

"Well, many people feel that he was a black racist," Mr. Pichon said, "pure and simple."

"Those people are blaming the messenger for the message," Professor explained. "You see, white folks want to throw a rock, then hide their hand, but Malcolm called them on that. He identified them for what they are, blue-eyed devils, and folks don't like it."

"Well, what's the difference in him calling all white folks devils and in white folks calling all black folks thugs and criminals?"

"Evidence."

"What evidence?"

"Mr. Teacher, are you a religious man?"

"Yes, I believe in God."

"Then you also believe in the devil."

"That's a fair statement."

"What is a devil?"

"A fallen angel."

"How would you describe him?"

"As a fallen angel."

"Would you say that God is great and God is good?"

"Yes, I would agree with that statement."

"Would you also say that the devil is powerful and evil?"

"Yes, I would agree with that."

"How would you describe white Americans—as great and good, or powerful and evil?"

"I wouldn't dare stereotype all white people. We cannot judge groups, only individuals."

"Didn't God judge Sodom and Gomorrah?"

"Yes, he did."

"And doesn't the Bible talk about a chosen people?"

"Of course."

"Ain't those groups?"

"I should think so."

"Well that's all Malcolm did."

"I believe that's a bit of a stretch."

"I believe it brings us back to my original question—are white people great and good, or powerful and evil?"

"The question can't be answered as it is posed."

"I don't see why not."

"Because it's an unfair question."

"Mr. Schoolteacher, is there such a thing as European history, African history, Russian history, German history, et cetera?"

"Of course."

"Then we can chronicle the behavior of groups of people."

"To a degree."

"But it can be done."

"As I said, to a degree."

"To the degree that we can answer the question, how have whites behaved toward blacks in America?"

"That's hard to say."

"What's so hard about it?"

"It depends on what white folks you are referring to."

"Would it be fair to say that, during the course of American history, white folks have enslaved, dehumanized, raped, lynched, castrated, beat, murdered, maimed, terrorized, harassed, and discriminated against blacks?"

"Yes, unfortunately those things did occur."

"Would it be fair to say that those acts were the rule rather than the exception?"

"It depends on the time period."

"How about during Malcolm X's time?"

"Perhaps."

"Now, would you describe those acts as good, or evil?"

"Of course they were evil."

"We have established the fact that God is good and the devil is evil, correct?"

"Correct."

"What color are most white folks' eyes?"

"They are a variety of colors."

"Would you say that blue eyes are common among white folks?"

"They are fairly common."

"So a lot of these evil acts could have been committed by white folks with blue eyes, correct?"

"That's a possibility."

"So how does calling white folks blue-eyed devils make Malcolm X a black racist?"

"Because all of them aren't."

"So the operative word is 'all.' "

"That's correct."

"You would feel better if Malcolm had said that *most* white folks are blue-eyed devils."

"We can't say that most are."

"Can we say some or many are?"

"Possibly."

"That makes you feel better?"

"I think it makes a lot of people feel better. That's why Malcolm X was more widely accepted after his change."

"Accepted by who?"

"Blacks and whites alike."

"You actually believe that?"

"History bears it out."

"That's why people like you still have delusions about a dream. Y'all are more interested in seeing some fictional change in Malcolm than in hearing what he was trying to tell you about race in this country."

"So you think we have been deceived?"

"That's right."

"Who deceived us?"

"White folks."

"Is that a fact?"

"They the ones who convinced you that Malcolm X was this evil, dangerous, violent black racist."

"No, Malcolm convinced me of that himself."

"That's what white folks want you to think."

"So white folks formed my thoughts?"

"That's right."

"And just how did they do that?"

"By getting inside your head with television shows like *The Hate That Hate Produced*."

"Sir, that's crazy."

"Is it?"

"I'm afraid so."

"Well, can you answer a question for me?"

"I can try."

"Name one thing that Malcolm X did to white folks."

There was a brief pause.

"I can't think of anything."

"Not one single act."

"Nothing."

"Take your time, Mr. Teacher," Professor said. "As evil as you say Malcolm was, he must have done something."

"I can't think of anything."

"Did he participate in any lynchings or castrations?"

"Not to my knowledge."

"Did he ever kill or attack any white person?"

"Not that I am aware of."

"Did he rape a white woman?"

"There is no record of that."

"Did he attempt to deny whites their citizenship rights because of their race?"

"No."

"Did he enslave anybody?"

"No."

"Then why label him a black racist?"

"Because of his incendiary words."

"What do you mean?"

"He preached hatred and violence."

"Mr. Teacher, if I am not mistaken he specifically stated that African-Americans should be violent with people who are violent against them. What's wrong with advocating self-defense?"

"What's right about spreading hatred?"

"It was whites who introduced racial hatred."

"And Malcolm X perpetuated it."

"Why should he like a people who hate him?"

"Because we should love everybody."

"Love those who brutalize and terrorize us?"

"Love them, disarm them, and change them—nonviolently."

"That's crazy."

"It's not crazy; it's who we are."

"No, it's where we went wrong."

"We chose the right road; we just didn't stay on it."

"You didn't choose Martin; white folks gave him to you."

"Now you're being ridiculous."

"It was either Martin or Malcolm."

"Please."

"It was either nonviolence or race war."

"Come on."

"Without Malcolm there was no Martin."

"Sir, you can't possibly believe that."

"Mr. Schoolteacher, believe it or not, it was the threat of violence that made nonviolence work."

"That's absurd."

"No, that's reality."

"So, now we're back to the issue of reality?"

"Reality never changed."

"You mean the reality of white folks in America?"

"I mean the reality of race relations in America."

"I guess we're back to the dream."

"There can be no dream without equality."

"No one said that there could. King understood that we had to get to a point where content of one's character is more important than the color of one's skin."

"I know that you believe in that possibility."

"With all my heart."

"The problem is that white folks have a different dream."

"And what dream is that?"

"The American Dream."

"I don't follow you."

"In their dream they're the master and we're the slave, they're superior and we're inferior, they're the boss man and we're the field hand, they ride in the front of the bus and we ride the back. We dream of a place where all is shared equally, and they dream of a place where all is reserved *For Whites Only*. They dreamed up America, and now black folks are trying to dream it away. The black man's dream is the white man's nightmare."

"Interesting."

"No, factual."

"I beg to differ."

"On what grounds?"

"Many of the things you mention no longer exist."

"Such as?"

"Slavery, *For Whites Only*, the back of the bus."

"Sometimes in wars you lose a few battles."

"So they've only lost a few battles?"

"And they haven't lost those yet."

"What do you mean?"

"They fought against the abolition of discrimination, and now they are fighting against the remedies."

"Affirmative action?"

"You said it."

"But I don't believe it."

"Well, that's the problem. African-Americans would rather dream than face reality."

"No, the problem is we can't let go of the past. We would rather view ourselves as oppressed, victimized African-Americans than as proud, loyal Americans. We are not Africans. We are Americans. We need to stop separating ourselves with this foolishness. How can we expect people to embrace us when we won't embrace the country?"

"Wait a minute, Mr. Schoolteacher. Are you suggesting that white folks have been more loyal to America than black folks?"

"That's exactly what I'm saying," Mr. Pichon told him. "They're proud to be Americans. They are more patriotic."

"If they're so proud and patriotic, tell me what that Confederate flag is all about."

"Many nations have had civil wars," Mr. Pichon told him.

"Come on, Mr. Teacher," Professor said. "You know good and well that America ain't had no civil war. That was a revolution. Anytime people rise up against their country, secede from the union, and form a new independent government, that's a revolution."

"Sho' it is," someone yelled in support.

"Hell, them white folks even call themselves rebels. Now, when black folks ever did anything like that?"

"Never," someone answered for Mr. Pichon.

"That's right, never," Professor said. "So, don't talk to me about no patriotic white folks. Them people trying to put us back in the cotton field and they counting on nigguhs like you."

"What you mean, nigguhs like me?" Mr. Pichon asked.

"Clarence Thomas, Armstrong Williams, Shelby Steele, you Uncle Tom Negroes. That's what I mean."

"Look out, Professor," someone yelled.

"You cooking with oil now," someone else exclaimed. "You cooking with oil."

"And Sonny," D'Ray whispered to himself, subconsciously conjuring an image of the man who he felt was simply a token black cop on an all-white force, with the authority only to arrest, ticket, or detain other black folks. Where was Sonny now? Was he still at the station, or had he gone home? Had he left, or was he still at D'Ray's house drinking coffee with his mother? Oh, how he hated that man.

"So anybody who thinks that black folks ought to get up off their butts and do something for themselves is an Uncle Tom?" Mr. Pichon said reprovingly.

"Black folks always been doing for theyself," Professor said. "And doing for white folks too!"

"If we doing so much, why we in this terrible situation?"

"Man, let me tell you something—"

Suddenly the door flew open and an elderly man stuck his head inside. It was Gus, the courthouse custodian.

"Y'all heard the news?"

"What news?" Fred asked.

"About Old Man Gunner's truck."

"What about it?"

"You knew it got stole last night?"

"Yeah I heard about that."

"Well, they found it."

D'Ray flinched. He sat up straight, staring at the old man and listening to his every word.

"Naw, I hadn't heard about that," Fred said.

"Well, they found it first thing this morning."

"Where?"

"'Round by the junkyard."

"They know who took it?"

"Naw," Gus said, "but they think he was black."

"What make 'em think that?" Professor asked angrily. "Do they have a witness?"

"They ain't got no witness that I know of."

"Well, how they figure he black?" Professor asked.

"They say the radio was on a black station."

D'Ray thought about the radio. He hadn't turned it back to the right station. How could he have been so careless?

"That don't mean nothing," Professor said. "White folks can listen to black music."

"That ain't the only thing."

"What else?"

"They think he from the projects."

"Why?"

"I guess because of where they found the truck."

"Don't white folks go to that junkyard?"

"I'm sho' they do."

"Well, then."

"Don't get mad at me," Gus said defensively. "I'm just telling you what I heard."

"They trying to say that somebody black went to a park full of white folks and stole a truck and ain't nobody seen him?"

"I guess so."

"That don't make no sense."

"Well, now, I didn't say it did."

"White man probably hid that truck out there hisself and lied and said somebody stole it."

"Sir, you don't know that," Mr. Pichon butted in.

"But I know them," Professor told him.

"By 'them' I suppose you mean white people?"

"You got it."

"You're no different than them."

"Why should I be?"

"Perhaps someone black did steal it."

"And perhaps they didn't."

"Well, we'll know soon enough," the old man said.

"How you figure?" Professor asked.

"They say they got fingerprints."

"Who say?"

"That's all right, who?"

Suddenly the door opened and a woman walked in carrying a paper plate wrapped in aluminum foil. Instantly, a strange quiet fell over the room.

"How you doing this morning, Fred?" she asked.

"Aw, Vanessa, I can't complain," he said. "And you?"

"Just working hard and paying bills," she said.

"Well, we all in that boat."

Gus moved to the door and grabbed the knob. He paused, looked at Vanessa, shook his head, then looked at Fred.

"Fred, I can't take it," he mumbled. "I going on back to the courthouse."

"Awright, Gus." Fred laughed.

"If I hear anything else, I'll let you know."

"Awright, don't you work too hard now."

"You know me better than that."

When Gus left, Vanessa moved closer to Fred.

"Mrs. Johnson sent you your lunch."

Fred glanced up at the large circular clock hanging in the middle of the far wall.

"You a little early today, huh?"

"I decided to run on over here before things got too busy."

"Well, I definitely appreciate it."

"Aw, I'm glad to do it."

"What I owe you?"

"You know your money ain't no good with us."

"Well, y'all got to make a living too."

"Aw, hush up, Fred, and tell me where you want me to put this."

"Just set it over there anywhere," Fred told her.

As she walked across the room all eyes were on her. She set the plate on the counter and then walked back to the door. She was a tall, shapely woman, about five feet, ten inches tall. She had long smooth legs, large athletic thighs, and a firm, protruding butt that danced seductively as she walked.

"You be sure to tell Joanne I said thank you."

"You know I will."

She turned to leave and one of the men called to her.

"Say, baby."

When she turned and looked, she recognized him.

"What you want, fool?" Her voice became hard and cold.

"When we gone get together?"

"Why you keep asking me that?"

"'Cause I wants to know."

"I done told you we cousins. With yo' mannish self."

"And I done told you goose is goose and guinea is guinea. Kinfolks stuff just as good as any."

The room erupted with laughter.

"You better stop disrespecting me."

"You know you like it."

"Huh, you too conceited for your own good."

"Baby, I ain't conceited, just convinced."

"Convinced you ain't never gone get it."

Again laughter filled the shop.

"Stop harassing my company," Fred ordered.

"Aw, Fred, she like it."

"You can't tell him nothing, Fred," Vanessa said as she was leaving. "He ain't nothing but a old dog with no home training."

"Lawd, it ought to be a sin for a woman to look that good."

Fred smiled, brushed the hair from a customer, and turned to the crowd. "Next," he said softly.

No one moved.

"And that body. My Lawd, that body."

"Whose next?" Fred asked a second time.

D'Ray was next but he wasn't paying attention. He was wondering, thinking. The police had a print. How long before they matched it to his? Would it take hours, or days? They would probably check the prints against possible suspects first. Surely they would suspect him. They always suspected him. Should he stay, or leave? If he left before getting his haircut, the men in the shop might become suspicious. But if he stayed and the police made a match while he was there, they would catch him for sure. If only he had worn gloves. He thought of something. He hadn't worn gloves during the robbery either. Had he touched anything in the store? He couldn't remember. The cash register. He had opened the cash register. He had to leave. He rose from his seat.

"You next?" Suddenly he was aware of Fred's voice.

"Yeah," he mumbled, "I guess so."

He walked to the chair and sat down. Fred draped the apron over his chest and pinned it behind his neck.

"The usual?" Fred asked.

"Yeah," D'Ray mumbled, "the usual."

He heard the clippers click on and he felt the tingle of the blades on the back of his neck. From the chair he could see out onto the streets. Everything seemed quiet. Everything looked peaceful. He wondered what was going on at the police station. He told himself to be calm. Gus had said that he would let Fred know if he heard anything else. He didn't have to worry. If he was still in the shop, he would know what the cops knew shortly after they knew it. He would have time to get away.

"Where did you take your degree from?"

D'Ray looked up. Mr. Pichon was talking to Professor.

"Angola State Penitentiary," Professor told him. "And you?"

"Tulane," Mr. Pichon said proudly.

"Fine school," Professor said.

"One of the finest in the country," Mr. Pichon boasted.

"Have you ever read any of Carter G. Woodson's books?"

"No, I can't say that I have."

"I think you should."

"Anything in particular?"

"Yessir."

D'Ray watched Mr. Pichon remove an ink pen and a small writing pad from his shirt pocket.

"Okay," he said. "What's the title?"

*"The Mis-Education of the Negro."*

# CHAPTER SIX

When he <sup>WALKED OUT OF THE BARBERSHOP AND</sup> <sub>ONTO THE PORCH, HE COULD FEEL IT IN</sub> the air. It was that same feeling you got when you played hide-and-go-seek. You had the perfect hiding place, yet you knew they were coming. You couldn't see them or hear them, but you knew they were coming. So you sat there, crouched in some uncomfortable position, fighting against your mind. Should you run, or stay put? Were they really onto you, or were you just being paranoid? Were they close by, and if so, would they see you if you moved? It wasn't a difficult game. Winning and losing was as simple as knowing when to stay put and when to run.

Yes, this was hide-and-go-seek, and he was it. And like any good player, he had tried to destroy the clues. He had hidden the truck, but they had found it. He had removed the gun, but he was sure by now his mother knew it was missing. He had burned the clothes, or so he thought. He hadn't gone back to check. Maybe they burned and maybe they didn't. How would he explain that away? How could anyone in the projects explain trying to burn up a perfectly good shirt and a pair of pants? The longer he thought, the clearer it became. He had to run. There were too many clues, and he was too easy to find.

When he turned the corner leading to his house, he knew that it was time to go. He only had the clothes on his back and the few dollars in his pocket; still, it was time to go. They were at his house. The police car was as visible as the nose on his face. Maybe they were only asking questions and maybe they were simply grasping for clues. He didn't know what they knew or what they were doing, but he did know they were getting too close.

He had a strange desire to move closer to the house. He wanted one last glimpse of his mother or a chance to make eye contact with Little Man. He needed to speak to him. He needed to say good-bye. He needed to make him understand why he, like the father he had never known, was abandoning him. He needed to make him understand that which his mother could not. He was poor and he was black, and the rules that worked for white folks in their world would not work for him in his. There was so much for Little Man to learn, but fate had cut their time short. Now he had to be a man. If he was going to survive, he had to be a man.

D'Ray saw two more police cars pull up in front of his house and stop. Now he knew. They were not asking questions; they were looking for him. He didn't know how they knew. Perhaps they had matched his prints with those they had found in the truck, or maybe someone had seen him. He didn't know how, but he was certain they knew. Now there was no more time. There could be no good-byes or any more advice. If he was to remain free, he had to leave now. He paused, pondering. Maybe he could hide out with someone until dark. No, that wouldn't work. The police would question his family; they would question his friends. He could already see Sonny Boy leading the way. Yes, Sonny would know just where to look and just who to ask. No, he couldn't confide in anyone. He wouldn't.

He made his way back to the slough, went into the woods, and retrieved the gun. He didn't know where he was going or how he was going to get there, but he knew that, as a fugitive, sooner or later he would need a gun. He followed the stand of woods north for two miles until he reached the backside of the parish livestock grounds, the site where public auctions were held. For a few minutes he lay on his stomach at the edge of the woods, watching as one truck after the other pulled up to the dock, unloaded its livestock, and pulled away. Self-preservation made him formulate a plan. He would leave town by stowing away in one of the empty trailers. But how would he know which one? And how could he know where the drivers were going? He watched several more trailers come and go. There were no discernible markings on any of them, save for the license tags.

He closed his eyes and buried his face in the palms of his hands, trying to think. He was only two miles outside of town, and sooner or later the police were going to close in on him. He opened his eyes and watched a tall, overweight white man drive his truck and trailer next to one of the offices, park it, get out, and then go inside the building. As he studied the trailer, he noticed a Wilmington High School bumper sticker stuck in the left corner of the rear fender. Wilmington was far enough away for him to feel safe, and it was large enough to have a bus station. If he made it there without being detected, he could catch a bus out of the state and then figure out what he wanted to do. He removed his wallet from his pocket and examined the money. It wasn't much, but it would be enough to tide him over until he could find a job. He jumped to his feet and jogged to the back of the trailer. It was a long, covered two-horse trailer with a large single rear door. Between the roof and the top of the door was a two-foot space. D'Ray climbed up on the rear bumper and looked inside. Near the front of the trailer, resting on the surprisingly clean floor, were several bales of hay.

When he was sure that he wasn't being watched, he pulled himself to the top of the trailer door, threw his right leg over, and dropped to the floor. He moved to the front of the trailer and crawled behind the hay. Although the space was cramped and a foul odor lingered in the air, he was relieved. Both the ceiling and the walls of the trailer were solid. He couldn't see out, but more important, no one could see inside.

He scooted to the left side of the trailer, turned his body parallel to the front, slid back against the wall, and stretched his feet in front of him. The space behind the hay was dark and cramped. His left shoulder was pressed against the hay and his right shoulder was pressed against the front of the trailer. He shifted his weight to a more comfortable position, then told himself that he had to be still lest someone should hear him. He tilted his head back, folded his arms across his chest, and closed his eyes. His mind began to wander from one thing to another. He thought about the thirty-mile trip to Wilmington. Then about his family, and then about the police. He became fixated on the police. Where were they? Were they looking for a thief, or were they looking for a murderer? The thought sent a chill down his spine. He was a murderer. He had taken someone's life. He tilted his head back, let out a deep sigh, and thought about Little Man. Because he had killed, Little Man had a chance. His life was lost and his daddy's life was lost, but now Little Man still had a chance. He reached down and rubbed his hand over the handle of the gun. Had pulling the trigger in that convenience store been the beginning, or the end? He had killed once; would he have to do it again? Could he do it again?

He didn't hear the man climb into the truck, nor did he hear him start the engine. It was the quick, violent, lurking motion of the trailer being jerked forward that had jarred him out of his sleep. Yes, he had fallen asleep. He had remained so still for so long in that tiny dark cramped space that his body had simply turned off. He leaned forward and listened intently. Although he couldn't see outside the trailer, the slow speed of the vehicle, the bumpy ride, and the sound of men talking told him that they were still on the auction grounds. As the truck moved forward, he leaned his head back against the wall of the trailer, closed his eyes, and followed the route in his mind. He measured every turn, every stop, every curve, and every bump, making certain that the driver stayed the course to Wilmington.

When he figured they had been on the highway for about half an hour, he eased from behind the hay, moved to the rear of the trailer, raised to a crouch, and peeped over the tailgate. From the back of the trailer he had a clear view of what lay behind him, but no idea of what was ahead. He was tempted to stick his head out of the trailer and peep around the corner, but thought better of it. If he stuck his head out just as someone was approaching from the opposite direction, they would surely see him.

On the far side of the highway, a street sign popped into view and quickly began to fade. He leaned forward, narrowed his eyes, and stared at the sign until it disappeared into the distance. Although he had only glimpsed the front of the sign, he was sure that it said, *Brownsville 25 miles.* He ran his hand deep into his back pocket, removed his wallet, and counted the money a second time. Yes, he only had $200 left. He put his wallet back into his pocket and took a seat on the floor. How much of the money could he afford to spend on a bus ticket? He quickly calculated the expenses mentally. Once he reached his destination, he would need enough money to buy food and find a place to stay. Today was Saturday. He couldn't even begin to look for a job until Monday. And once he found one, it would be at least two weeks before he received his first paycheck.

Suddenly he felt the truck begin to decrease speed. He pulled to his feet and peered over the tailgate. He saw the large, two-story brick school building sitting on the left side of the highway. They were inside the city limits. He crouched back down behind the tailgate. "Fifty dollars," he mumbled to himself. He would travel as far as $50 would carry him. Then he would get a job and move on after he earned more money. Now the truck was barely moving. He rose to his feet again, peeped over the top, and quickly kneeled. They were downtown on Main Street. There was a line of cars behind them, and from the pace of the traffic he assumed there were vehicles in front of them as well.

As he sat listening to the sounds of the city he realized that he had no idea of how to get to the bus station. He had traveled through Wilmington before, but he had never stopped there. As the driver of the truck turned left onto a side street, D'Ray leaped to his feet and looked over the tailgate. When he was sure that the coast was clear, he threw his leg over the gate, slid down to the back bumper, collected himself, and stepped from the truck onto the side of the road. As his numb right foot made contact with the ground, his legs buckled and a sharp, tingling pain raced down the heel of his foot and exploded into the tip of his toes. His foot had gone to sleep. Instinctively he lifted his foot and began to rotate it in a slow circular motion until the numbness began to subside. Then he gingerly lowered it to the ground and wiggled his toes until all of the feeling returned. When his feet could again support the full weight of his body, he brushed the dirt from the seat of his pants and walked back toward Main Street.

Main Street in Wilmington was no different from Main Street in any other small north Louisiana town. Various stores and businesses lined both sides of the street. In the center of downtown was the courthouse square. On the west side of the huge, multistoried courthouse was the post office. On the back side was a newspaper office. On the east side was a toy store. Next to the toy store was an ice cream stand. And directly across the street was the bank. Farther down, there were two hardware stores, a dry cleaner's, a shoe shop, a barbershop, several gas stations, a restaurant, a catfish house, a café, and several different types of fast food places.

When D'Ray turned the corner, he paused in front of the drugstore and watched the people moving up and down Main Street. Some of them carried shopping bags, while others just carelessly strolled along, occasionally pausing to look at some item of interest staring at them from behind one of the huge glass store windows. He needed to ask someone for directions. He turned and looked through the window of the drugstore. A small, frail-looking white child was sitting at the counter on a bar stool licking a large vanilla ice cream cone. Suddenly he became aware of the uncomfortable hunger pains churning in his lower abdomen, a loud rumbling noise bellowing up from the pit of his stomach. Instinctively he sucked in his gut and flexed his stomach muscles taut. He hadn't eaten since yesterday. He stared at the cone, contemplating whether he should spend some of the money or not. Again his stomach rumbled. He reached down, folded his arms over his stomach, and squeezed tightly. He had to eat something. He moved closer to the window to see what else they served and to see if any other black people were inside. He cupped his hands around the outside of his eyes to block out the glare of the sun and pressed them against the window. No sooner had he pressed his face against the window than he heard the sound of a deep, angry voice.

"You looking for something, boy?"

Startled, he wheeled around and stared into the eyes of a large, overweight white policeman.

"I'm just trying to find the bus station."

The policeman looked at him, then slowly placed his right hand over the handle of his gun. D'Ray looked at his hand, then thought about the gun in the waist of his pants. What if the policeman searched him? How would he explain the gun? A surge of nervous energy swept over his body. He felt his legs begin to shake and his left eye began to twitch.

"The bus station?" the policeman asked, in a loud, intimidating voice.

"Yessir," D'Ray said trying to steady his voice.

"Why you looking through that window?"

"I was looking for somebody."

"I thought you said you was looking for the bus station?"

"Yessir, I was."

"Do that look like a bus station?"

"No sir."

"Then why was you looking through that window?"

"I was going to get something to eat."

"I thought you just said you was looking for somebody."

"Yessir, I was."

"Who?"

"Sir?"

"Who was you looking for, boy?"

D'Ray didn't answer. The police officer grabbed him by the arm and pushed him into the doorway.

"Show me who you were looking for."

"I don't see him."

"You was looking at that white woman, wasn't you?"

D'Ray looked toward the counter. A tall, blond white woman wearing blue jean shorts and a tight-fitting halter top was leaning suggestively against the end of the counter.

"No sir."

"You like looking at white women, don't you?"

"No sir."

"If you wasn't looking at that white woman, then who were you looking at?"

"Nobody."

"You just said you was looking at somebody."

D'Ray didn't answer.

"What's your name, boy?"

"D'Ray."

"D'Ray what?"

"D'Ray Reid."

"Well, D'Ray Reid, do I look like a fool?"

"No sir."

"Why are you trying to tell me you wasn't looking at nobody and I saw you looking at that white woman?"

"I wasn't looking at no white woman."

"You want to go to jail, boy?"

A single tear fell from D'Ray's left eye and wound it's way underneath his chin.

"No sir."

"Well, you better stop lying to me."

"I ain't lying."

The police officer looked at him with a hard, cold stare. D'Ray lowered his head and looked at the floor.

"You got any identification, boy?"

"Yessir."

"Give it to me."

D'Ray removed his wallet and handed it to the police officer.

"Step outside."

D'Ray stepped outside and moved to the right of the doorway.

"Go on over there next to my car."

D'Ray crossed the walkway, descended the step, and moved next to the squad car. Then he watched the police officer open his wallet and remove the money.

"Where you get all this money from, boy?"

"My mama gave it to me."

"Your mama! What she give you all this money for?"

"A bus ticket."

"What your mama's name?"

"Mira."

"Y'all ain't from 'round here, are you?"

"No sir."

D'Ray watched the officer remove his driver's license, examine it, and put it back.

"So you headed to the bus station?"

"Yessir."

"You walking or driving?"

"Walking."

"How did you get over here?"

"Someone brought me."

"Why didn't they take you to the station?"

"They didn't know where it was at."

"So they just let you out in the middle of the street?"

"They were in a hurry and I told them this was good enough."

The officer looked D'Ray in the eyes.

"Where your bags?"

"I ain't got none," D'Ray told him.

"You going on a trip, but you ain't got no bags?"

"Yessir."

"You must not be going far."

"No sir, not too far."

"You must not be staying long."

"No sir, not too long."

"Exactly where you going?"

"New Orleans."

"When you coming back?"

"Monday."

"But you ain't taking no clothes?"

"No sir."

"Why is that?"

"I already got clothes at my auntie's house."

"So you going to visit yo' auntie?"

"Yessir."

"Where she live?"

"In New Orleans."

"Where in New Orleans?"

"Sir?"

"On what street?"

"Saint Charles Avenue."

"She must be well off."

"She a teacher."

"Where?"

"At one of the universities."

"Which one?"

"Xavier."

"One of the colored schools?"

"Yessir."

"What she teach?"

"English."

"White English or black English?"

"I don't know."

The officer closed the wallet and handed it back to D'Ray.

"You got anything else in your pockets?"

"No sir."

"Pull your front pockets inside out and let me see."

D'Ray pulled the lining out of his front pockets.

"You got anything in your back pockets?"

"No sir."

"Turn around and lean against the car and spread your legs."

D'Ray closed his eyes, turned around, and leaned against the car. He bit down on his bottom lip and held his breath as he felt the officer's hands move across his back pockets, down the back of his legs, around his ankles, and up the front of his legs. He sighed softly and opened his eyes as the officer stopped just below his front pockets. He hadn't detected the gun.

"I ought to take you to jail."

"What for?"

"Lying to a officer."

"I ain't lying, sir."

"You just want to know how to get to the bus station?"

"Yessir."

There was a pause.

"What time yo' bus leave?"

D'Ray hesitated. He knew the officer was trying to trap him.

"Four o'clock."

The officer looked at D'Ray, then looked at his watch.

"It's three-thirty now."

"Yessir," D'Ray said, lowering his eyes. "I sho' don't want to miss my bus."

"So if I call over to the bus station, they'll tell me that a bus is leaving for New Orleans at four o'clock."

"Yessir, that's what the man told Mama when she called."

After a brief silence the officer turned and pointed to the far end of the walkway.

"Go over yonder around that corner. Walk about two or three blocks until you come to the Dodge place. You gone see a little old narrow one-way street that run right behind it. Go down that street about a block and you'll see a place called the Chicken Shack." He paused. "You like fried chicken, boy?"

"Yessir."

"You wouldn't be colored if you didn't, now would you?"

"No sir."

"Now when you see the Chicken Shack, go left for about a half a block and the bus station is on the other side of the road. You can't miss it."

"Yessir. Thank you, sir."

D'Ray turned to walk away.

"Boy."

D'Ray turned around and faced the officer.

"Sir?"

"You stay out of trouble now."

"Yessir."

Again D'Ray turned to leave.

"Boy."

He stopped and faced the officer again.

"Sir?"

"I'm gone be watching you. You hear?"

"Yessir."

As D'Ray walked away, he could feel the officer's eyes on his back. He could hear his cold, threatening words ringing inside his head. "Boy, I'm gone be watching you." He had been too careless. He had drawn too much attention to himself. If he was going to survive, he couldn't afford to have the police aware of his presence. He had to blend in and be that which he had not been born to be, an honest, hardworking, law-abiding citizen.

When he reached the Dodge place he turned and looked back. The police car was about twenty yards behind him, moving in his direction at a very slow speed. D'Ray began to wonder why the policeman was following him. Maybe he had called the bus station to verify D'Ray's story. He knew his name and where he was from. Maybe he had radioed the station and they were checking him out. What if the Brownsville police had put out a bulletin on him? D'Ray began to panic. He started to run but thought better of it. That would only give the officer a reason to chase him. He told himself to relax. He put his hands in his pockets and began to whistle softly to himself. Then he turned onto the street as he had been instructed, and picked up his pace. When he had gone about a block, he turned and looked back a second time. The police car was still behind him. D'Ray paused and looked at the Chicken Shack. He could feel his stomach rumbling. He desperately wanted to go inside and get something to eat, but the policeman was making him nervous. He turned left and continued on his way. When he saw the bus station on the opposite side of the street, he stopped, looked both ways, then dashed across.

At the door, he turned and looked over his shoulder. The police officer had driven his car across the street and stopped in front of the station. Their eyes met, and the corner of the officer's mouth turned up, forming a wide, cryptic smile.

"You have a good trip now, you hear."

After he had driven away, D'Ray pushed the door open, stepped inside, and glanced around. The officer had unnerved him. He wanted to board a bus and leave as soon as possible. He saw the large schedule board hanging on the center wall. He walked over, looked at the schedule board, then at the clock, and back at the board. There were two buses leaving the state within fifteen minutes. One was going to Houston and the other was going to Jackson. For a moment he stared at the board, pondering his decision. Houston would be ideal. It was far enough for him to feel safe, large enough for him to be anonymous, and diverse enough for him to find work. But could he afford the ticket? He looked back at the board. It listed departure and arrival times, but not fares. How could he find out? He couldn't ask the ticket clerk without making him suspicious. Out of the corner of his eye he saw two police officers walk into the station. Their presence revived in him a sense of urgency. He decided on Jackson. He moved over to the counter, purchased a one-way ticket for $45, and exited the station.

When he boarded the bus, he went directly into the bathroom, locked the door, and removed his right shoe. Then he took all the money from his wallet, except for $20, and stuffed it in the heel of his sock. After he had slid his foot back into his shoe and put his wallet in one of his front pockets, he went back into the cabin, moved to the center of the bus, and took a seat next to the window. As he sat, staring out into the afternoon, he was unaware of the other passengers piling onto the warm, musty bus.

He was unaware of the little old lady who sat next to him, clutching the moderate-size tote bag resting on her lap as if it contained her most sacred possessions. He was unaware of the two young children holding hands in the seats directly across from him, fighting against the fears and anxiety of taking their first bus trip without the comfort of their parents. He was unaware of the interracial couple, a black man and a white woman, sitting two rows back, whose trip to God knows where had brought them through a region of the country where such unions were still greeted with the cold, hostile stares normally reserved for weirdos, freaks, and criminals. And he was unaware of the short stocky bus driver, who had boarded the bus, slid into his seat, and pulled the door shut. But when the bus began to move and he felt himself being transported farther and farther away from all that he had ever known, he was overcome by a strange, eerie feeling rooted in the harsh reality that he was all alone. He was a fugitive. How would he live? Where would he stay? What kind of life could he expect to have? He had lost his family, his friends, his home, everything.

For a long time he sat staring out the window, fighting back tears.

He had closed his eyes a number of times, but the uncertainty of his situation would not let him sleep. So, for hours he sat listening to the aimless chatter of strangers telling one another their life stories— where they were going, who they were going to see, how long they were staying, and when they were coming back. Two young guys, one black and one white, were minor league baseball players. They had just been traded to the Braves and were on their way to a farm system in Birmingham. One older lady was on her way home; she had gone to Shreveport for a family reunion, but the gangs and violence had gotten so bad there that she was cutting her trip short. She couldn't wait to get back to the peace and quiet of her northern Alabama home. One man worked on the pipeline. He was going to meet a friend in Starkville, and together they were going to drive to a job site in Tennessee. A young blue-eyed, blond-haired newlywed was already having marital problems. She had secretly left home during the night while her husband of two months was asleep on the sofa. She was returning to her parents, in Ridgeland, to tell them that they had been right; marrying John was a big mistake.

Behind him he heard the sound of paper rattling. Soon his nose told him that which his eyes could not. Someone had determined that it was time to partake of the meal they had packed for the trip. From the noisy commotion he could tell that it was a family of two or three small children and a young mother. From the mother's threats of "When we get to Mississippi, I'm gone tell yo' daddy just how you acted if you don't hurry up and straighten out," he could tell that theirs was a trip taken to reunite the family. And from the scent of the food he could tell they were eating, among other things, fried chicken, corn on the cob, and some type of baked bread.

In spite of his valiant efforts to ignore the delicious aroma emanating from behind him, the scent of the food caused a loud, long, involuntary noise to erupt from his stomach. Embarrassed, he quickly clutched his stomach and turned his face toward the window. He could still feel the uncomfortable churning underneath his shirt. He sucked in his midsection and secretly prayed that he could control the growls until the next stop. Suddenly the little lady sitting next to him reached into her tote bag and removed a smaller brown paper bag, the contents of which were not visible.

"Honey, you hungry?" she asked him.

"No ma'am," he lied.

"You sure?" she asked.

He started to answer her, but when he relaxed to speak, the muscles in his stomach betrayed him and a loud, growling sound answered her question for him.

"Honey, why don't you have a sandwich?" she said, extending a sandwich toward him. "Lawd knows I can't eat 'em all."

"Ma'am, are you sure?"

"Yeah, baby," she smiled warmly. "Go'n and eat it. I got mo' sandwiches than I know what to do with."

D'Ray took the sandwich from her hand, thanked her, removed the plastic wrapping, and began eating. The sandwich told him a lot about the little lady. She was very meticulous. The sandwich had been so perfectly wrapped that it was as fresh as if she had just made it. The lettuce, tomatoes, and pickles told him that she had been or was a mother. The meat, which tasted like some type of steak, told him that she was accustomed to preparing food for a man. And the hot, spicy seasoning told him that she was either Creole or from south Louisiana. As he ate, slowly chewing his food and secretly hoping that she would offer him more, his body began to react to the spices. His eyes began to water and his nose began to run. He began to sniffle. Then he began to cough. Out of the corner of his eye he watched the little lady reach into her bag and remove a can of soda.

"I should have warned you, yeah," she said, handing him the can. "I forget that everybody can't eat their food hot and spicy like we do at home."

He took the drink, tilted his head back, and took a long swallow. After the cold liquid had cooled his burning palate, he turned to her and smiled.

"I like it hot like that."

"Sho' nuff?" She laughed.

"Ma'am, that's 'bout the best sandwich I done had in a long time," he told her.

A wide smile spread across her face.

"You want another one?" she asked.

"I don't want to eat up all yo' food," he told her.

"Well, aren't you a polite one?" she said, handing him another sandwich.

"Not me, ma'am," he said. "You."

"You remind me of my oldest grandson," she told him.

"Do I?" he asked.

"You sure do," she said, smiling up at him warmly. "He in the army. You want to see a picture?"

"Yes ma'am, I do."

As she leaned forward to search through the bag, he unwrapped the sandwich and began to eat it. As he chewed, he secretly observed her through the corner of his eye. She was a petite, neatly dressed lady who appeared to be in her late fifties or early sixties. Her comely round face, which was void of any makeup except for a lightly applied coat of red lipstick, was set off by a pair of high well-defined cheekbones and a pair of large brown eyes. Her long, slightly gray hair was pulled back into a bun and partially covered with a multi-colored scarf. Attractive as she was, D'Ray could only imagine what she must have looked like in her prime.

When she found the picture, she handed it to him. Her grandson was dressed in green military formals, standing in front of a mounted full-length American flag. His left arm was pressed tight against his leg, and his right hand was pressed against the brim of his hat in a salute. For the next half hour, she talked about her family. As she spoke of them her voice was filled with gentleness and her large, beautiful brown eyes sparkled with a mixture of love and pride. While D'Ray sat listening to her talk it was as if she were transformed from a complete stranger to someone he had known all of his life. She was the grandmother that he wished he had, and hers was a family like none that he had ever known.

They talked until the bus driver announced the next stop. Then she gave him a bag with several more sandwiches and another soft drink and told him this was where she was getting off. When the bus pulled into the station, she reached over, hugged him for a long time, and told him to be good and to be safe. Then she stood and began collecting her things. As D'Ray watched her he had a strange desire to hold on to her. He was alone, and her kindness had revived him and given him hope. For a few minutes she had been his friend and his family. She had made him believe that maybe everything would be OK. She had revealed to him that life's greatest gift was simply a kind word or a loving act performed by a family member, a friend, or an occasional stranger.

At each stop, in every small town along the route, he watched a new host of travelers board the bus with new tales, new problems, and new plans. At each stop he watched the joy and excitement demonstrated by those who had reached the end of their journey. As they disembarked, he observed the wide, infectious smiles etched across their faces as they fell into the arms of their waiting friends and loved ones. Each time he witnessed this scene, a small piece of him died. Those wonderful, beautiful, heartwarming greetings were a constant reminder of what he had given up. When he reached his destination, no one would be there anxiously anticipating his arrival. On the contrary, he would simply be a stranger in a strange place with nowhere to go. But now the kindness of a little old lady had given him hope. He would be a stranger only as long as he chose to be. Friendship and kinship were only a word away.

As the bus pulled off, he stared at the little lady standing next to her family, smiling and waving back at him. He watched until he could no longer see her. Then he placed the bag of sandwiches in his lap, leaned the side of his head against the window, folded his hands across his chest, closed his eyes, and, finally, went to sleep.

# CHAPTER SEVEN

The bus PULLED INTO THE JACKSON STATION, AND D'RAY MOVED HIS FACE CLOSER TO THE WINDOW AND stared out into the night. On edge and worried, he watched a dirty, shabbily dressed man push a shopping cart filled with odds and ends past the station and disappear into the darkness. Disturbed by the sight, he closed his eyes and concentrated. What was he going to do? Where was he going to go?

The bus driver's voice interrupted his thoughts.

"Jackson!"

D'Ray opened his eyes, took a deep breath, and slid out into the aisle. As he made his way toward the front, he thought of something. Maybe he could spend the night in the station. Yes, he could sleep there and figure out a plan of action in the morning. Relieved that he had thought of something, D'Ray stepped from the bus and walked toward the small, one-room terminal. Once inside, he moved to the last row of seats, sat down, and propped his legs on the chair directly in front of him. No sooner had he tilted his head back and closed his eyes than he heard someone shout, "Hey!"

Startled, he snapped his head forward and looked in the direction of the voice. A short, overweight black man was staring at him from behind the ticket counter.

"You talking to me?" D'Ray asked, surprised.

"You see anybody else in here?" the man asked.

D'Ray looked around slowly. The room was empty save for an elderly black man sweeping in the far corner.

"I guess not."

"Well, then I must be talking to you, huh?"

"Guess so."

The man looked at him with a blank expression on his face. "What you think you doing?"

"Just sitting down, that's all."

"For what?"

"Just crashing here till morning."

"Naw, you ain't."

"Why not?"

"'Cause I said so, that's why."

"Son," the second man interrupted.

D'Ray turned and looked at him.

"What?"

"You just got off that bus?"

"Yeah."

"That was the last one tonight."

"So?"

"Son, the station fixin' to close."

"Close!" D'Ray shouted, rising to his feet.

"That's right," the old man told him. "And we don't open back up till in the morning."

"What time in the morning?" D'Ray asked.

"Eight o'clock."

There was silence.

"What time is it now?"

The man pointed to the large clock on the wall behind the ticket counter. It was fifteen minutes until eleven.

"You got somebody you can call to come git you?"

"Naw."

The old man looked at him compassionately.

"You from 'round here?"

"Naw, I'm from Louisiana."

"You got someplace to stay?"

D'Ray shook his head.

"Well, that's your problem," the agent yelled from behind the counter. "I done told you, you can't stay in here."

"You got any money?"

D'Ray paused before he answered.

"Little bit."

"Why don't you go to a hotel?"

"Where one at?"

"They everywhere."

"How I'm gone git there?"

"Catch a cab."

"Where?" he asked.

"Come see," the man said pushing the door open.

D'Ray walked to the door, stuck his head out, and looked in the direction that the old man was pointing. In the distance he could see a lone yellow cab parked next to the curb.

"That's Lonzo sitting out there, sleeping," the man told him. "He can carry you where you want to go."

D'Ray thought about his limited funds.

"How far is the closest hotel?"

"Not far."

D'Ray stepped through the door then stopped.

"How far are the cheap hotels?"

"Not too far."

D'Ray turned to leave, then paused.

"Is the neighborhood safe?"

"Son, you better go on befo' Lonzo wake up and drive off."

D'Ray walked to the car and knocked on the window. Startled, Lonzo snapped forward, clutched the steering wheel, and looked up at D'Ray.

"I need a cab." D'Ray spoke first.

"I was just 'bout to pull off," Lonzo said, stepping out of the car and opening the back door. "Where you headed?"

"Hotel," D'Ray said, sliding in the backseat.

"Which one?"

"The cheapest one in town."

Lonzo slid under the wheel, laughing. He buckled his seat belt, started the engine, and looked back at D'Ray in the rearview mirror.

"You sho' you want the cheapest?"

"I'm sho'," D'Ray said without hesitating.

"Well," Lonzo said, pulling the car in gear and turning onto the highway, "your wish is my command."

"You don't have to go the scenic route either," D'Ray told him. "The shortest way will be fine."

Lonzo threw his head back and laughed at the top of his lungs.

"You ain't from 'round here, are you?"

"Naw, but my kinfolks are."

"If you got kinfolks, why you going to a cheap hotel?"

"They don't know I'm coming."

"Aw, this a surprise visit?"

"That's right."

There was a brief silence.

"What your people name?" Lonzo asked. "Maybe I know 'em."

"You ever hear of the Pughs?" D'Ray made up the name.

"Naw, can't say that I have."

"Well, them my people."

"Huh," Lonzo exclaimed loudly. "I guess you can't know everybody."

"Guess not," D'Ray agreed. "'Specially in a big city like Jackson."

When they made it to the hotel, Lonzo pulled over to the shoulder of the road and stopped.

"There she is," he said. "The E&M Motel."

D'Ray looked at the old single-story building and frowned.

"You said you wanted cheap," Lonzo reminded him.

"That's right," D'Ray said. "How much I owe you?"

"Five dollars will do it."

D'Ray leaned back and removed his wallet from his front pocket.

"Here you go," he said passing the money across the front seat. "Five dollars for the ride and two dollars for your company."

"I sho' appreciate it," Lonzo said.

"Don't mention it," D'Ray said, exiting the car.

"Hey," Lonzo called to him.

"Yeah," D'Ray answered.

"Tell Emma that Lonzo sent you. She'll do you right."

"I'll be sho' to do that. Thanks."

D'Ray walked into the hotel lobby, rang the bell, and waited. When no one responded, he rang the bell a second time and leaned over the counter to see if he could see through the partially open door directly behind the counter.

"Hold your horses. I'm coming," he heard a woman's voice call from behind the door. Soon a short, robust black woman wearing an old housecoat and slippers entered the room, yawning.

"You Ms. Emma?" D'Ray spoke first.

"That's right."

"Mr. Lonzo say you got rooms."

The woman looked at him appraisingly.

"How old are you?"

"Eighteen."

"Uh-huh!" she said, looking him in the eye. "Lonzo brung you here?"

"Yes ma'am. He just let me off."

There was silence.

"What kind of room you wanting?"

"Single."

"How long you staying?"

D'Ray hesitated before answering. "How much is the room?"

"Ten dollars a night."

"One week."

"How you paying?"

"Cash."

"That a five-day week or seven-day week?"

"Seven."

She paused and looked him in the eye.

"You have to pay in advance, you know."

"Yes ma'am, that's fine."

"That'll be seventy dollars even," she said, sliding D'Ray an old writing tablet that she used as a register. "I don't charge Lonzo's friends no tax."

D'Ray signed the name André Pugh on the tablet and removed the money from his sock.

"You can't be too careful these days," he said as he paid her.

"You sho' can't," she said, handing him the key. "Your room is around back. Checkout time is noon."

When D'Ray made it to his room, he pushed the door open, entered the room, and clicked on the lights. Instantly the dull glow from the single bulb hanging from the ceiling illuminated the room, and scores of tiny roaches scampered across the filthy, rugless floor and disappeared into the wide crevices separating the floor and the baseboard. Astonished, he entered the room, walked over to the bed, pulled back the spread, and checked the bed for bugs. Satisfied that there were none, he leaned over and sniffed the sheets. Although they appeared to be clean, he detected a distinct foul, nauseating scent. Baffled, he removed the right pillow, pulled back the sheet, and looked. A large pear-shaped stain stretched from the top right corner to just below the center of the old worn mattress. Disgusted and unwilling to sleep in what he thought was dried urine, D'Ray removed the remaining covering from the bed, flipped the mattress over, and examined it. Although there were several small, dark smudges ground into the fabric of the moderately soiled mattress, it was a grave improvement over what he had seen on the opposite side. Once he had made the bed, he removed the gun from his waist and the money from his sock and placed them underneath one of the pillows. Then he removed his pants and his shirt and placed them on top of the small rickety table in front of the window. After this, he locked the door, crossed the room, and climbed into the bed. No sooner had he turned out the lights and pulled the bedspread up underneath his chin than he became aware of a strange sound in the next room. Wide eyed, he lay perfectly still, curled in the fetal position, concentrating. Soon the screeching became louder. Then there was the sound of something knocking against the wall, softly and slowly at first, then faster and harder and louder. He heard the high-pitched moan of a woman, followed by the dull, low grunt of a man. Suddenly he felt light-headed and dizzy as he lay listening to the intoxicating cadence of the woman's erotic pant. He heard her cry out something, but he couldn't understand what. Frustrated, he leapt from the bed, raced into the bathroom, and grabbed the drinking glass from the sink. With glass in hand, he returned to the bedroom, climbed onto the bed, and placed the glass against the wall. He closed his eyes and pressed his left ear against the glass, listening.

"Oooh! Oooh! Oooh, baby!" He heard her clearly.

As he listened to her soft sensuous cries, keeping perfect time with the rhythm of the bedsprings, the image of two hot, sweaty, naked bodies pressed hard against each other, swaying and gyrating in love underneath the flickering flames of romantic candlelight, danced in his head. Suddenly the creaking of the springs became faster. Her moans were transformed to screams. The tap-tap-tapping of the headboard against the wall was now a loud, violent banging. "Yes! Yes! Yes!" he heard her shout at the top of her lungs. "Ooooh!" he heard the man scream. Then there was silence.

D'Ray closed his eyes and listened intently. Then, sweating heavily with his heart pounding rapidly, he removed the glass from the wall, stretched out on the bed, pulled a pillow tight against his body, and stared into the darkness of the room.

# CHAPTER EIGHT

At exactly 5 A.M., D'RAY ROLLED OVER ON HIS BACK, CLASPED HIS HANDS BEHIND HIS head, and stared at the ceiling. What was he going to do? He had no clothes, no food, no job, nothing. He ran his tongue over his dry, dingy teeth. What he wouldn't give for a toothbrush, a pair of clean underwear, and a stick of deodorant. He reached under the pillow, removed the money, and recounted it. Where had it all gone? He began to replay yesterday in his head. A bus ticket, a taxi ride, a hotel room. He slid the money back underneath the pillow, lay back, and closed his eyes. If only Kojak hadn't been so unreasonable. If he had only given him more time. He inflated his jaws and blew the air out of his lungs. It was probably common knowledge by now, Papa World's boy had killed somebody. No one was surprised. They all knew that he would, sooner or later. He was rotten just like his no-good daddy. How many times had he heard his own mother say so? He buried his face in the palms of his hands and slowly massaged his eyelids with the tips of his fingers. He was sure that the police were still watching his house. Undoubtedly they knew by now that he had fled.

Suddenly he heard a soft, steady tap on his hotel door. Startled, he sat upright. Who could that be? No one knew he was here. Maybe the police had tracked him down. He eased out of bed, tiptoed to the table, and stepped into his pants. The knock came again. He fastened his pants, leaned against the door, and looked through the peephole. It was a woman, a young, beautiful, sexy woman. He quickly clicked on the light and opened the door.

"You want some company?"

He looked at her with wide, lustful eyes.

"How much?"

She smiled, walked in, sat on his bed, leaned back, and crossed her legs. The slit in the side of her long blue dress opened, exposing her large, shapely thigh.

"What's your name, sugar?" she asked.

D'Ray closed the door and composed himself.

"André," he lied. "What's yours?"

"Folks call me Peaches," she said, slowly licking her top lip with the tip of her tongue and gently caressing the inside of her naked thigh with her hand.

"Why?" D'Ray asked.

She answered his question with one of her own. "You ever ate a peach?"

"Yeah."

"How it taste?"

D'Ray hesitated, thinking.

"Sweet," he said.

"And?" she asked.

"Juicy," he said.

"And?" she asked.

"Delicious," he said.

She leaned forward, smiling.

"Any more questions?"

D'Ray stared at her, imagining himself holding her, caressing her, kissing her.

"How much are your peaches?"

She smiled coyly and looked around the room.

"I saw you when you came in this morning."

"You did?" D'Ray asked, surprised.

"Yeah. A fine, young, good-looking black man traveling light and traveling alone." She paused. "What brings you to Jackson?"

"Just passing through."

"Job related?" she asked.

"Something like that," D'Ray replied.

"What kind of work you do?"

Suddenly D'Ray understood. She was trying to figure out how much money he had.

"Little of this, little of that."

She smiled and patted a spot on the bed. D'Ray crossed the room and sat next to her. She reached over and began to gently massage the back of his hand.

"You ever had company before?" she asked.

Her question caught him off guard.

"Plenty," he answered deceptively.

"Then you know."

"Know what?"

"Good company ain't cheap."

D'Ray looked at her.

"How much?" D'Ray asked a second time.

She reached over and began gently massaging the side of his face with her hand.

"What do you want to do to me?" she whispered seductively.

D'Ray could feel his body react.

"Be good to you," he whispered.

She removed her hand from the side of his face and began to move the tip of her finger slowly across his top lip.

"Do you think I'm pretty?"

"Yes," D'Ray said.

"Do you think I'm sexy?"

"Very."

She leaned back and placed her hand on the bed behind her. The thin strap of her dress slowly fell off her shoulder and slid down her arm.

"Do you like me?"

"Yes."

"What do you like most?"

D'Ray lowered his eyes, staring.

"Your thighs."

She sat up straight, slipped her arms through the straps, and let her dress fall about her waist. D'Ray watched wide-eyed as she arched her back and began fondling her large, full breasts.

"Don't you like my breasts?"

D'Ray could feel the blood rush to his head. He reached over and gently ran his finger across the tip of her right breast. Instantly he could feel her nipple responding to his touch.

"Oooh." She let out a sensuous moan. "That feels so good."

Encouraged, D'Ray removed his finger, leaned forward, and touched her with the tip of his tongue. She closed her eyes, tilted her head back, and clutched his shoulders.

"Please don't stop," she whispered.

"I want you," D'Ray responded.

"I'm all yours, baby."

D'Ray dropped to his knees, placed his fingers in the waist of her dress, and pulled. She gently clutched his wrist and looked deep into his eyes.

"Baby, business before pleasure."

He looked up at her.

"How much?"

"Fifty dollars and I'm at your mercy."

"Fifty dollars!" D'Ray exclaimed. "Baby I just want to rent it, I don't want to buy it."

"Fifty dollars," she moaned seductively. "And worth every penny."

D'Ray raised to his feet, reached under the pillow, removed the money, and placed it on the nightstand.

"You'll get your pay after we play."

Without speaking, she rose to her feet, stepped out of her dress, removed her underwear, and gently pushed D'Ray across the bed. As he lay looking up at her, she climbed onto the bed, straddled his body, and whispered: "Alright, baby, let's play."

As he lay pinned beneath the weight of her body, listening to her soft, seductive moans and feeling the slow, titillating roll of her hips against his groin, his world had been made perfect. It was as if all of his fears and anxieties had been drowned in the depths of her passion. He placed his hands about her waist, gently pressing his fingers against her soft, smooth skin while holding her body tight against his own. He desperately needed to touch her, to see her, to hear her, in order to convince himself that she was real. Last night, as he had lain in a strange bed in a strange town, comforted only by the familiar sounds of two faceless people enjoying each other's company in the adjacent room, he had struggled with the reality of his situation. Then, it had all seemed like a bad dream from which he would awaken at any moment. But now, the pleasure and the passion that she was arousing in him was all the confirmation that he needed. His situation was real; he was very much alone. For the second time since he had left the only home that he had ever known, a stranger had entered his life giving him temporary relief from the horror and fear that was now so much a part of him. As he thought of the old lady on the bus and the sinking feeling that swept his body when she departed, he was overcome by a strong desire to hold on to Peaches, to make their time together last. He closed his eyes and fought against the passion that he felt rising within himself. Mentally he wanted to slow the moment down. But with each sway of her body he could feel his own response until he could no longer control his movements. Soon, his mouth was opened wide, panting. His fingers were digging into her skin; his shoulders were bouncing off the bed. Then, with a violent shudder of the hips, and a loud, orgiastic scream, it was over.

Peaches collapsed forward, exhausted. He placed his arms around the small of her back and drew her close. He could feel her chest rising and falling as she struggled to gain control over her breathing. Through the window he could see the tiny rays of sunlight shining through the plain, coarse curtain. Outside was the strange, uncertain world that he dreaded facing. He loosened his grip and began to gently run his finger through Peaches's long, silky hair. Her presence calmed him. As she moved her head with the motion of his hand, he raised his mouth to her ear and softly whispered, "Stay awhile."

"I can't," she said softly.

"Just to talk," he pleaded.

"I can't," she repeated herself.

D'Ray watched her roll out of bed, put on her dress, and step into her panties. He hated her for rejecting him and he hated himself for needing her. How had he allowed himself to sink so low as to plead with a prostitute? He quietly slipped his hand under the pillow and removed the gun and pointed it at Peaches's head.

"You got yo' clothes on, now git on up out of here."

"What?"

"You heard me; git to stepping!"

"Gladly," Peaches said, reaching for the money.

"Leave that alone," D'Ray shouted.

"But it's mine."

"I ain't gone tell you again."

"But you owe me."

"Send me a bill."

"I ain't going nowhere without my money."

"Ain't nobody playing with you."

"OK. I'll stay with you. Just give me my money."

"Woman, you trying to find out what death feel like?"

"I already know."

Her comment stunned him.

"What?"

"Mister, I'm in a bad way."

"You a crackhead, ain't you?"

"Naw! I don't even smoke."

"Then you must be fifty-one, fifty."

"What?"

"You know, loco."

"Ain't nobody crazy."

D'Ray looked at her, puzzled.

"Then what's yo' problem?"

"André, I'm desperate."

D'Ray dropped the gun to his side, averted his face, and burst into a long, loud laugh. Maybe it was the tone in her voice or the strange sound of the name she had called him or the irony of the situation or a combination of the three, but whatever the reason, he couldn't stop laughing.

"Peaches." He called her name while trying to compose himself.

"What?" she answered, confused.

"Why you so desperate?"

"My folks put me out the other night. Everything I own is over there in the alley in a suitcase."

"Suitcase!" D'Ray screamed and fell back on the bed, clutching his stomach, laughing. His body shook, and a single tear fell from the corner of his eye and disappeared underneath his chin.

"I say something funny?"

"Not really."

"Then why you laughing?"

"It's a long story."

"Mister, I just want my money."

"How long you been on the street?"

"Just one night."

"I'm yo' first trick?"

"Second."

"Then you got money."

"Naw, that bastard didn't pay me neither."

D'Ray sat up and looked at her, thinking.

"Y'all got busy over here?"

"Right next door."

"So that was you?"

"Mister, I'm hungry and I ain't got no place to stay. Please give me my money."

"Is he still over there?" D'Ray asked, ignoring her comment.

"I don't know."

"Is he from around here?"

"He didn't say."

"He black or white?"

"White."

"How much he owe you?"

"One hundred."

D'Ray laughed and began to dress.

"I got the discount."

"No, you got the basic package. He wanted extra."

"Come on. Let's go git yo' money."

They exited the room and walked next door. The curtains were still drawn but the light was on. D'Ray placed his ear against the door and listened. He could hear someone moving around. He moved to the side, leaned back against the wall, and motioned for Peaches to knock. She knocked, paused, and knocked again. The chain rattled and the door creaked opened.

"What do you want?"

"My money," Peaches said.

"I told you I'm not going to pay you."

D'Ray sprang in front of the door, pushed his way inside, and jammed the barrel of his gun against the man's temple. "Now that's where you wrong, partner," he said, dragging the man back into the room. "You gone pay."

Peaches followed them inside and closed the door.

"You make one sound and I'm gone blow your brains out," D'Ray warned. His words were cold and hard.

"I won't. Just don't hurt me. Please don't hurt me."

"Just do like I tell you."

"Yessir." The man submitted to D'Ray.

His reaction fired the anger lodged deep within D'Ray, and he had a strong desire to dominate and humiliate the man. The tables were turned; the oppressor was now at the mercy of the oppressed. When D'Ray slid his hand in the man's back pocket to remove his wallet, he could feel the man's leg trembling.

"Yo' name Gene Washington?"

"Yes."

"What?"

"Yessir."

"That's better, Gene." D'Ray's voice was filled with mocked paternalism. "I'm so happy to make your acquaintance, Gene." He paused. "Gene, you happy to meet me?"

"Yessir."

"That's good, Gene. Real good."

D'Ray continued to thumb through the wallet. "This must be your wife." D'Ray reached the wallet over Gene's shoulder so that they both could see the picture. Gene glanced at the picture.

"Yessir," he mumbled.

"She ain't bad, Gene. Ain't bad at all." D'Ray studied the picture. "Got a nice set of hooters too. Huh, Gene?"

D'Ray paused, watching the back of Gene's neck flush red with anger. "What's wrong, Gene? She ain't puttin' out?" He paused again, but Gene didn't answer. "Don't you hear me talkin' to you, Gene?"

"Yessir."

"Yessir she is, or yessir she ain't?"

"Yessir, she is."

"How often you git it, Gene?"

"That's personal," Gene mumbled through clenched teeth.

D'Ray pulled the cock back on the pistol.

"You ready to die, Gene?"

"Please. Don't hurt me."

"How often you git it, Gene?"

"Couple of times a week."

"That ain't bad, Gene. D'Ray paused. "I don't understand, Gene. What's the problem? Don't git me wrong. We appreciate your business, but what's the problem?"

"There's no problem."

"Aw, you just like nigguh meat, don't you, Gene?"

D'Ray felt Gene cringe.

"Like a hog like slop?" Peaches interjected.

"What you say, Gene?"

"Mister, I don't talk like that."

"Like what?"

"Use the N-word."

"You ain't never said the word 'nigger'?"

"Never."

"You's a good ole boy, ain't you, Gene?"

"I got black friends."

"They the ones got you hooked on nigger meat?"

"Sir, I'm not hooked on anything."

"But you do like nigger meat?"

"I like all women the same."

"You had big fun last night, didn't you, Gene?"

"Yessir."

"Y'all kept up just some racket last night."

"Sorry, sir."

D'Ray held the picture of his wife up again.

"Do your wife holler like that when y'all doing it?"

"No sir," Gene whispered.

"What she do?" D'Ray asked. "Just lay there?"

"Sir, please. Just take the money and let me go."

"You telling me to shut up, Gene?"

"No sir."

"Good. I wouldn't advise that. No sir, I wouldn't advise that at all. I'm just curious, Gene, that's all. They tell me white women just lay there. I was just wondering if it was true. Is it true, Gene?"

"I don't know."

"Yo' old lady sho' got some fine, smooth-looking legs," D'Ray said, drawing attention back to the picture. As he talked, he moved his thumb back and forth across the picture, finally letting it rest on the woman's crotch. "Wonder do they feel as soft as they look." He paused. "Huh, Gene? Do they?"

Gene swallowed, closed his eyes, and averted his head. A tear rolled down the side of his face.

"Yessir."

"You a lucky man, Gene, ain't you?"

"Yessir."

D'Ray pulled the wallet to him and examined the currency.

"Wow! Gene. What you do for a living?"

"I'm a businessman."

"Is that a fact?"

"Yessir."

"Must be two or three hundred dollars in here."

"Something like that."

D'Ray turned to Peaches.

"Sweetheart, what he owe you?"

"A hundred dollars."

"Is that right, Gene?"

"Yessir."

"You know it's a little more now, right?"

"Yessir."

"There's the late fee. The collection fee. And of course the carry-ing charges." He paused. You understand the carrying charges, don't you, Gene?"

"No sir."

"That's what you gone pay me for letting you carry yo' sorry self on up out of here, you understand?"

"Yessir."

"According to my calculations, that just about cleans you out," D'Ray said. "To avoid such costly penalties in the future, please pay on time."

"Yessir."

"You still live on Jackson Avenue?"

"Yessir."

"You rent or own?"

"Own."

He reached the wallet back over Gene's shoulder.

"These your children?"

"Yessir."

"Both of them?"

"Yessir."

"You love them?"

"More than life itself."

"You know, I would hate to see anything happen to them or the little lady. You know what I mean?"

"Please, don't bother my family."

"Gene, I tell you what. You don't mess with me, I won't mess with you. Is that a deal?"

"Yessir."

He slid the wallet back in Gene's pocket and walked into the far corner of the room, face first. "Now, Gene, we gone have to go. I want you to know that I really enjoyed spending a little time with you. Now this is what I want you to do. Close your eyes and count to a hundred real slow. When you finish, git your things and git out of here. If you're smart, you'll forget the whole thing. If you cause me or any of my girls any trouble, I promise you, I'll kill you. Now, you have a blessed day, you hear?"

When they made it back to the room, D'Ray stood in the window and watched Gene get in his car and speed away. Then he crossed the room, stretched out on the bed, and stared at the ceiling.

"Peaches."

"Yeah, André."

"You can stay here with me from now on."

"For how long?"

"As long as I say."

"I thought you was just passing through."

"What just happened changed thangs. You understand?"

"Yeah, I understand."

"Just so that you do."

# CHAPTER NINE

D'Ray SPENT THE REST OF THE DAY SHOPPING FOR A CHANGE OF CLOTHES AND OTHER NECESSITIES IN THE LOCAL thrift shop. He was frugal, for he needed to save enough money to leave town as soon as possible. He was lucky that he had met Peaches. Now, not only could he make money and still lie low until he was able to leave town, but he also had a companion and a guide. It was something about her. Maybe it was her soft, sexy voice or her cheerful, childlike disposition or her unmistakable eagerness to please him. Whatever it was, its impact was such that he had to constantly tell himself, Don't like her too much. She was simply a means to an end. Her love, regardless of how sweet, how juicy, how delicious, was not for keeps but for sale. He wanted to be cold and distant with her, keep theirs strictly a business relationship. But she kept getting in the way. She kept looking at him softly and lovingly with those big, beautiful brown eyes. She kept doing for him. She kept selling herself and giving him all the fruits of her labor. She kept shopping for him. Cleaning for him. And she bought him things. Not big things but little, thoughtful things. Sweet treats to eat. A stylish shirt or a pair of pants that she had noticed on sale. A girlie magazine. A cold drink on a particularly hot day. And those notes. She was always leaving notes. Under the pillow. In his shoes. In the bathroom cabinet. Just-thinking-about-you notes. I-missed-you-today notes. And yes, I-love-you notes.

Maybe that's why he was so angry when she returned all battered and bruised. He told himself it was because someone had the audacity to shake down his girl. This was business, not personal. He had to protect her in order to protect his interest. But when he stormed out of the room, looking for the perpetrator, he knew in his heart that he was angry because someone had harmed her, not because someone had stolen from him. Somewhere, somehow, he had allowed himself to feel for her what a man feels for a woman. It didn't make sense and he knew it. But somehow, someway, it had happened.

When he found the man sitting in the alley behind the old mom-and-pop store drinking a can of beer, he still had her money in his pocket and her blood splattered on his clothes. They hadn't talked long before he knew. It was the cold look in the man's eyes. It was the way he held his body, real relaxed in what was a very tense situation. It was the slow, deliberate manner in which he rose to his feet. It was the speed with which he admitted beating her down and taking her money. It was the unspoken addendum, Yeah I did it, now what you gone do about it?

The man knew that she was D'Ray's girl, but he didn't care. He didn't respect him. That's when D'Ray knew. It didn't matter who saw him. In fact, it would be better if someone did. He had to send a strong, clear message. The price for crossing him was death. He had no choice. Before Peaches could do her job, he had to do his. D'Ray pulled his gun, but he never intended to fire it. The noise would alert the store owner. He simply pulled it to get the man's attention, to make him hand over that which he had taken from Peaches. He used it to make him kneel against the wall of the store, face first. He used it to make the man remain silent while he removed the short steel rod from the trash bin and bashed in his skull.

When he killed him, he didn't know who he was, nor did he care. He was simply dealing with someone who had wronged him. He didn't know his reputation. He didn't know how others feared him. He didn't know how dangerous or how ruthless he was. Had he known, maybe he wouldn't have gone after him. After all, no one else had. But in his moment of anger, he slew the mighty Goliath. And because he had, people were talking. They didn't know him. Most had never and would never see him. But they knew he was the killer and they knew why he had killed. Peaches saw to that. And because they knew, they feared him. And because people feared him, women who lived by selling themselves sought him out. They needed a protector. The day he killed Breeze he had one woman, Peaches. Two days later he had five.

He wasn't happy that he had killed again, but he didn't regret it either. Unlike the boy in the store, Breeze deserved to die. He had been a predator who had simply stalked the wrong prey. He had attacked D'Ray by attacking Peaches; D'Ray had simply defended himself by defending her. No, he didn't regret what he had done, but he did regret the attention. He was getting too big, and things were moving too fast. There were too many women, too many johns, and too much activity. He lay beside Peaches listening to the sound of her heavy breathing. He couldn't sleep. Instinctively he knew it was time to go. He had been thinking about leaving ever since the killing, two weeks ago. But each day he talked himself into staying a little while longer. With five women working and more money coming in than he could have ever anticipated, it was difficult to just leave. But now there was something in the air warning him that Jackson was no longer safe.

Finally convinced that now was the time, he crawled out of bed, pried opened the floorboard, and removed the glass jar containing the money that he had collected from the girls. It was dark. Not too dark to see how to get the money, but too dark to count it. He moved over to the table near the window, clicked on the light, and took a seat. As he slowly removed the money from the jar, he made plans. As soon as it was daylight, he would go buy a car. He had seen one parked in a yard not too far from the hotel. According to the sign in the window, the owner was asking fifteen hundred, but he was sure that he could get it for a thousand. Once he had a car he could leave. But where would he go? Chicago? The thought rose from nowhere. No, he had people there. His aunt Peggy. If she discovered him, she would tell his mother, and if she told his mother, she would tell Sonny, and if she told Sonny, he would turn him in or advise her to. That's the kind of man that Sonny was. An Uncle Tom cop who would do anything to prove to white folks that he was a good Negro.

It was a long time since he had thought about his family. But now there bloomed in his mind a memory of the day that he left. His watching the police watching his house, all the time longing to catch one last glimpse of his mother's face or to hear one last time the sound of his brother's voice. The thought of his people troubled him. It was as though something was affirming in him that it was indeed time to go. Detroit. The thought came to him suddenly. Motown. He had never been there, but it was just as good a place as anywhere else.

Detroit it was. His mind was made up. He would buy the car and go to Detroit. He began to focus on the pile of money lying on the table. The total should have been a little more than $6,000. He began counting the money, then paused. Where was Detroit? He should know, but he didn't. He would have to get a map. What else would he need?

When he leaned back to contemplate the answer, he accidentally knocked the jar off the table. Instantly he looked over toward the bed. Peaches had risen to a sitting position and was looking directly at him.

"Honey," she yawned, "what you doing?"

"Nothing," D'Ray said offhandedly. "Go'n back to sleep."

He reached down and picked up the jar. It wasn't broken in two, but it was cracked. He placed the jar on the table in front of him and looked over at Peaches. He loved her. He had known it was true for some time, but he had never been able to admit it to himself. She calmed him and made him feel that everything was going to be all right. She made him dream about tomorrow. For him, starting over wasn't such a frightening thought if his new beginning included her. He knew what she was but it didn't matter. Like him, she had only done what fate had forced her to do. She was a good person caught up in a bad situation.

When he went to look at the car the next day, he didn't take any money with him. He wanted to give the owner the impression that he was just passing by and happened to see the *For Sale* sign in the window. He wasn't looking to buy, but he was willing if the price was right. Like most of the boys in Brownsville, he had been tinkering around under the hood of cars long before he could legally drive them. When he popped the hood and started the car, he knew by the quiet, steady hum that the car had been well maintained. He checked the odometer. The mileage was reasonable for a car of that age. He made several inquiries: Did the car use much oil? Had it ever been in an accident? What kind of gas mileage did it get? Had anyone else ever owned it? Then he test-drove it. Satisfied with the car's history and performance, he asked for the best offer. The owner wanted fifteen but said he would let it go for fourteen. D'Ray countered with nine. They settled for twelve.

As he made his way back to the hotel, he made plans to leave. He would wait until just after dark to pick up the car. That way, if anyone saw him, they would have a difficult time making out the color or make of the car. In the meantime, he would stop by the store and pick up a road map. When he made it back to the hotel, he would pack, map out the route, and talk to Peaches. He had never discussed his plans with her for fear that she would say the wrong thing to the wrong person.

When he turned the corner to the hotel, he saw them. Stunned, he stopped and ducked behind the building. He took a deep breath, composed himself, and peeped. Peaches was spread-eagled against the car with her hands cuffed behind her back. He pulled his head back, thinking. Were they after her, or him? He looked again. There were too many policemen. They wouldn't send three cars after a hooker. He could feel his heart pounding. He turned to leave, then stopped. The money. All of the money was in the hotel room. He looked a third time. Several of them had gathered around Peaches. She was crying and shaking her head from side to side. The door of his hotel room was open. They were searching his room. What were they looking for? Maybe they had tracked him down. He had to leave.

He turned and slowly walked back in the direction from which he came. He wanted to run, but knew better. He would only draw attention to himself. He decided to avoid the street. He turned to leave, then paused. In the distance, he saw the bus coming. He ran his hand into his pocket, removed some coins, and hurried to the bus stop. When the bus arrived, he didn't check the number or the destination. He simply boarded, dropped the fare in the box, and found a seat near the back. He wondered if they had gotten Peaches to talk. Even if they did, what could she tell them? She didn't even know his name.

He stayed on the bus until the driver yelled, "Last stop!" When he stepped from the bus, he had no idea where he was. He knew they had passed downtown Jackson and that it had taken approximately forty-five minutes to reach their destination. He followed the main street to the first intersection, then turned onto the side street. As he walked, he looked for clues that would tell him where he was. He was in a residential area, but was the neighborhood black, or white? The farther he walked, the more uneasy he became. The houses were too large and the lawns were too nice. This had to be a white neighborhood. He stopped, petrified. His eyes fell on the neighborhood-watch sign displayed in one of the large bay windows. Maybe someone had already called the police. How would he be able to explain being in a white neighborhood after dark on a Sunday night? He was about to turn back when he heard a familiar sound. He paused, listening. "Amazing Grace." He recognized the tune. He relaxed and walked toward the music.

He followed the street to the intersection. To his right, one block away, he could see the church's steeple. He decided to go inside. He had no desire to pray. He wasn't even sure that he believed in God. But if the police were trying to find him, church would be the last place they would look.

He entered the building, took a seat near the back, and tuned everything out. He wondered if they had found the money. Surely Peaches hadn't shown them where it was hidden. He buried his face in his hands and sighed. He needed to leave town tonight, but how could he? He ran his fingers across the hotel key in his pocket. Maybe he could go back, sneak into the hotel room, and retrieve the money. No. They were probably watching his room. He had to wait a few days. But where could he stay?

He was pondering that question when he suddenly became aware of the preacher's powerful voice. "Come unto me, all ye who are heavy laden, and I will give you rest." D'Ray leaned back into the hard wooden bench. The preacher had given him the answer. He waited patiently for church to end. Then he remained seated as the reverend positioned himself in the door and bid each member of the congregation good night. When the last person had exited the church, D'Ray approached the preacher.

"Reverend, did you mean what you said?"

The preacher looked at him and smiled warmly. "If I said it, I meant it."

"Well, sir, I am heavy laden and in need of rest."

The preacher placed his arms about D'Ray's shoulder. "What's troubling you?"

"I'm a alcoholic."

The preacher looked at him, stunned. "Son, how old are you?"

"Nineteen," D'Ray lied.

"How long you been drinking?"

"Since Mama and Papa died."

"Your parents dead?"

"Yessir."

"My Lawd."

"Sir, I'm at my wit's end."

"Son, let's go on back in my office and talk," the reverend said, pulling the door closed behind him.

D'Ray followed him into the chapel and through a door at the front of the room. As he walked, D'Ray tried to piece together a story in his mind. If he wanted the preacher to help him, he would have to move him. He would have to convince him that he was a lowly sinner seeking salvation from the throes of this wicked world. He had to appeal to his Christian compassion.

He entered the office and stood near the door while the preacher removed his robe and hung it on the coatrack in the corner behind his desk. He unbuttoned his suit jacket, loosened his tie, and took a seat.

"Please, have a seat." The reverend pointed to the chair positioned closest to his desk.

"Thank you, sir," D'Ray said softly.

"How long your parents been dead?"

"Two years last month," D'Ray said with downcast eyes.

"What happened to 'em?"

"Cancer," he said, making up the story as he went along. "I was with them when they died."

"They died at home?"

"Yessir. When the doctors said there wasn't nothing else they could do, my grandmama wanted me to put 'em in a home. But I wouldn't. I know she thought I wouldn't be able to handle 'em all by myself. But Mama and Papa hated that nursing home."

"So, you took care of them all by yourself?"

"For the most part." He paused to let the preacher absorb the full effect of the idea. He could tell by the preacher's reaction that he was getting to him. "A nurse came by every other day to make sure that everything was alright, and then an aide came by every morning to give 'em a bath. But other than that, it was just me."

"What about your relatives?"

"Didn't have but one or two close by," D'Ray told him. "And they were old or sick themself."

"No brothers or sisters?"

"No sir."

"My Lawd." The preacher sighed and leaned back in his chair. D'Ray decided to milk the moment.

"I guess that's why I took it so hard. They were really the only close family that I had. Seem like when they died, I died."

"Well, that's understandable," the preacher sympathized.

"They died on the same day," D'Ray continued.

"Is that right?" the preacher asked in disbelief.

"Yessir," D'Ray replied. "Papa died first."

"God bless his soul," the preacher mumbled softly.

"I don't know exactly when he died. I heard a strange rattling noise. Sound like it came from Mama's room. But I was so used to checking on Papa first that when I got up, I just went to his room. I don't know why, I just did."

"Old habits are hard to break," the preacher explained.

"When I went in, I bent over and kissed him on the forehead like I always did. Soon as I kissed him, I knew. He was so cold." D'Ray paused, took a deep breath, and closed his eyes. "I didn't want to believe it, so I put my head on his chest and listened. When I didn't hear his heart beating, the first thing I thought about was Mama. I didn't want her to know. I just didn't think she would be able to handle it. So I pulled the sheet over his head and went to Mama's room. When I sat next to her bed, she took my hand, smiled, and said, 'Everything is gone be alright.' Then she closed her eyes and left here." D'Ray paused and looked at the preacher. "Reverend, do you think she knew?"

"Possibly."

"But how?"

"I don't know, son."

"You think she could see it in my face?"

"Maybe."

"Then it was my fault?"

"No."

"I knew she couldn't take that kind of news."

"Son, you can't blame yourself."

"Maybe I shouldn't have gone in there so fast."

"No."

"I should have pulled myself together first."

"Son."

"But I wasn't crying. How did she know? I wasn't crying."

"Son."

"How, Reverend? How did she know?" D'Ray closed his eyes and began to sob heavily. Crying wasn't difficult. He simply thought about his situation. "I didn't say anything, Reverend." He continued the charade. "I didn't say anything at all."

The reverend moved around the desk and took D'Ray in his arms. Slowly he began to rock him back and forth, whispering softly: "It's alright, son. It's alright."

"I didn't say anything, Reverend," D'Ray mumbled, his voice shaking. "I swear I didn't say anything."

"I know you didn't, son," the preacher said, gently patting D'Ray's back. "It was just her time, that's all. It was just her time."

Suddenly D'Ray pulled away and took a deep breath.

"I'm sorry, Reverend."

"Nothing to be sorry about."

D'Ray rose and walked to the corner of the room.

"I don't know what came over me."

"You just allowing yourself to feel, that's all."

D'Ray cupped his hands over his face, inflated his jaws, and exhaled. "That has never happened to me before."

"Good that it finally did."

"Sir?"

"It's a good sign."

"Sir?"

"That everything's gone be OK."

"Sir?"

The preacher laughed softly.

"Son, you got to cry before you heal."

"I guess."

"Aw, don't be ashamed. Even Jesus wept."

"Reverend."

"Yes."

"Some folks say Mama just didn't want to live without Papa." D'Ray paused and looked the preacher in the eye. "Reverend, is that so?"

"It could be."

The reverend moved back behind the desk, removed a tissue from the drawer, and handed it to D'Ray. He took it, wiped his eyes, and sat down.

"Everybody say it was romantic the way the end came," he said softly. "To them it was like a love story. But I just couldn't see it like that."

"Why not?"

"Guess I was just too close to it."

"So how did you see it?"

"Just that my parents were dead and I was all by myself. Reverend, I ain't never felt so lonely in all my life as I did the day they died."

"You still feel that way?"

"Yessir."

"That's why you took to drinking?"

"Reverend, I just want to feel better or not feel at all. Soon as that funeral was over, I got a hold of some liquor and I didn't stop dranking until I was too drunk to drank anymore. And Reverend, I been on the bottle ever since."

"Drinking still makes you feel good?"

"It makes me feel nothing."

"Is that good?"

"I thought so for a while."

"But not anymore?"

"No sir."

"Why not?"

"It cost too much."

"Money."

"No sir. Everything."

"What do you mean?"

"When I started dranking, I stopped living."

"I don't understand."

"I just started living from one drank to the other."

"Oh, I see."

"I quit school and just started walking the streets." He paused and smiled. "You know I was gone go to college."

"Really."

"Yessir," D'Ray replied deceitfully. "Actually went for a semester."

"What happened?"

"Mama and Papa got sick."

"That's when you quit?"

"No sir. I just took a semester off. They wouldn't let me quit."

"But you never went back?"

"No sir. They died during the summer. That's when I took to the streets."

"You from Jackson?"

"No sir, Texas."

"How did you end up in Jackson?"

"Well, after a while them streets in Texas just got too familiar. Everywhere I turned I saw something that reminded me of my folks. After a while I just couldn't take it no more. So I started hitchhiking."

"How did you live?"

"From hand to mouth. Begging and piddling."

"That's no life."

"Most of the time I was drunk. So what did it matter?"

"How did you end up at Mount Calvary?"

"To be honest, Reverend, I don't know why I came in here tonight. I was just walking and before I knew it, I was inside. I ain't never talked to no preacher before and I wasn't planning on talking to you. But when you said that you could give me rest I knew I had to talk to you." D'Ray slid to the edge of his seat and leaned on the desk. "Please help me, Reverend. I don't want to drank no more."

The reverend reached over and took D'Ray's hand.

"Son, do you believe in the power of God?"

"I want to believe, Reverend," D'Ray told him. "I really do. But I just don't know."

"Seek and ye shall find."

"I'm seeking, Reverend."

"Knock and he will answer."

"I'm knocking, Reverend."

"Son, he will deliver you."

"I wish I could believe that."

"You can."

"How, Reverend?"

"With faith."

"Faith!"

"Yes, the faith of a mustard seed."

"I don't know, Reverend."

"Son, Jesus loves you."

"If he loves me, why he take my folks from me?"

"No man knows the Master's plan. But you can be sure that he has a plan for you."

"For me?"

"Yes, he sent you in here tonight."

"Who?"

"The Lord."

"The Lord!"

"Oh, he works in mysterious ways."

"Sir?"

"Of all the churches in Jackson, he sent you to mine."

"Sir?"

"Son, my ministry caters to the youth."

"So, you can help me?"

"If the Lord say the same."

"Reverend, are you serious?"

"Have you heard of American Teen Challenge?"

"No sir."

"It's a church-sponsored rehabilitation center set up to help teens deal with drug, alcohol, and behavior problems."

"Reverend, I ain't got no money."

"The program is free."

"Free!"

"Yes, but you will have to pay your fare there."

"Where?"

"The first four months in Hot Springs, Arkansas, and the last ten months in Cape Girardeau, Missouri."

"Fourteen months!"

"That's right. Is that a problem?"

"No sir."

"Now, I have to warn you. It's a very strict, demanding program. It's no picnic."

"Sir, I don't expect it to be."

"So, you're interested?"

"Yessir."

"Good. I'll give them a call first thing in the morning to get the ball rolling. It takes a few days to get everything in order. I'll also talk to the deacon board about assisting you with your fare."

"Thank you, Reverend."

"Don't mention it." He paused. "Do you need someplace to stay while you wait?"

"Yessir."

"OK. I know just the place." The preacher reached for the phone, then hesitated. "I don't even know your name."

"Damien," D'Ray lied. "Damien McDaniel."

D'Ray sat quietly watching as the reverend lifted the receiver. He called a woman. By the way he spoke to her, she was an older woman. Somebody named Ms. Dorothy. He told her he had a young fellow who needed a place to stay until he could get him into the teen program. "No," D'Ray heard him say, "he's not dangerous, just has a little problem with alcohol. No ma'am, he's from Texas. Yes ma'am, that's right. No ma'am, they both passed a couple of years ago. Cancer."

D'Ray smiled as he heard the preacher repeating the embellished story. He had convinced him. He would stay with the old lady for a couple of days. Then he would go back to the hotel, get the money, buy the car, and go to Detroit.

When they arrived at the house the preacher pulled to the shoulder and stopped.

"This is it," the preacher told him.

"Yessir," D'Ray said softly.

The preacher turned and looked at him. "You nervous?" he asked.

"Yessir. A little bit."

"Don't be. Ms. Dorothy is good people."

"She live by herself?"

"Yes and no."

"Sir?"

"She takes in people like you."

"Like me?"

"Young people who need a place to stay."

"Why?"

"Just out of the goodness of her heart."

"I hope she likes me."

"Don't worry," the preacher reassured him. "She will."

Just as they mounted the steps, the porch light flashed on and the door flung open. A gray-haired heavyset woman greeted them with a smile.

"Reverend, I thought I heard your car door shut," she said jovially. "Is this the young man you was telling me about?"

"This is him."

She looked at D'Ray. "What's your name, sugar?"

"Damien McDaniel, ma'am."

"Well, it's good to meet you, Damien," she said, extending her hand to him. "Folks 'round here just call me Ms. Dorothy." She pushed the door open wider and stepped to the side. "You men come on in."

They followed her down the hallway and into a spacious living room. A young girl was lying on the sofa watching television. When they entered the room, she leapt to her feet, raced to the reverend, and fell into his arms. D'Ray stared at her. He couldn't tell if she was black or white.

"I want you to meet somebody," the reverend told her. They turned and faced D'Ray. "Sparkle, this is Damien."

"Hi," D'Ray said shyly.

"Hi," she responded in kind.

"He gone be staying with us for a few days," Ms. Dorothy informed her.

"Yes ma'am," Sparkle answered.

Ms. Dorothy looked at D'Ray.

"Honey, you hungry?"

D'Ray started to answer, then hesitated.

"You ain't shy, is you?" Ms. Dorothy teased.

"No ma'am," D'Ray said, then lowered his eyes.

"Sparkle, take him in the kitchen and fix him a plate," Ms. Dorothy instructed.

"Yes ma'am," Sparkle said. She turned to the preacher. "Reverend, you want me to fix you one too?" she asked.

"No thank you, sugar. I'm gone have to make it on home."

She smiled and turned to D'Ray.

"Come on. The kitchen this way."

# CHAPTER TEN

The house WAS A LARGE WHITE TWO-STORY PLANTATION-STYLE HOME. D'RAY'S room was on the second floor, directly off the stairs. It was a spacious room beautifully decorated with old, well-preserved French Provincial furniture. Fully dressed, D'Ray stretched out on the large comfortable bed but did not sleep. He tossed the entire night, contemplating his next move. He resolved that he would return to the hotel, retrieve his money, and resume his original plan. His mind cautioned him to wait, but instinct warned him that the dangers he sought to elude were nearby. The preacher worried him. He was a good man with honorable intentions; but in order to help D'Ray, he would require more information: a birth certificate, a social security card, a high school diploma, some official documentation verifying his identity. There would be registration forms to fill out and in-depth interviews. Yes, there would be more questions requiring answers that he could not afford to give. That thought made him uneasy. He slid off the bed, moved to the window, and pulled back the curtain. The sun had risen. He raised the window and poked his head out, measuring the distance to the ground. Suddenly he heard a knock. Startled, he pulled back inside. The door opened and Sparkle entered. She looked at the neatly made bed and then at him. He was fully dressed, including his shoes.

"Breakfast ready," she said dryly.

"Alright," he answered quickly. Almost too quickly. He didn't want to seem nervous. He moved away from the window, careful to avoid looking in her direction but sensing her eyes upon him. He glanced at her, then lowered his eyes. Yes, she was still staring. "Is something wrong?" he asked.

"Did you go to bed last night?"

"Yeah."

"What time you get up?"

"Early."

"How early?"

"Real early."

She parted her lips to say something else, but instead turned and left the room. After the door closed, he stood motionless, listening to the sound of her house slippers sliding across the hardwood floor. He could tell that she was suspicious of him. No, she didn't say it, but it was evident by the way she looked at him and by the short, terse manner in which she spoke.

By the time he made it to the dining room, Ms. Dorothy, Sparkle, and three other young women were already sitting at the table eating. As he approached, Ms. Dorothy spoke first.

"Come sit right here by me."

"Yes ma'am." D'Ray slid the chair back and sat down.

"How did you sleep?" Ms. Dorothy wanted to know.

"Fine," D'Ray answered. Sparkle looked at him with a long, cold stare. Instinctively, D'Ray averted his eyes.

"Let me introduce you to everybody," Ms. Dorothy said eagerly. "You met Sparkle last night, remember?"

"Yes ma'am," D'Ray said, forcing a faint smile.

"Well, that's Veronica," Ms. Dorothy said, looking at the young lady sitting at the far end of the table. "Next to her is Kathy, and across from Kathy is Sarah. "Y'all say good morning to Damien."

"Good morning." The voices blended in perfect unison. D'Ray smiled, nodded his acknowledgment, then lowered his eyes.

"Lord, I still believe you call yourself shy," Ms. Dorothy teased him.

"No ma'am," D'Ray corrected her. "Just quiet."

"It's those quiet, sneaky ones you have to watch." Sparkle spoke up.

"Quiet and sneaky is two different things," Ms. Dorothy explained. "No, this one ain't sneaky quiet, he shy quiet. Look at him sitting there blushing. God bless his little heart."

Embarrassed, D'Ray began to fill his plate with food.

"How long you gone be with us?" the girl Ms. Dorothy had identified as Veronica asked.

"I don't know exactly," D'Ray told her.

"A few days," Ms. Dorothy answered for him. "Just until Reverend Sims can get him in the program."

D'Ray looked at her wide-eyed.

"Aw, don't be embarrassed," Ms. Dorothy said warmly. "Everybody in here has one type of problem or another. We don't hide that from each other and we don't make a big deal out of it."

"Yeah, I been in that same program," Kathy confessed.

"Me too," Veronica echoed.

"I guess you kind of scared?" Kathy said. "Lord knows I was."

"A little bit." D'Ray played along.

"Don't be," Kathy advised. "It's a nice place."

"Good people too," Veronica added. "I made a lot of friends there."

"That's good to know," D'Ray said.

"So, you from Texas?" Sparkle butted in.

"That's right," D'Ray answered.

"What part?" she wanted to know.

"Small town. You probably never heard of it."

"Try me."

"It's close to Dallas," D'Ray was intentionally vague.

"How close?" she pushed him.

"About a hour away."

"Is it east of Dallas or west of Dallas?"

"East." D'Ray arbitrarily picked one.

"So, it's between Shreveport and Dallas?"

"That's right."

"Is it—"

"Sparkle!" Sarah interrupted.

"What?"

"Stop sweating him."

"Whose sweating 'im? I'm just talking to him."

"Talking! Try 'interrogating.' "

Thankful for the temporary reprieve, D'Ray slid his fork underneath the pile of scrambled eggs and lifted them to his mouth, fully conscious of the awkward silence that had engulfed the room.

"Don't pay Sparkle no mind." Ms. Dorothy broke the silence.

"She comes across like a pit bull but she's the biggest little pussycat you ever did see."

"Don't you believe that," Veronica warned, pushing away from the table. "Sparkle is vicious."

"Meaner than a junkyard dog." Sarah seconded the observation.

One by one they left the table until D'Ray, Sparkle, and Ms. Dorothy were the only ones remaining. Two of the girls were in summer school, and the other had a job.

"Baby, what you gone do today?" Ms. Dorothy asked Sparkle.

"Pamper myself," Sparkle said enthusiastically. She was beginning a two-week vacation from work. "First, I'm gone take a long, hot bubble bath. No quick shower this morning." She paused and tilted her head back, smiling. "Then I'm gone go git my hair and nails done. After that, who knows?" She looked at Ms. Dorothy. "Why do you ask?"

"I was wondering if you could do me a little favor sometime today?"

"Of course," she said without hesitation. "Just name it."

"You going downtown?" Ms. Dorothy asked.

"Little farther," Sparkle said. "I'm going to Rene's."

"You think you could stop on the way back for me?"

"Sure. No problem. What you need?"

"I want to buy this child a few things."

Sparkle looked at D'Ray and frowned.

"What kind of things?" she asked.

"Suitcase. A few clothes. You know, just some things to tide him over until he can get on his feet."

"No ma'am," D'Ray interrupted. "I can't let you do that."

"You just try to stop me," Ms. Dorothy said playfully.

"Ms. Dorothy, I'll be alright. I can't take your money."

"You ain't taking it, I'm giving it to you."

"No ma'am, I can't."

"Honey, you don't have a choice."

"I won't."

"Why you want to deny me my blessing?"

"Ma'am?"

"Don't you know that every time you do a good deed, the Lord blesses you?"

"Yes ma'am, I heard that."

"Well, I'm trying to do a good deed, but look to me like you ain't gone rest till you done cheated me out of it. Why is that?"

"Ma'am, I ain't trying to cheat you."

"Well, that's exactly what you doing."

"No ma'am, that's what I'm trying not to do."

"What?"

"I don't want to take advantage of your kindness."

"Well, if that don't beat all."

"You done already done more than enough for me."

"Why don't you let me be the judge of that?"

"Ma'am, I'll be alright."

"You got any more clothes?"

"No ma'am," D'Ray lied.

"You got any toiletries?"

"No ma'am."

"You got any towels or washcloths?"

"No ma'am."

"How you planning on going halfway cross the country with little or nothing?"

"I don't know," D'Ray said, "but I'll figure something out."

"Pride can be a terrible thing," Ms. Dorothy warned.

"I'll manage," he said. "I ain't looking for something for nothing."

"Tell you what. You can pay me back when you get on your feet. Would that be alright?"

"Yes ma'am. If you'll take a IOU."

"Ain't no need for that. Your word's good enough for me."

"Yes ma'am."

"Well that settles that," Ms. Dorothy said, smiling and turning her attention to Sparkle. "Honey, what time can you take him?"

"Why don't I drop him off on the way to the hairdresser and pick him up on the way back?"

"Well, I would hate for you to get out of pocket like that," Ms. Dorothy said, concerned. "What if he need you?"

"I'll be alright," D'Ray assured her.

"How long you think it's gone take Rene to do your hair?"

"No more than two or three hours."

"What's that child gone do all that time?"

The solution to his dilemma pierced his consciousness. He could go to the hotel and retrieve the money while she was at the beauty shop. He spoke up before they decided to alter the plan.

"It'll probably take me that long to find everything."

"You sure?"

"Yes ma'am," D'Ray tried to reassure her. "Couple of hours ain't nothing when you shopping."

"But what if something happens?"

"Ms. Dorothy, how about I give him my pager number?" Sparkle suggested. "That way he can page me if he needs me. Would that make you feel better?"

"A lot."

While Sparkle took her bath, D'Ray helped Ms. Dorothy clear the breakfast dishes. Then the two of them retired to the living room. While they waited, he watched fixated as Ms. Dorothy unbuttoned the top of her blouse, reached into her bosom, and removed an old sock that had been pinned in the cup of her brassiere. She methodically peeled back one sock after another until she had reached the object of her efforts, a small tight roll of money. She counted out $150, handed it to D'Ray, and pinned the rest back inside her bosom. To D'Ray she was the epitome of contradictions, a walking, breathing paradox—a highly complex, urbane woman with all the social graces of the most refined sophisticate, who simultaneously possessed the subtle crudeness normally exhibited by the lowliest commoner. Her unconditional kindness, while appreciated, was deeply disturbing. She had freely bestowed upon him a trust that he had no choice but to violate. As he slid the money into his pocket and uttered what appeared to be a heartfelt thank you, he hated himself.

When Sparkle emerged, he followed her out of the house to the car. After he was inside, he pulled the buckle over his shoulder, snapped it closed, and sank into the softness of the seat, vowing to remain silent. His conversation with her had to be guarded. As she turned the key in the ignition switch, he stared blankly out the window, secretly hoping that she too was void of any desire to engage in trivial chatter with someone she obviously despised.

A hastily depressed accelerator, and the instant pull of the car on the open highway made him cock his head back. He dug his fingers into the seat and braced himself. He glanced at Sparkle out of the corner of his eye. She was gripping the steering wheel with both hands, staring straight ahead, seemingly oblivious to his presence. He focused his eyes on the street, noting the route and looking for familiar markers, anticipating the time that he would have to travel this route solo. They were farther in the country than he had realized. Soon he saw the church. Automatically he began calculating in his mind the distance they had traveled. It was more than a mile, but not quite two. Thoughts of his imminent escape made him imagine what would happen tomorrow. He would sneak out of the house while everyone was sleeping—somewhere around 5 A.M. It shouldn't take more than twenty minutes to arrive at the bus stop. Once there, he would take the early bus to the hotel, walk back to the car owner's house, buy the car, and be on the road before anyone realized that he was gone. There was only one possible problem with his plan—the money. What if the money was missing? "Peaches!" He called her name out loud.

"What?" Sparkle asked, looking directly at him.

"Huh?" He played dumb.

"What did you say?" she asked.

"Aw, nothing," he said, turning his head and looking out the window.

"You said something," she mumbled underneath her breath.

D'Ray ignored her. Downtown Jackson came into view.

"What store you want to go to?" Sparkle asked.

D'Ray hesitated before answering. He wanted to go as close to the hotel as possible.

"Is there a thrift shop around here?"

"Thrift shop?" She repeated his question.

"I don't need nothing fancy." He felt the need to explain.

"Whatever," she said absently.

"Well, is there?"

"It's one a little farther up."

She guided the car off the freeway and down onto a narrow, two-lane highway. D'Ray recognized the street. It was the same one the bus had traveled the previous day. He leaned back, relaxed.

"You ain't fooling me," she said bluntly.

"Ain't trying to," D'Ray responded calmly.

"Oh, you slick now. Cool as a cucumber. Smooth as silk. Got everybody eating out of your hand. Bending over backwards to help the poor orphan boy. But I ain't buying it. I seen your type before."

"My type." D'Ray chuckled. "Woman, you don't know nothing about me."

"Yeah, I know you, alright. You a lying, smooth-talking, good-for-nothing hustler. But if you think you gone hustle Ms. Dorothy, I'm telling you right now, it'll be over my dead body."

"Have I asked that woman for anything?"

"No, but your kind don't operate like that. You conned her into believing that she's giving things to you freely—forcing them on you."

"Maybe you the con artist."

"What?"

"I'm just passing through," D'Ray explained. "Be gone in a couple of days. But what about you? How long you gone keep your feet under Ms. Dorothy's table?"

"You don't know what you talking about."

"You pay rent?" D'Ray's question caught her off guard.

"No, but—"

"This your car, or hers?"

"Hers, but—"

"You pay utilities?"

"No, but—"

"Is she your mama?"

"What?"

"Did she birth you into this world?"

"No, but—"

"But what?"

"But she the only mama I've ever known."

"Aw, she adopted you?"

"No. Not exactly."

"Not exactly." D'Ray laughed. "What kind of con you running?"

"Don't you dare say that to me!"

"Say what?" he asked, hunching his shoulder. "You doing all the talking. I'm just asking a few questions. You like questions, don't you? God knows you ask enough of 'em."

"You turning everything around. Making it sound ugly."

"Ain't you doing that to me?" D'Ray asked. "I don't know how y'all feel about it over here, but in Texas we got a old saying: 'What's good for the goose is good for the gander.' "

"Look, I love Ms. Dorothy."

"I'm sure you do. But that don't give you the right to badmouth me. I'm just a little down on my luck, but that don't make me no

criminal. Girl, you need to check yourself." D'Ray averted his face to
keep from laughing at himself.

"Ms. Dorothy is too trusting."

"Ms. Dorothy is grown."

"Ms. Dorothy is old."

"So, you her guardian angel?"

"I owe her my life."

"Your life!"

"That's right," she said, turning her face toward D'Ray. "My life.
Look at me!" she ordered.

"What?"

"Look at me and tell me what you see."

"Woman, I don't know you."

"I saw how you looked at me last night when you were with the
reverend."

"And how was that?"

"With those curious eyes."

"Woman, what you talking about?"

"Is she black, or is she white? That's what you were thinking."

"You crazy."

"I seen that look all my life."

"Sounds like a personal problem."

"That's why they didn't want me."

"They who?"

"My people."

"Why you telling me this?" D'Ray pretended to be uninterested.

"Because you need to understand."

"Understand what?"

"Ms. Dorothy."

"I'm confused."

"My mama was white and my daddy was black. She was from a
prominent, upper-class family and he was from the hood. Needless
to say, my mama's folks didn't approve of them seeing each other."

"Yeah," D'Ray said, "needless."

"But Mama was in school, so wasn't nothing they could do about
it. Anyway, she fooled around and got pregnant. Grandpapa told her
to have an abortion. But Grandmama wouldn't hear of that. She said
that killing that child was just as wrong as Mama getting pregnant.
Well, Grandmama decided to send Mama away until the baby was

born. She was supposed to go away and have the baby and put it up for adoption, then come on back home and finish school and forget about the whole thing. So that's what she did. She went away. I believe they told everybody that she was gone to study abroad for a year. And she had the baby. But when she came back, she brought the baby, me, with her. When Grandmama questioned her, she said that she was going to give me away just like they had planned. But after she had me and the nurse let her hold me, she just couldn't do it. I was her flesh and blood and she couldn't do it.

"Well, all hell broke loose. Grandpapa went to swearing and cussing and saying that he would die before he allowed a white nigger to live under his roof. Well, they say Mama kept me in the house for three days until Grandpapa said either that baby was going or he was going. Mama wasn't gone let Grandpapa leave Grandmama, so she packed to leave, but Grandpapa told her that if she was grown enough to go against him, then she was grown enough to make it on her own. He wouldn't let her take nothing out of that house that she didn't work and pay for herself, except the clothes on her back. And that's all she had because she hadn't worked a day in her life. Grandmama got in it, but Grandpapa wouldn't back down.

"So, that's when Grandmama called Ms. Dorothy. They had been friends since they were children. Ms. Dorothy's mama had kept house for my grandmama's mama. Everyday when she'd come to work, she'd bring her child, Ms. Dorothy, with her. My grandmama was an only child too. So her and Ms. Dorothy played together. That's how they came to be so close. Ms. Dorothy say that her and Grandmama was so crazy about each other that for the longest time, they thought they were sisters.

"Well, Ms. Dorothy said that she would take the baby, but Mama still wouldn't agree to give me up for adoption. So, to keep the peace, Ms. Dorothy agreed to keep me as long as need be, but not to adopt me. I was still my mama's baby. I was just living with Ms. Dorothy. And of course none of my mama's people would know that I was her child. To this day I don't know how Ms. Dorothy explained me to other folks. The only thing that I can figure is that she was taking in so many kids that most folks just thought that I belonged to one of the runaways.

"Boy, that Ms. Dorothy is something else. From day one, she wouldn't let me call her Mama. I knew my mama. Ms. Dorothy saw to that. She let her come by and visit with me until I was thirteen. Then I told her that I didn't want her to come by no more. I got tired of her slipping around like I was some dirty little secret. I knew it was my grandpapa who had called me that ugly name—white nigger. But after a while, it was Mama who made me feel like that's what I was. So one day I just decided to cut my ties to all white folks, including my mama, and just be a nigger. To me, she wasn't no kin to me no-how. Ms. Dorothy is my mama, even if she won't allow me to say so. She know it, I know it, and my mama know it. I don't need her or none of 'em. What they ever do for me, anyway?" She paused. Her voice was beginning to shake. "That's why you or nobody else ain't gone hurt Ms. Dorothy unless it's over my dead body."

"Touching," D'Ray said sarcastically. "But, sweetheart, just in case you don't know it, we all got a story."

"I ain't your sweetheart," Sparkle snapped.

"Tushhog." D'Ray called her a name.

"And don't you forget it." Her tone was threatening.

"Whatever." D'Ray dismissed her.

She pulled the car to the shoulder and stopped.

"Thrift shop over there," she said, pointing. "Now git out."

"Where?" D'Ray asked, feigning ignorance. This was the same shop he and Peaches had patronized.

"Right there." Sparkle raised her voice. "Can't you see?"

D'Ray leaned forward, staring.

"Oh yeah, I see it."

Sparkled opened her purse, removed a pen, and scribbled a number on a piece of paper.

"Here." She handed him the paper. It was her pager number. "Don't bother me unless it's important." She started to turn away, then paused. "And another thing. I ain't your chauffeur and I ain't your friend, so you better be standing here when I get back, or you can walk back to Ms. Dorothy's house."

"Yes ma'am." D'Ray saluted, threw his head back, and laughed.

"Don't be here when I get back and see if I'm playing."

"You'll wait," D'Ray said with assurance. "Or Ms. Dorothy'll have your high yeller hide."

"Git out!" she screamed. "I mean it. Git out!"

D'Ray slid out of the car, laughing. Not only had he made it within a stone's throw of the hotel, but Sparkle of all people had brought him there. As he watched her speed away, he raised his hand and mockingly waved good-bye, thinking the person who liked him least had unknowingly helped him most.

He ambled toward the hotel, ever conscious of his surroundings. He placed both hands in his pockets and tried to look innocent. He still did not know why the police had gone to his hotel room or even if they were looking for him. But if they were, surely they would not expect to see him leisurely strolling along in broad daylight. When he turned the corner, he sighed, relieved that he had made it onto the property undetected, but quickly feeling the anxiety of the night before as he stood in the exact spot where he had watched the boys in blue ransack his room and terrorize his woman.

He thrust his hand deep into his pocket and removed the hotel key. Instinct made him check his surroundings a second time. Satisfied that the parking lot was empty, he eased to the door, lifted the key to the lock, then paused. What if someone was inside? He placed his ear to the door, listening. He heard nothing save for the sound of his own breathing. He knocked, paused, then knocked again. No answer. He turned the key in the lock, pushed the door open, and silently advanced into the dim room. He reached to click on the light but thought better of it. The glow through the curtain would make his presence known. His eyes adjusted, and he saw his belongings scattered upon the bed. Stunned, he slowly advanced. "What were they looking for?" he mumbled to himself. Maybe they thought he was a drug dealer. His eyes fell on Peaches's bra and panties. Someone had arranged them in the center of the bed. "Perverts," he mumbled as he imagined the white police officers standing by, gawking at her underwear, trying to visualize how they would look squeezing her large, firm breasts and hugging her trim, curvy waist. Suddenly, he heard the sound of approaching footsteps. Terrified, he dropped to the floor and, lying flat on his stomach, pulled himself underneath the window. Through the small slit in the curtain he saw the outline of a man standing outside the door. Feeling trapped, he removed the gun from his waist and eased to his feet, standing with his back against the wall. He wanted to reach over and chain the door, but feared being betrayed by the noise. He heard the knock. Instantly he drew in his breath, raised the gun, and pulled back the cock. A second knock. He swallowed, aware of the tiny beads of sweat gathering in the center of his concentrated face. He stood stone still, planning his next move. Someone must have seen him arrive. But who? He had been so careful. He had checked twice. He shouldn't have come back. He wouldn't go to jail. No, he would die first.

He closed his eyes, preparing himself to kill. Shuffled footsteps on the concrete made him relax. He sank to the floor and peeked through the curtain. He saw the back of a short, modestly dressed black man move away and disappear around the corner. He lowered the gun, released the cock, and placed it back in his pants. "A john," he mumbled. "Had to be a john."

Unnerved, he rushed across the room, slid the bed over, pried the floorboard loose, and quickly fished out the jar. Once he had it, he replaced the floorboard and slid the bed in place. Clutching the jar tightly, he started to leave, then stopped. It was too bulky. He could never sneak the jar past Sparkle. He needed something else. He found a small paper bag in one of the drawers, dumped the money inside, and dropped the jar in the trash. As he walked, he formulated a plan. When he made it to the thrift shop, he would hide the money in one of the bags of clothes. Anxiety was making him hyper. He had to make it to the house, buy the car, do his shopping, and be at the agreed-upon meeting place before Sparkle returned. He had to pass through a maze of barking dogs before reaching the house. He ambled on, picking up a rock here and a small stone there, slipping them into his pocket, readying himself in case of an attack. He knew better than to run from a charging dog. Experience had taught him that a visible stick, carried by the best traveler, or a cocked arm amply loaded with a sharp stone normally sufficed to deter the most ferocious yard dog. He reached into his pocket and pulled out a stone, imagining a charging dog and picturing it fleeing in pain, whining uncontrollably as the sharply hurled stone dug deep into its unsuspecting flesh.

When he ascended the steps, he walked toward the front door, feeling that his nightmare was almost over and longing for the time that he would be on the road, putting even more distance between himself and his suffocating past. He was tired of running and hiding and changing identities at the drop of a hat. He resolved to reinvent himself and create a new person whose life and personality could be easily adapted to whatever circumstance with which he found himself confronted.

A woman, not the man with whom he had spoken the previous

day, answered the door. She must have been his wife, for she was too young to be his mother and too different looking to be his sister. Stunned and feeling the need to quickly explain his presence, D'Ray turned and pointed to the car.

"I came by yesterday to buy the car."

"I don't know nothing about that," she said abruptly.

"I was supposed to come back yesterday, but—"

"I told you, I don't know nothing about that."

"Is the man here who I talked to?"

"No, he ain't."

D'Ray waited for her to explain, but she offered no additional information.

"When will he be back?" D'Ray asked.

"Tomorrow morning. Seven o'clock."

"Seven o'clock!" D'Ray exclaimed, stunned.

"He working graveyard tonight. Won't be back until tomorrow. If I was you I'd git here before he go to bed."

"He ain't sold it to nobody else, is he?"

"How many times I got to tell you? I don't know."

"Tell him—"

"Mister! Whatever business you got with him, you gone have to handle it yourself. Now, I'm busy."

She closed the door and D'Ray turned to leave, then stopped. Maybe he should leave a deposit. He raised his hand to knock, then reconsidered. She probably wouldn't take it.

He made it back to the thrift shop, purchased a few items, and was waiting outside when Sparkle returned. Her nails were freshly manicured and polished, and her hair was cut and styled.

"Hi, beautiful," D'Ray teased her.

She rolled her eyes and furrowed her brow.

"Don't talk to me," she ordered.

D'Ray pulled the door open and slid into the car. Instantly, Sparkle stepped on the accelerator. The tires screeched and the car sped forward.

"Where you learn how to drive?" D'Ray asked sarcastically.

"You don't like it, git out and walk!" Sparkle countered.

"At least I'd git there."

Sparkle pulled to the shoulder and stopped.

"Git out, Mr. Big Stuff!"

"Meaner than a junkyard dog." He repeated Sarah's earlier description.

"Git out!"

"Girl, stop clowning."

She pulled back onto the highway and headed home.

"You got a boyfriend?" He continued to spar with her.

"What's it to you?"

"Just looking for answers."

"Don't bother."

"Got to be a reason why you so mean."

"Maybe I just don't like you."

"Maybe you need a man."

"What?"

"To release some of that pressure."

"Please."

"Please, nothing. Every woman needs a good—." He paused, looked at her, and raised and lowered his eyebrows several times. "Every now and then."

"Shut up."

"Don't ever underestimate the power of some good loving."

"Typical."

"What?"

"Typical black man."

"What's that's supposed to mean?"

"Don't know a woman long enough to know her before you're talking under her dress."

"Aw, white women don't like that?"

"I ain't white."

"Well, stop acting like it."

"Bastard."

"I been called worst."

"I'm sure you have."

"At least I know my daddy."

"Well, you know one nigger, you know them all."

"What are you? Aw, I forgot. You a white nigguh. You a little bit better than us regular old black nigguhs."

"Don't you dare call me that!"

"What? White, or nigguh?"

"Just leave me alone."

"Naw, somebody need to tell you about yourself."

"Leave me alone."

"You ain't God's gift to this world."

"Never said I was."

"Well, stop acting like it."

"And how am I acting?"

"High and mighty."

"Please."

"Look at you. Lay you down and spread your legs and you ain't no different than no other woman."

"Shut up with your nasty self."

"Well, that's what you made for."

"So you say?"

"So it is."

"Just shut up."

"You get off my back, I'll get off yours."

"Fine."

"Fine."

When they arrived at the house, D'Ray carried all of his purchases into the living room and sat quietly as Ms. Dorothy examined, first, the suitcase, and then the clothes. The small bag sitting on his lap contained personal items: underwear, toothpaste, and other toiletries. At least, that's what he told her. He inclined his head against the back of the chair, trying to appear at ease, patient. The money was worrying him. He rolled the top of the bag closed, silently wishing that she would finish her inspection so that he could hide the money.

"You got some nice things."

"Thank you ma'am." He acknowledged her compliment.

"Anything else you need?" she asked.

"No ma'am," he said, smiling. "This is fine."

"If you think of anything, let me know."

"Yes ma'am," he said, rising, sensing the perfect opportunity to make his exit. "I'm gone put these things in the room."

"OK, baby," she said, letting the lid of the suitcase fall shut. "This is a fine piece of luggage. Should last a long time."

He climbed the stairs, clutching the bags and lugging the suitcase, shunning all offers of help. He needed to be alone. He dumped everything on the bed, sat down, and began unfolding the bag. He decided to count out $1,200 on the slight possibility that time would not afford him the opportunity later. Most of the money was in large bills. As part of his routine each week, either he or one of the girls would take $100 worth of currency to a store and exchange it for a large bill. That way there were fewer bills to conceal.

No sooner had he laid his wallet on the bed than Sparkle barged into the room. In his haste, he had neglected to lock the door.

"Don't you know how to knock?" he said, stalling, trying to think.

"I knew you was trouble," she said, eyeing the money. She grabbed the wallet before he had time to react. "D'Ray Reid." She read his name off the license. "Who are you and what do you want?"

D'Ray leaped to his feet, covered her mouth with his hand, and pulled the gun from his waist.

"You just couldn't keep your nose out of my business, could you?" he growled. She began frantically shaking her head from side to side, whimpering. He pressed the barrel of the gun tight against her temple. "Don't make a sound unless you want to die and carry that old lady with you. You understand?"

Terrified, she nodded her head yes. D'Ray pulled her back across the room and closed the door. This time he made sure that it was locked.

"I'm gone turn you loose. Don't do nothing crazy or I swear, I'll kill you."

He removed his hand and shoved her hard onto the bed. She looked up wide-eyed, trembling.

"Please, don't hurt me," she begged.

"Shut up," D'Ray ordered. His voice was forceful, angry. "Let me think."

"I won't say a word. Please, just let me go."

He raised the gun and pointed it at her head. She closed her eyes, squinting.

"I told you to shut up."

"OK," she pleaded. "I'm sorry."

D'Ray grabbed his wallet, tucked the $1,200 inside, and placed it in his back pocket. Then he put the rest of the money back in the bag and stuffed it in the waist of his pants.

"I got to git out of here and you gone help me, understand?"

"Yeah, just tell me what to do."

"You gone tell Ms. Dorothy that you gotta take me back to the thrift shop to git my wallet. Tell her you called and they say they found it. Then we gone leave. Got it?"

"Where we going?"

"Don't worry about it."

"You ain't gone hurt me, are you?"

"Not unless you make me."

"I won't. I won't do nothing."

"When we talk to that old lady you better be convincing or I'm gone kill you both. Right here and right now." He motioned toward the door. "Let's go."

She rose to her feet, trembling.

"Girl, pull yourself together," he said through clenched teeth, "or so help me God, I'll kill you."

Sparkle took a deep breath and exhaled.

"I'm trying."

"That ain't good enough," he said, placing the gun in the back of his pants. "Do it."

"I'm doing my best."

Wondering, full of doubt, he followed Sparkle down the stairs and back into the living room, where Ms. Dorothy was watching television.

"Got everything put away?" she asked.

"Yes ma'am," D'Ray said calmly.

"That's good," Ms. Dorothy said, not suspecting a thing. "Y'all come on 'round and keep me company."

"We need to run back to the store." Sparkle spoke up.

"What for?" Ms. Dorothy wanted to know.

"He left his wallet," Sparkle told her.

"Lord, I hope and pray it's still there."

"I called the manager," Sparkle lied. "They found it lying on the counter. I told him I would take him to get it."

"See," Ms. Dorothy said, "I told you she was a pussycat." She looked at D'Ray and smiled.

"Yes ma'am. You sure did."

"Well, Ms. Dorothy, we better go."

"OK, honey. Y'all be careful now, hear."

"Yes ma'am, we will," Sparkle said, leaning over and kissing her on the cheek.

As soon as they were in the car, D'Ray removed the gun from his waist and placed it in his lap.

"Just in case you get any ideas."

"I won't," Sparkle assured him. "Just tell me where to go."

"Drive toward town," D'Ray said, looking in the direction of the house. "Just in case she's watching."

Sparkle backed out of the driveway and headed toward town.

"Don't speed or do anything to attract the cops. You hear?"

"Yeah, I hear."

D'Ray looked at her. She was leaning forward, gripping the wheel with both hands.

"Relax," he said calmly.

"I'm scared."

"Well, don't broadcast it to the world. Lean back. Take one hand off the wheel." She complied. "That's better," he said quickly, focusing his attention on the road. "Git on the freeway."

"OK" was her nervous response.

"Drive out into the country."

"You ain't gone hurt me, are you?"

"Just do like I tell you."

Tears began to stream down her face.

"Stop that!" His tone was threatening.

She dried her eyes on the arm of her blouse.

"Take me where there ain't no people or houses." He paused and looked at her. "Do you know a place like that?"

"Yeah," she whispered. "The Trace."

"Look, I ain't gone hurt you. Just relax."

"OK, I'm trying."

"You did real good at the house."

"I'm trying."

"You fast on your feet."

"I'm trying."

"Telling her that you talked to the manager. That was good. Real good." Suddenly his tone changed. "Why did you have to come in my room?"

"I don't know."

"Why did you have to look at my license?"

"I don't know."

"Now you know my name, don't you?"

"I won't tell anybody. I swear I won't."

"You knew I was gone leave in a few days. Why couldn't you just leave me alone?"

"I don't know."

"Well, it don't matter now no way," he said, looking out of the window. They were passing through a wooded area.

"How far have we gone?"

"About ten miles."

"What's out there?" he asked, pointing.

"Nothing," Sparkle said softly. "Nothing but trees."

Ahead, he noticed a narrow dirt road jutted out from the highway and disappeared into the woods.

"Turn right there," he said, pointing.

Sparkle turned off the highway, steered onto the road, and drove into the woods. She had driven no less than four miles when D'Ray told her to stop. Startled, she turned, staring at him wide-eyed, trembling.

"Please don't hurt me."

"Git out!"

"What you gone do?"

"Just git out," he shouted.

She eased out of the car, crying.

"Please don't hurt me," she begged.

D'Ray got out, walked to the driver's side, pulled the door open, and climbed inside.

"You gone just leave me out here?"

"You'll be alright."

"How am I supposed to get back?"

"Walk, princess. Walk."

He backed into a clearing, turned the car around, and sped away. When he reached the freeway he had a strong compulsion to head to Detroit. But he fought against it with every fiber of his being. Soon the police would be looking for him. To attempt such a lengthy trip in a stolen car would almost certainly ensure his capture. No, he would return to the thrift shop, abandon the car somewhere along the bus route, perhaps in one of the department store parking lots, then take the bus back to the house where the car was and hide until morning. If the owner was back by seven, he could be on the road by seven-fifteen.

It was a good plan, but fear made him change his mind. The thrift shop parking lot was too small and it was too close to the house. Surely they would focus their search where they found the car. He diverted his course and headed in the direction of the mall. As he drove, he stared into the bright sky, trying to imagine how he would survive until nightfall. He felt tense. Instinct was telling him they were close. He had to hide, but where? He took the next exit, not knowing what he expected to find but sensing that the freeway was too dangerous, too open. He felt too exposed.

He had driven no more than a quarter of a mile when he saw the mall. He began to relax as his way became clear. He could bury the car in the sea of cars in the mall parking lot. He entered the lot cautiously, cruising up one aisle and down the other, eventually deciding to abandon the car in the center of the lot, not too close to any particular building. When he exited the car, his initial inclination was to lock the keys in the trunk, but caution prevented him. Should the unexpected occur, dictating a hasty escape, he wouldn't be trapped. He slid the key into his front pocket and proceeded toward the mall, wondering what he would do to pass the time and wishing that he could somehow make himself invisible. He followed the sidewalk around the building, then stopped, staring as the solution materialized before his eyes. Outside, on the wall, encased in glass, were several full-length posters promoting several movies. Relieved, he perused them, anticipating the peaceful solitude of the dark theater and appreciating the additional time to mull over the tenuous situation in which he found himself.

A thousand times before he had entered a darkened theater motivated by something other than a desire to be entertained by a thriller unfolding on the big screen. To the contrary, his had been a scheme not unlike the ones hatched in the minds of so many of his young contemporaries, who, like him, had not too recently come into the knowledge of women. The theater was their place for courtship. Somewhere—a couple of seats in an empty row, preferably in a dark corner near the back—would provide the perfect place to steal a kiss or to cop a long, slow rub of a soft, young thigh or a gentle groping caress, however brief, of a firm, aroused breast. It was a ritual in which little was accomplished but much was attempted. Any success, regardless of how meager, was fodder for the ensuing locker room talk and incentive for another hunt on another day.

After the movie, D'Ray spent a few hours in the mall. He had a long quiet dinner in the cafeteria, traversed the wide mall corridors window-shopping, and he spent a significant period of time playing video games in the arcade. He had formulated a plan of action and was simply waiting on the proper time to execute it. He was in no hurry. By now the consensus of the local authorities had to be that he had skipped town. That was the only logical conclusion. He had a car, an exorbitant amount of cash, and knowledge that his cover had been blown. Surely, he had fled.

At ten-fifteen, he called a cab. By eleven o'clock, he was standing on the sidewalk, staring at the small junior high school. As the cab pulled away, he looked around, making sure that he was not being watched. Across the street he saw a single light burning in a lone window. He decided to walk north one block and double back to the school. He casually moved down the narrow sidewalk, finally feeling that everything was going to be OK. The car that he would purchase the next morning was on the adjacent street, two blocks over. By the time the rest of the world stirred, he would be in his own car, en route to Detroit.

On the backstreet, hanging on a clothesline behind a house, he spied a string of clothes blowing in the cool night air, waving, beckoning to him. His eyes fell on the thin bedspread draped on the end of the line. He smiled. Yes, everything was going to be alright. Cautiously he approached the line, removed the spread, doubled it over, and placed it underneath his arm. Then he removed a shirt, smiling. Yes, everything was going to be OK. Fate was smiling on him.

The campus was dark and sullen. He navigated his way between several buildings, finally stopping in front of a large structure near the back of campus. He slowly circled the building, examining it carefully. Next to it, on the back side, was a long narrow metal pipe extending well beyond the roof. He removed the bedspread, wrapped it about his waist, and tied it. He stuffed the shirt between the bedspread and his body, moved next to the pole, paused, and looked up. He spit into his hands, rubbed them together, readied himself, then shimmied up the pole and swung onto the roof. He walked to the front of the building and looked. From the top of the building he could see into the surrounding neighborhood. Convinced of the security of his hideout, he spread the bedspread on the roof, rolled the shirt into a pillow, stretched out, and closed his eyes.

He had just dozed off when he heard the noise. Startled, his eyes flew open and he rose onto his elbows. The sound was faint but clear. A helicopter. He struggled to his feet and looked. The sound was getting stronger. It was moving toward him. He spun in circles, searching the sky. When he spotted it, his first impulse was to get off the roof, but there wasn't time. Feeling trapped, he dropped to his belly and crawled underneath the bedspread, praying that the helicopter would pass. The bedspread was a dark color; surely they wouldn't be able to see him. He lay motionless, holding his breath and staring out into the darkness of the night. Now the noise was deafening. To his dismay, the helicopter was directly above him, hovering. He wanted to look, but fear prevented him from moving. A light clicked on and the entire building was illuminated. D'Ray eased his head under the bedspread, hoping they would not be able to tell that what they saw was a person. He felt the wind from the blades. The helicopter was slowly descending. A voice boomed over the public address system.

"This is the police. Stand up with your hands above your head."

A lump of terror lodged in his throat. He could feel the blood pulsating in his arm, hear the sound of his heart echoing off the surface of the roof. He made a decision to flee. He leaped to his feet, running wildly toward the edge of the roof. He jumped, crashing hard against the pole, feeling the excruciating pain race through his groin. He slid down the pole, landing hard on his feet. Adrenaline numbed him, strengthened him. He raced toward the streets, ducking between buildings, hearing the helicopter above, seeing the spotlight illuminating the ground, following him like a shadow. In the residential area, he jumped a fence, ran through a backyard, and hid underneath a car, waiting. He saw the spotlight pass over, then come back, pausing—illuminating the car. He gave up his hiding place. As he ran, he heard doors opening and closing, saw lights clicking on, heard shouts: "There he is. He went that away."

Tired and panting, he darted into the street. In the distance he heard sirens. He began to struggle against the tiredness in his legs. His breathing was labored. His lungs burned. He saw a police car round the corner. He left the street, cut through a yard, and raced behind the house. The helicopter was still above him. He tried to think. He heard more sirens. Behind him. In front of him. He angled away from the street. He heard a dog barking. He looked over his shoulder.

He saw those eyes, wide, glowing, bearing down on him. He stopped, pulled his gun, and raised it to fire. But he was too late. He felt the animal's force knock him to the ground. Saw the gun fly from his hand. Felt the teeth boring into his flesh, ripping, tearing, mauling. He doubled his hand into a fist, drew back, and pounded the animal's head. The animal paused and released his grip; then, in the blink of an eye, sunk his teeth into D'Ray's neck, clamping down hard, restricting his airway. D'Ray's body began to jerk, his arms began to flutter; he gasped for breath, suffocating. He felt a painful tightness about his eyes. He became dizzy, light-headed. He felt himself losing consciousness, when suddenly the dog abated. Through hazy, unfocused eyes, D'Ray saw a policeman holding the dog back and two others standing over him with guns drawn.

"Roll over on your stomach and move your hands away from your body," he heard the officer command through heavy, labored breathing. D'Ray complied. Instantly he felt a knee in the center of his back, his arms being jerked behind him, and the cold, steel cuffs digging into his wrists.

"Got any weapons on you?" he heard another officer ask.

"No sir," he replied. The gun was lying just outside the circle of light cast by the hovering helicopter. He felt the officer's hands moving over his body, stopping first on the wallet. The officer pulled it from his pocket and handed it to his partner. D'Ray angled his head and watched him remove his flashlight from his belt, click it on, and hold it above the wallet.

"D'Ray Reid," the officer read his name out loud. "You D'Ray Reid?"

D'Ray didn't answer. Why hadn't he gotten rid of that license?

"You ain't got to say nothing," the officer informed him. "I can see it's you."

While he talked, the other officer continued to frisk him. D'Ray felt the officer's hand move up his back, under his arms, down his stomach, and pause at his waist. The officer reached his hand inside the waist of D'Ray's pants, removed the bag, and handed it to his partner. D'Ray watched him open the bag and look inside.

"Where you get all this money?"

D'Ray didn't answer.

"Naw, you ain't got to answer." The officer mocked D'Ray. "You got rights." D'Ray watched as he brought the bag around to his partner. "Charlie," he heard him say, "I believe we done apprehended ourselves a thief."

"Or a pusher," Charlie offered as another possibility. "Did you see him toss anything?"

"No, but that don't mean he didn't," he said, scanning the ground with his flashlight. "Bingo!"

D'Ray turned and looked. He had found the gun.

"Charlie, I believe you were right," he said, holding up the gun. "We got ourselves a thief. Any stores been burglarized?"

"Don't know. Read 'im his rights while I call it in."

D'Ray focused his attention on the second officer while Charlie read him his rights. He knew them already, but even if he hadn't, he wouldn't have been any more interested. He saw the officer hold the wallet up, glance at it, then speak into the walkie-talkie. He had moved a considerable distance away, and D'Ray couldn't hear him. He saw Charlie wave to the helicopter. He watched the pilot kill the spotlight, then guide the machine into the heavens and out of sight. He felt an arm in his back pushing him toward the highway. When they caught up with the second officer, he heard Charlie ask the question.

"Got any warrants?"

"Yeah," the other officer said nonchalantly.

D'Ray felt his heart racing uncontrollably.

"Here?"

"No, Louisiana."

"How many?"

"Three. Burglary. Grand theft auto."

"What else?"

"Murder one," he said, smiling. "Look like we got ourselves a real outlaw."

"Huh," Charlie said matter-of-factly. "Chalk up another one for neighborhood watch."

# CHAPTER ELEVEN

It wasn't A LONG TRIAL; THE WHOLE THING LASTED ONLY THREE AND A HALF HOURS. HE WAS there and he was conscious, but none of it seemed real. It was like a dream. It wasn't a particularly bad dream. He wasn't frightened or nervous. Nor was he hopeful. Of course, there was the slight possibility that the prosecution might make a mistake or that his attorney might be able to create reasonable doubt in the mind of the judge, but he wasn't hopeful. He had committed the crime and he knew that most people were already convinced of his guilt. Maybe if he weren't Papa World's boy or if he hadn't been in and out of trouble most of his life, he would be hopeful. But he was who he was, and that had always worked against him. Besides, he had known this day was coming. It was his birthright. Like his daddy and his daddy's daddy before him, he had been born to do time. No, he wasn't hopeful or fearful; he only wanted to know how much time and where.

When they led him into the courtroom he paused in the doorway. Standing there in a bright orange jumpsuit with his hands cuffed behind his back and his feet chained together, he surveyed the small, crowded room. Besides the pitying glances of the stenographer and the shameful stares of his family, the eyes of hate were upon him. They peered at him from the prosecution table, from the family section, from the witness stand, and even from the judge's bench. No, as he sat next to his court-appointed attorney, he wasn't hopeful or fearful; he only wanted to know how much time and where.

Once the trial started, everything seemed hazy. It was as though he was a casual observer viewing the whole thing through a pair of unfocused binoculars. People moved in slow motion. Their words were terse and deliberate. Some were calm, some cried, some shouted, but all were angry. The two old women from Mr. Clem's store broke down on the stand, but not before they told the court that he was the person that they had seen in the store. An officer testified that he had discovered fingerprints on the cash register and on an unopened bottle of soda sitting on the counter. They were D'Ray's.

A criminalist testified that the bullet that killed young Stanley Earl was fired from the gun found in D'Ray's possession. The ballistics report confirmed that fact. The two arresting officers from Jackson testified that D'Ray had thousands of dollars on him at the time that he was apprehended, $1,200 in his wallet and $3,800 concealed in a paper bag stuffed in the waist of his pants. No, they didn't prove that it was the same money that was taken from the cash register on the day of the robbery, but that's what was being intimated. That's what they wanted the judge to infer.

When the prosecution rested, his guilt seemed clear and irrefutable. But it could have been worse. Like his daddy, he could have been on trial for killing a white man. Or his could have been a capital offense case, with him facing execution, as opposed to time in an institution for boys. No, things weren't as bad as they could have been. And no, he wasn't angry at anyone for his situation. Not Little Man for smoking Kojak's crack. Not Kojak for demanding his money. Not himself for doing what he had to do. Not at his friends, who would not testify on his behalf. (What would their testimony have meant anyway? What could they say about his character that his rap sheet didn't?) Not at his mother for refusing to provide him with an airtight alibi. Sure, she testified that she had seen him shortly before the estimated time of the murder and shortly afterward, but she couldn't be sure of his whereabouts during the murder. No, she wouldn't lie, not even to save her son.

When he took the stand he knew it was up to him to do what the others had not. He sat up straight, looked his attorney in the eye, and spoke in a clear, steady voice filled with confidence but void of arrogance.

"Did you kill Stanley Earl?" His attorney's first question was short and to the point.

"Absolutely not." His response was immediate. A low rumble

swept through the courtroom. The judge pounded his gavel. "Order! Order! Order in the court. One more outburst and I will clear this courtroom."

"Wouldn't you say that things look bad for you?" His attorney asked his second question.

"Yessir."

"But you didn't kill Stanley Earl?"

"No sir, I didn't."

D'Ray watched his attorney move to the evidence table and remove the unopened bottle of soda.

"Please tell the court what I am holding in my hand."

"A bottle of soda pop."

"Have you ever seen this bottle before?"

"Yessir."

"Where?"

"In Mr. Clem's store."

"When?"

"Friday."

"Do you remember the date?"

"Yessir."

"What was it?"

"July seventh."

"What time was that?"

"Early afternoon."

"Do you remember the exact time?"

D'Ray paused, thinking.

"No sir."

"But it was afternoon?"

"Yessir."

"How can you be sure?"

"Because of the weather."

"What was the weather like that day?"

"Hot."

"Why were you in the store?"

"I went in to buy a pop."

"Did you?"

"Did I what?"

"Buy a pop?"

"No sir."

"Why not?"

"I didn't have enough money."

"So you left the store?"

"No sir."

"What did you do?"

"I tried to talk the cashier into letting me have it on credit."

"Did he?"

"No sir. He said he couldn't."

"Then what happened?"

"I told him to lend me thirty-five cents until I could do better."

"Did he?"

"No sir. He said he was flat broke. That's why he was working."

"What did you say?"

"I told him I knew he had plenty money."

"What happened next?"

"He patted his front pockets and said if I could find it I could have it."

"Then what happened?"

"I reached across the counter and rang the cash register open and stuck my hand inside."

"What did he do?"

"Slammed the drawer on my hand."

"Then what happened?"

"I laughed and told him don't sell my soda 'cause I would be back for it in a few minutes."

"Then what did you do?"

"I went outside and tried to beg some money."

"Did you?"

"No sir; I asked, but people just looked at me like I was crazy."

"What did you do?"

"I went home."

"And what time was that?"

"Six o'clock."

"How do you know?"

"I asked the man I hitched a ride with."

"Who was he?"

"I don't know. Just some truck driver."

"Where was the bottle of soda the last time you saw it?"

"I left it on the counter."

"Is this the bottle?"

"Yessir. It looks like it."

"So, you did handle this bottle?"

"Yessir. I took it out of the cooler and set it on the counter." D'Ray paused, looked up at the judge, and smiled. "Sir, could I please have some water?" The judge nodded and the bailiff handed D'Ray a glass of water.

"Do you own a gun?" his attorney continued.

"No sir."

He watched his attorney cross to the evidence table and remove the gun.

"This is not your gun?"

"No sir."

"Wasn't it in your possession when you were apprehended?"

"Yessir. But it's not mine."

"Can you tell the court who it belongs to?"

"Yessir."

"Who?"

"My mama."

"What were you doing with your mother's gun?"

"I snuck it out of her room."

"Why?"

"I always sneak it out."

"Why?"

"Protection."

"Protection from who?"

"Everybody."

"Somebody threatened you?"

"Everybody is a threat."

"Why do you say that?"

"Because everybody packing."

"What do you mean, 'packing'?"

"Carrying a gun."

"Is that what you believe?"

"No sir, that's what I know because that's how we live."

"What do you mean by 'we'?"

"Black folks in the projects."

"Were you aware that that gun killed Stanley Earl?"

"No sir, I wasn't."

"But you heard an officer from the crime lab testify to that fact, correct?"

"Yessir."

"Do you understand that there is no doubt that this gun killed Stanley Earl?"

"It might be the right gun, but I'm the wrong person."

"Did you give the gun to someone else?"

"No sir."

"On those occasions that you removed the gun from your mother's home, did you keep it on you at all times?"

"No sir."

"What did you do with it?"

"I hid it."

"How often did you take the gun?"

"All of the time."

"Could you be more specific?"

"Just about every day."

"Did you take the gun on July seventh?"

"Yessir."

"Did you hide the gun on July seventh?"

"Yessir."

"Did you take the gun to the store with you?"

"No sir."

"Why not?"

"I don't carry it everywhere I go."

"How do you decide when to carry it and when not to?"

"If I think it's gone be trouble, I carry it."

"But you didn't anticipate trouble?"

"No sir; I was just hanging out."

"Could you please tell the court why you went to Lake Providence on July seventh?"

"To go to the beach."

"Do you normally do that?"

"Sometimes when it's hot. Ain't no lake in Brownsville. Ain't nothing in Brownsville."

"When did you decide to buy a soda?"

"After I left the beach."

"How long did you stay on the beach?"

"A couple of hours."

"Did you drink anything on the beach?"

"No sir. Nothing."

"Not even water?"

"No sir. Ain't no water out there except in the lake, and that ain't fit to drink."

"What did you do on the beach?"

"Just sat on the bank under a tree and watched the boats."

"Did you talk to anybody?"

"No sir."

"Did anybody see you?"

"I don't know. Could have."

"Let's go back to the gun for a moment. Did you always hide it in the same place?"

"Yessir."

"Was the hiding place a secret?"

"Not really."

"Are you saying that there were others who had knowledge of where you hid the gun?"

"Yessir."

"Who?"

"A lot of people."

"Could you be more specific?"

"All of my friends. All of their friends. And people that just heard us talk about it. A lot of people."

"So you bragged about having a gun?"

"Yessir."

"Why?"

"So folks would know I was packing."

"Why was that important?"

"If they knew, they wouldn't hardly mess with you."

"Why didn't you just carry it with you?"

"That's just asking for trouble."

"What do you mean?"

"Police'll get you for packing."

"But didn't you say that everybody was carrying a gun?"

"Yessir, but not on them. Most of them hide 'em someplace or keep 'em in the car if they got a car. They don't carry 'em unless they know it's gone be trouble. Like in a club or something. Then they might have it on 'em. But most times you just need to have it close by."

"Where did you keep your mother's gun?"

"In the junkyard across the railroad tracks."

"Where in the junkyard?"

"Under a old car."

"The same car every time?"

"Yessir."

"Who do you think took it?"

"Objection, Your Honor," the prosecutor shouted. "Calls for speculation."

"Sustained," the judge said.

D'Ray's attorney paused, collected his thoughts, and then resumed.

"Has anyone ever removed the gun without your consent?" he asked.

"Yessir."

"On more than one occasion?"

"Yessir."

"How did you get it back?"

"They put it back when they were finished."

"How do you know this?"

"They told me."

"What time did you hide the gun on July seventh?"

"That morning."

"Do you remember the time?"

"A little after seven."

"When did you retrieve it?"

"That evening after I made it back to Brownsville."

"What time was that?"

"A little before six."

"Then what did you do?"

"I headed home."

"Do you recall your mother's testimony?"

"Yessir."

"She testified that you made it home that evening around six P.M. Do you remember that testimony?"

"Yessir."

"She also testified that you were out of breath. Had you been running?"

"Yessir."

"Why?"

"Right before I made it to the house somebody told me that my little brother was over at the café and I wanted to hurry up and go get 'im before something happened."

"Did you have reason to believe that he was in danger?"

"Not really. But it was Friday night. Folks had got paid and I knew they was gone be over there drinking and gambling. I just didn't want him around there."

"Why did you go in the house?"

"I wanted to put the gun back befo' Mama noticed it was missing."

"Did you?"

"Yessir. She went out on the porch to see if Little Man was coming, and when she did I went in her room and put the gun back under her mattress."

"What did you do next?"

"I went to look for Little Man."

"Did you find him?"

"Yessir."

"Where?"

"He was over there. But he wasn't inside, though. He was sitting out back under a tree, watching the people going in and out and listening to the music. They play it so loud on Friday and Saturday nights that you can hear it clear outside."

"What did you do after you found him?"

"We talked a little then we went home."

"What time was that?"

"Around seven."

"How long did it take to find him?"

"A little while, because I looked inside first."

"What did you do after you made it home?"

"Visited with my aunt Peggy, from Chicago. Ate supper and went to bed."

D'Ray watched his attorney move to the evidence table and remove the clear plastic bag containing the money that he had in his possession the night that he was arrested.

"Please tell the court what I am holding in my hand."

"A bag of money."

"Several officers testified that this money was on your person at the time you were apprehended. Is that testimony accurate?"

"Yessir."

"This money was in your possession."

"Yessir."

"How much money was in the bag?"

"About five thousand dollars."

"Please tell the court where the money came from."

"I found it, sir."

"You found five thousand dollars?"

"Well, I took it out of a truck."

"And where was this truck?"

"In the junkyard across the railroad tracks."

"And what time was that?"

"Around seven o'clock in the morning."

"And what day was that?"

"Saturday, sir."

"What were you doing in the junkyard that early?"

"I went to hide the gun."

"Was your mother at home?"

"Yessir."

"And she keeps the gun in her bedroom?"

"Yessir."

"Well, how did you remove the gun from her bedroom at such an early hour without alerting her?"

"She got up to answer the door. Her boyfriend came by and they went in the kitchen to drank some coffee. That's when I got the gun and went out the back window."

"Did you go directly to the junkyard?"

"Yessir."

"Then what happened?"

"I saw the truck."

"Were there other trucks in the junkyard?"

"Yessir."

"Then why did you notice this particular truck?"

"It was new looking."

"What's strange about a new-looking truck?"

"Nothing. I just wondered why someone would leave a new truck in a junkyard."

"What did you do?"

"I looked in the window."

"What did you see?"

"The keys were still in the switch."

"Then what did you do?"

"I got inside to see if it would crank."

"Did it?"

"Yessir."

"Then what did you do?"

"I started messing around with the gadgets."

"Why did you do that?"

"It was a fancy truck and I wanted to see how everything worked. I turned on the lights, the windshield wipers, the radio. You know, everything."

"Then what did you do?"

"I looked through the glove compartment."

"Why?"

"I don't know. I just did."

"What did you do next?"

"I looked under the seat."

"And what did you see?"

"A crumpled-up brown paper bag."

"What did you do?"

"I got it and looked inside."

"What did you see?"

"Money. More money than I ever seen."

"Then what did you do?"

"I reached in and took some out."

"What were you thinking?"

"Drug money. I figured it must be drug money."

"Then what did you do?"

"I stuffed it in my pants and started running."

"Where were you going?"

"I didn't know."

"So where did you go?"

"To one of my friends' house."

"Did you tell your friend about the money?"

"No sir."

"Why not?"

"He wasn't home."

"Was anybody home?"

"Just his little sister."

"Nobody else?"

"I asked her if anybody else was home."

"What did she say?"

"No."

"What did you do?"

"I asked her why she was eating a raw potato."

"What she say?"

"Because she was hungry."

"What did you do?"

"I went and bought her some groceries."

"With the money you found in the truck?"

"Yessir."

"Then what did you do?"

"I started to go home."

"Did you go home?"

"No sir."

"Why not?"

"Because Mama still had company."

"How did you know that?"

"Because I saw the police car in front of the house."

"Your mother's boyfriend is a police officer?"

"Yessir."

"But why did that stop you?"

"I wanted to talk to Mama, not him. Besides, me and him don't get along. I wanted to ask her what to do, not him."

"Did you want to keep the money?"

"Yessir."

"Why?"

"Because we needed it."

"Did you think taking the money was wrong?"

"No sir, not if it was drug money and they were hiding it in the junkyard and I found it."

"Where did you go when you left your friend's house?"

"I went to the barbershop."

"Why?"

"I figured that by the time I got my haircut, Sonny would be gone and then I could go home and talk to Mama."

"Sonny is your mother's boyfriend?"

"Yessir. His name is Benny, but everybody call him Sonny."

"When you made it to the barbershop did you get your haircut immediately?"

"No sir."

"Why not?"

"The shop was already full. There were people ahead of me."

"So what did you do?"

"I waited."

"Did someone visit while you were waiting?"

"Yessir."

"Please tell the court the visitor's name."

"Mr. Gus."

"Do you know his last name?"

"No sir, we just call him Mr. Gus."

"Where does he work?"

"At the police station."

"What does he do at the police station?"

"He's the janitor."

"Did he come to the barbershop to get his hair cut?"

"No sir."

"Why did he come?"

"To tell Fred that the police had found the stolen truck."

"Was that the first time that you had heard that a truck had been stolen?"

"Yessir."

"What else did Mr. Gus say?"

"He said that they didn't know who took it, but they had finger-prints."

"Did he say where the police had found the truck?"

"Yessir."

"Where?"

"In the junkyard."

"When?"

"He said they had just found it."

"What time was that?"

"I don't know exactly."

"Approximately."

"Somewhere around eight o'clock."

"Did he say anything else?"

"Yessir."

"What did he say?"

"He said that as soon as they had matched the prints he would come back and tell whose they were."

"What did you do?"

"I didn't know what to do."

"How did you feel?"

"I was scared."

"Why were you scared?"

"Because I knew my fingerprints were on the truck and they would say that I stole it."

"Why didn't you just go tell them the truth?"

"Because they wouldn't believe me."

"Why not?"

"Because I'm my daddy's son."

"Who is your daddy?"

"D'Marco Reid."

"Is he here today?"

"No sir."

"Where is he?"

"Angola."

"Does he work at Angola?"

"No sir."

"Is he incarcerated there?"

"Yessir."

"For how long?"

"Life."

"For what?"

"Murder."

A dull rumble raced through the courtroom. The judge tapped the gavel against the small wooden block sitting on his desk, and instantly all was quiet.

"Where did you go after you left the barbershop?"

"I went home."

"What happened when you made it home?"

"I saw the police at my house."

"How many officers did you see?"

"Three or four."

"Where were you?"

"I was across the street."

"So when you state that you went home, you don't mean that you literally went inside your mother's house, do you?"

"No sir, I was across the street."

"What did you do when you saw the officers?"

"Nothing at first."

"What did you think?"

"I thought that they had found my fingerprints on the truck and had come to arrest me."

"What did you do?"

"I didn't know what to do."

"But what did you do?"

"I ran."

"You thought they wanted you for auto theft?"

"Yessir."

"Did you steal that truck?"

"No sir."

"Then why did you run?"

"Because I was scared."

"If you didn't do anything, why were you scared?"

"Because I'm my daddy's son."

"Did you kill Stanley Earl?"

"No sir."

"When you ran, did you know that he had been killed?"

"No sir."

"You thought you were an accused thief, not an accused murderer, correct?"

"Yessir."

"When you left Brownsville, where did you go?"

"I went to Jackson."

"Why didn't you go farther? You had over five thousand dollars."

"I just wanted to figure out what to do. They had the truck back. I didn't think they would come all the way to another state looking for a car thief."

"When did you learn that you were wanted for murder?"

"When they caught me in Jackson."

"Did you kill Stanley Earl?"

"No sir."

"What about the witnesses?"

"What about them?"

"They say they saw you do it."

"No sir, they couldn't have."

"Why not?"

"I was in Brownsville at the time of the murder."

"Why would they lie?"

"I'm not saying that they are."

"What are you saying?"

"That they are mistaken."

"Are you familiar with the phrase 'consciousness of guilt'?"

"No sir."

"Do you know what it means?"

"No sir."

"Did you kill Stanley Earl?"

"No sir."

"Did you run because you were guilty?"

"No sir, I ran because I was scared."

"Why were you scared?"

"Because I'm my father's son."

"Nothing further, Your Honor."

"Your witness, Counselor."

"No cross, Your Honor," the prosecuting attorney said, staring at D'Ray. "I see no need to waste the court's time."

A murmur swept over the room.

"Mr. Reid, you may step down."

Stunned, D'Ray made his way back to his seat. His attorney gripped his arm, bent close to his ear, and whispered, "I've done all I can do." Then he stood and faced the judge. "Your Honor, the defense rests."

Again D'Ray heard the uneasy murmurs from the small gathering of people sitting behind him.

"We'll adjourn for lunch and reconvene at a quarter till one for closing arguments."

D'Ray turned to his attorney. "Why didn't he ask me any questions?"

"The same reason that he did not object while you were testifying."

D'Ray looked at him, trying to understand.

"It's just an old tactic, that's all."

"But what does it mean?"

"That they have proven their case and your testimony is irrele-
vant. At least that's the impression they are trying to give the judge."

"So they're saying I'm lying?"

"Exactly."

"That's what they think."

"It doesn't matter what they think. We have to convince the
judge, not them. Understand?"

"Yessir."

"Son, the best thing that you can do for yourself right now is to
get some rest and try to remain positive. I know you're scared and I
know it looks bad. But this thing is a long way from over. We still
have closing arguments."

Two policemen walked on either side of him, leading him handcuffed out of the courtroom and guiding him through the small
crowd of people milling about in the hallway. D'Ray felt their eyes
fastened on him. He stood stolidly, trying not to let them detect any
fear in him. As he passed they were silent, but as soon as he was some
feet away, he heard their voices rise. He didn't look at them. He
didn't react. He maintained contact with the guards, following them
through a side door and out into the bright sunlight. The jail was
only a short distance from the courthouse. They crossed the parking
lot and paused in front of the large steel door. The sun felt good.
D'Ray tilted his head back and felt the warm rays on the side of his
face. Freedom had a distinct feel, a distinct taste, a distinct smell. He
drew in a deep breath, inhaling the fresh air, enjoying its scent, all
the time wishing that he could store enough of it in his lungs to help
him survive the time in his tiny, cramped, musty cell. A series of soft,
rapid taps and the door flung open. He was guided down the short,
narrow hallway to his cell. He was pushed inside, the handcuffs were
removed, and the door clanged shut. He lay on the cot and stared at
the ceiling. He wouldn't allow himself to feel hope. What could his
lawyer say that hadn't already been said? He closed his eyes and the
darkness soothed him. But no sooner had he begun to relax than he
heard the steel door open.

He opened his eyes and saw a white man with a tray of food. He
sat up and the man brought the tray to the cot, placed it beside him,
and left. D'Ray picked up the plastic fork and twirled it about slowly.
He stared at the food. Was this what he had to look forward to? He let
out a deep sigh. Why was this happening to him? Why did . . .? No,

he wouldn't do this. He dug the fork deep into the pile of mashed potatoes. He raised the food to his mouth and pulled it off the fork with his lips. It tasted bland, but he didn't care. He filled the fork a second time. No, he wouldn't regret. He wouldn't question. He wouldn't expect. He and the Earls were strangers. They were two different versions of black folks. His fate had been sealed the day he emerged from his mother's womb and entered a world that despised his presence. He was a feared animal, born to be hunted, born to be caged. Born to live a life in which he was dead long before he died.

He finished eating, then lay back on the cot and rested his eyes. He didn't think. He wouldn't allow himself to. He lost himself in complete silence, not moving a muscle until he lifted his head when he heard footsteps.

"Time to go." The guards were back.

He was handcuffed, led down the hall and back outside. Across the street he saw several people standing near the ice cream stand, looking. They saw him.

"There he is."

"Murderer."

A paper cup filled with soda sailed through the air and splattered at his feet. He ignored it. He never looked and he never broke stride. His mind was on what awaited him inside. He wasn't hoping for anything except for it to be over.

Once inside, he was led to his seat and freed of his handcuffs. His lawyer was already there. He pushed D'Ray's chair back and D'Ray sat next to him.

"Get some rest?"

"Yessir," D'Ray answered and leaned back in his chair.

"Good." He smiled and tried to act at ease, but D'Ray could see that he was tense, nervous.

"This shouldn't take too long."

"It don't matter. I ain't going nowhere."

Feeling awkward, his lawyer averted his face and began thumbing through the stack of papers on the table in front of him. The judge entered and the bailiff moved to the center of the courtroom. "All rise."

The court stood as the judge climbed behind his desk and sat in the large high-back chair.

"Please be seated." He spoke with authority.

On cue the entire court obeyed his command.

"Is counsel present?"

"Yes, Your Honor," both attorneys answered in unison.

"Is the State ready to present closing arguments?"

The prosecuting attorney rose.

"The State is ready, Your Honor."

"Please proceed."

The state attorney stepped from behind the table and positioned himself between the judge and D'Ray.

"Your Honor, at the beginning of this trial I promised you that we would prove beyond a reasonable doubt that the defendant, D'Ray Reid, did maliciously and savagely murder young Stanley Earl in cold blood. Your Honor, the counsel for the defense has followed a line of questioning designed for the sole intent of having the court believe that the defendant is on trial because of his name. They would have the court believe that the defendant is a victim. No, Your Honor, this is not about a name. And no, Your Honor, the defendant is not a victim. Mr. Henry Earl is the victim, and the defendant is the one that victimized him. No, this is not about a name. This is about murder. This is about justice. In this country, this wonderful land of opportunity, we raise our children to believe in a dream. We tell them if they work hard, and follow the rules, and live by the laws of the land, and develop character, and exhibit integrity, and learn how to love their fellow man, that the world will be their oyster. That's all that Mr. Earl tried to teach his son. No, Your Honor, this is not about a name. This is about a young man who had never been in trouble a day in his life. A young man whose record of citizenship is not blemished by so much as a traffic ticket. He was a church member. He was an honor student. No, it's not about a name. It's about a child who had his whole life ahead of him until this . . . this . . . this sorry excuse for a human being decided to snuff it out because he wanted to take that for which he refused to work.

"And yes, Your Honor, he is guilty. We have established motive. We have provided compelling forensic evidence. We have produced the murder weapon, which was found in the possession of the defendant. We have the defendant's fingerprints at the crime scene. We have provided not one but two extremely credible witnesses, who have sworn under oath that they saw the defendant murder young Stanley Earl in cold blood. We have the money that he stole from Mr.

Clem's cash register, which was retrieved from his person. And then, Your Honor, we have the defendant's own actions. Innocent men don't run, but the defendant did. Further evidence of a consciousness of guilt.

"Yes, Your Honor, he did it. And how did he do it? He stole the truck, drove to Lake Providence, killed young Stanley Earl, robbed the store, drove back to Brownsville, hid the truck in the junkyard, went home, and sat down to a joyous dinner with his family. He ate dinner, Your Honor, with no remorse for the life he had just taken and no regard for the pain that his murderous act would wreak upon the Earl family.

"Your Honor, we don't come seeking revenge. For 'Vengeance is mine, saith the Lord.' We simply come seeking justice. We simply come asking that you do what is right. Find the defendant, D'Ray Reid, guilty of murder in the first degree."

D'Ray continued to stare straight ahead, unaffected by what he had just heard. The state attorney passed close to his seat, but D'Ray didn't look at him. He could feel his eyes on him, glaring, trying to intimidate. His attorney reached over and gently patted him on his knee, but D'Ray didn't respond. He had retreated deep within himself to a place that was warm and safe and peaceful.

"Is the defense ready?" the judge called from the bench.

"Yes, Your Honor."

"You may proceed."

"Thank you, Your Honor," his attorney said, rising and stepping out parallel to the side of the table.

"Your Honor, we do not come before the court this afternoon seeking a favor, nor do we come expecting anything other than that which is just. Your Honor, we come simply asking that you right a wrong by doing what is mandated by the laws of this great country; set my client free.

"Your Honor, in this country the law is clear. No person for whom there exists a reasonable doubt to his or her guilt shall be subject to incarceration. In this case, Your Honor, not only is there reasonable doubt, but there is reasonable certainty that D'Ray Reid did not and could not have committed this crime. You might ask why I would make such a statement. Could it be because of the exemplary life that my client has lived? No, Your Honor. D'Ray Reid cannot boast of an unblemished record of citizenship. D'Ray Reid is guilty of many things. He is guilty of poor judgment. He is guilty of being stubborn. He is guilty of being hardheaded. He is guilty of being stupid. He is even guilty of having run afoul of the law on any number of occasions. But, Your Honor, he is not guilty of the crime for which he has been charged. No, Your Honor, he is not guilty, because he was not there. And since he was not there, he had no opportunity. And since he had no opportunity, he could not have committed the crime.

"What proof has the State offered of my client's guilt, Your Honor? Fingerprints on a gun that my client handled daily and to which any number of people had access. Two witnesses who were so distraught that when questioned only minutes after the crime, they could offer no description of the assailant other than the clothes he was wearing (clothes which, I might add, were never found in my client's possession). Money on my client's person in excess of five times the amount that Mr. Clem estimates he had in his cash register at the time of the alleged robbery. No, Your Honor, D'Ray Reid did not rob Mr. Clem's store. He found that large sum of money under the seat of a truck he thought abandoned. And no, Your Honor, D'Ray Reid did not murder Stanley Earl. He was in Brownsville at the time of the murder, not Lake Providence.

"I submit to you, Your Honor, that this case is indeed about a name. Look at my client, Your Honor. Why was he charged with the crime? Could it be because he is a poor, black high school dropout from the projects who happens to be the son of a convicted murderer? He has an alibi, Your Honor. *He was not there.* He is not guilty.

"Your Honor, if this is about truth, if this is about integrity, if this is about justice . . . now that due process has run her course and the evidence of my client's innocence is clear, I urge the court to follow the only reasonable and just course of action: set my client free."

As the verdict was being read, D'Ray stood next to his lawyer, staring straight ahead. He was not stoop-shouldered, nor were his muscles taut. He felt relaxed. There was in him no anxiety or worry, only a resolve that from this day forward he would go to bed at night and get up in the morning. He would expect nothing more, nor would he desire anything less.

"In the above entitled act the court finds the defendant, D'Ray Reid, guilty as charged."

He was aware of the sounds in the courtroom. "Yes," he heard the shout of one of the victim's relieved relatives. "You bastard," he heard someone else say. "I hope you rot in hell," came a wish of eternal damnation from another. The word "hell" penetrated his skull and rattled around in his brain. Hell is where he had always been. It was the place into which he had been born. It was the home where he resided. It was the streets where he fought for his survival. It was all that he had ever known in this world and all he ever expected to find in the next. Yes, they were emotional, but not him. He heard the judge pound his gavel against the desk, yelling: "Order! Order! Order in the court." Through it all, he stood perfectly still, staring straight ahead, looking calm and feeling relaxed. No, he wasn't surprised or afraid. He only wanted to know how much time and where.

# CHAPTER TWELVE

After THE TRIAL, D'RAY WAS ESCORTED BACK TO HIS TINY CELL IN THE LAKE PROVIDENCE JAIL. INSIDE, TIME HAD NO meaning. There was no need to look back and no reason to look ahead. The future was now some faraway thing that the present wouldn't allow him to see. In his small, windowless cell there was no day and there was no night. There was no early morning sun searing through the window introducing the dawning of a new day. Nor was there the loud, shrill sound of some faraway horn blowing in the noon hour. Neither was there the sight of the moon glowing majestically in the still, starlit night. His world was now a bed, a toilet, and a sink crammed into a small, six-by-nine-foot space. His sun and his moon were one and the same, lights outside in the corridor that burned both day and night. His company was himself.

Not once during the four and a half weeks since his capture had he received a single visitor, save for his court-appointed attorney and the few officials who had interrogated him. But he didn't allow himself to think about that, or what he had done, or what he faced. He had learned to pass the time by listening. Since his arrival, he had been housed alone in a cell on a corridor isolated from the adults. He couldn't see them and they couldn't see him, but he could hear them. By now he could recognize their voices. As he moved to and fro, going back and forth to court, he stole an occasional glimpse of some of them, trying to match the faces that he saw peering out from behind the bars with the voices ringing in his head. Some were difficult, but not White Boy. He knew him as soon as he saw him. That long, stringy blond hair. Those dark blue eyes set deep into that small, perfectly shaped head. Those wiry, tattoo-covered arms dangling from those bony, square shoulders, all made the more noticeable by a too flat chest that was a perfect match for that high-pitched, whiney voice that filled the corridors both day and night. It was ironic, but White Boy, the lone Caucasian confined amongst a sea of blacks, had been his saving grace during the first few days of his incarceration.

Like him, White Boy was confined. But neither the cement nor the bars nor the wrath of his captors seemed to dull his spirit. He was caged, but he sang. All through the day and all through the night, he sang, he yelled, he shouted, he talked, he blasted his radio, he performed. But for White Boy, every day began and ended the same. Friday looked like Saturday. Saturday looked like Sunday. Sunday looked like Monday. Nothing to look forward to save for White Boy and his antics.

D'Ray had come to depend on him. Listening to him had kept his mind off the trial and his troubles. But right now everything was quiet. Too quiet. He didn't want to think about what had just happened in court or about what would happen because of what had just happened. He had just pulled the pillow over his face when he heard the keys in the door. He lowered the pillow abruptly and watched a guard pull the door open and step aside.

"Go on in, Henry," he heard the officer say. "Holler when you through."

It was Henry Earl, the dead boy's father. Stunned, D'Ray snapped upright and watched him walk over to his cot and pause. He was carrying a thin brown paper bag, which he held in a tight embrace against his chest. Suddenly the tiny cell seemed even smaller. D'Ray had a strong desire to flee, but the realization that he was trapped, caged, held him firmly in place. In his mind he saw himself frantic, pressed in a corner, clinching the steel bars, pulling, struggling, screaming as the man whose only son he had murdered bore down on him. As he approached, D'Ray turned his body toward the cell door, focused his attention on the corridor wall, and waited to hear the man's angry words. He wouldn't look at him no matter what he said and no matter what he did. In his mind he was a stone, hearing nothing, seeing nothing, feeling nothing.

"Son, do you recognize me?" His voice was sad and soft and compassionate, but not angry. D'Ray felt a strong compulsion to furrow his brow and look at him, but he didn't. He sat perfectly still, staring at the gray concrete wall, wishing that he was alone and trying to stifle his feelings, which in an instant had been transformed from fear to something akin to remorse. He didn't want to feel, he didn't want to think, he didn't want to listen. What did Mr. Henry want from him, anyway? He had been caught, he had been tried, he had been convicted. D'Ray felt the bed give as Mr. Henry sat on the cot next to him.

"I'm Henry Earl and this is my boy, Stanley," he said, shaking the bag rattling the contents. D'Ray clamped his teeth and swallowed, but he didn't look. A bloody image of the dead boy's body lying in a pool of blood flashed before his eyes. The image was clear, but he couldn't recall if it was the result of what he had actually seen that night or if staring at those gruesome crime photos had imprinted it on his brain. D'Ray focused on the wall. He was a stone, void of feelings, void of emotions.

"Ya'll know each other, right?"

D'Ray couldn't believe his ears. He held firm, sitting very still, staring straight ahead, but only, now, he saw nothing. He concentrated on the words ringing in his head. He tried to block out the question. But how could he? No, he hadn't known the boy, but what did it matter now? The boy was dead and he was incarcerated. He heard the sound of paper being ruffled. He glanced at Mr. Henry out of the corner of his eye, then quickly looked away. He saw him remove an item from the bag, then lay it on the floor halfway between the two of them.

"Ain't he a fine-looking boy?" D'Ray heard Mr. Henry ask. Involuntarily, his eyes fell on the picture. It was a graduation picture. Cap and gown. D'Ray's eyes found the wall again. He stared at it, concentrating. He didn't want to see the boy. He didn't want to know him. That would make everything too real. That would cause him to feel, and what good would that do? No, he wouldn't allow himself to feel someone else's pain. Sure, the man had lost a son. And he had taken his life. But what choice had he? It was either Mr. Henry's son or his brother.

"Yeah, he's a good boy." Again Mr. Henry's words pierced D'Ray's imaginary shield and seeped into his consciousness. "Ain't never gave me one minute's trouble."

Honor thy mother and thy father, that thy days may be long

upon the earth. The thought came searing to the fore of D'Ray's mind from some remote place in his brain. Not his adult brain, but his childhood brain. Back at a time when Sunday school was mandatory and the ways of the world seemed clear. A time before the time he learned that you had to fight the world for life. A time when he honestly believed that bad things only happened to bad people. But now he knew better. Good and bad had nothing to do with living and dying. That's what he knew and that's what he had to believe. A good boy died in a bad situation. It was unfortunate, but so was much of life in his world.

"And he was smart too." Again he was aware of Mr. Henry's words as well as the sound of the bag being ruffled. He felt himself struggling against the temptation tugging at his eyes. No, he wouldn't look.

"Ain't never made a B in his life." He heard the pride in Mr. Henry's voice. "Said he wanted to be like Thurgood Marshall. A credit to his race. Can you believe that?"

D'Ray didn't answer.

"In this day and time, when it look like everybody is interested in stealing, dealing, and killing, he dreaming about being the next Thurgood Marshall. Just might do it, too. Lord knows he got the brains. What you think?"

D'Ray heard a thud as Mr. Henry dropped what he was holding to the floor. He glanced down, then quickly looked away. Lying on the floor at his feet was a thick stack of report cards bound together with a single rubber band.

"Yeah, he's a smart boy," D'Ray heard Mr. Henry say in a low, raspy voice. To D'Ray it almost seemed that Mr. Henry had ceased talking to him and was now talking to himself. Again he heard the sound of Mr. Henry's hand inside the bag moving about, searching. From the corner of his eye he saw him remove a single piece of paper and hold it out in front of him. "Scored sixteen hundred on the SAT." Mr. Henry hesitated, chuckling. "Boy, you should have been there the day he opened that letter. You'd thought the house was on fire the way he was running and jumping and hollering.

"By the time I got use to him doing so well on that test, I found out that he had done won this." Mr. Henry paused, dropped the test scores on the floor at D'Ray's feet, then busied himself searching through the bag. "Here it is," he heard him say after a long, awkward pause. "National Merit Scholarship." He paused again, then chuckled softly to himself. "I ain't never heard of no National Merit Scholarship. His teachers tell me it's a big deal. They say it's a high honor, but I wouldn't know. I never made it past the seventh grade myself. So I wouldn't know about such things. But I made it far enough to know about merit. Can't nobody say he won that scholarship for no other reason than he earned it. That's what I like about it. Couldn't nobody talk against his accomplishments. No sirree bob. Neither the blacks or the whites. Couldn't say he progressed 'cause he was rich, 'cause we sho' ain't that. Couldn't say he progressed 'cause we give him some kind of advantage—truth be told, I ain't been able to give him much of anything 'cept love and understanding. Couldn't say he progressed 'cause he black. All they can say is he progressed because of his own merit. That's what this here paper say." D'Ray felt the bed give as Mr. Henry turned toward him. "Yeah, this made it all seem worthwhile. All the hard work. All the sacrifices. All the trips back and forth to that school. This makes it all worth it."

D'Ray fought to keep his eyes focused on the wall. Though he did not turn his head or move his eyes, he still saw Mr. Henry raise the paper above his head and release it. He watched it slice through the still, stale air until it too, like the others, rested on the floor at his feet.

"Just when I was so proud that I thought I would pop wide open, this here come." He reached into the bag, removed a long white envelope, opened it, and removed the contents. "It gives us—" He paused and took a deep breath. His voice had begun to shake. D'Ray glanced at him, then looked away, but not before he saw that his hands were trembling. "It gives us great pleasure—" He sighed and paused a second time. Now he was sobbing heavily. He resumed. "—to inform you that you have been admitted to the University of Chicago." He pulled the paper to his chest, embraced it with both arms, then let it drop to the floor. "My boy going to the University of Chicago. What do you think about that?" He paused.

D'Ray didn't answer.

"Gits mighty cold up there, you know."

D'Ray still didn't answer.

"Told 'im to git hisself some of them long johns with the flap in the back. And some boots too. The kind that's insulated." He paused. "You ever been to Chicago?"

D'Ray didn't answer.

"You got any people up there?"

D'Ray thought about aunt Peggy. She lived in Chicago. He wondered if she had heard about the killing.

"The night he got the letter, I went in the back bathroom, locked the door, and kneeled down right between the bathtub and the commode. And I talked to God. I told him right then and there that I didn't know if I could stand any mo' good news. I was trying to be humble and fight off all them prideful feelings. 'Cause you know what the good book say, 'Pride goeth before a fall.'" He reached into the bag and removed his son's diploma. It was still in its original leather case. He held it firmly in his hand, running his fingers back and forth across the smooth cover. "Not long after I prayed that prayer, he graduated. When they gave him his diploma, he walked right over to where I was sitting and gave it to me. I know he wasn't supposed to do that. But when he said, 'Daddy, this is as much yours as it is mine,' and handed it to me, look like I just got full. Full of joy. Full of happiness. Full of pride. He didn't have to do that, but he did. That's just the kind of person he was. Good through and through. That's how he ended up working at Mr. Clem's. Said he wanted to make some college money. Didn't want me to have to buy all his clothes or bear all his expense back and forth to school. I ain't never let him work before. You know how you young boys are. Ya'll start piddling around on them old jobs while ya'll still got your feet under your daddy's table, y'all get to thinking that's something big. First thing you know you want to buy a little old car. Then you got to keep piddling to keep a little gas in it. Then before you know it, y'all call yourself courting. Then you want to quit school and git married. Then when you get out on your own with a family, you find out that that little old money ain't enough to do nothing with but be po'. So I wouldn't let 'im work. But when he started working for Mr. Clem, he already had his future planned." He paused. "University of Chicago."

He reached into the bag and pulled out a crumpled piece of paper. "June third, nineteen seventy." He read the date out loud. He paused. "That was the happiest day of my life." He tossed the paper onto the pile and reached back into the bag. D'Ray lowered his eyes, glanced at the paper, then looked away. It was a birth certificate. "And this was the saddest," Mr. Henry said, kneeling to the floor and gently placing the paper on the top of the stack. *"Honor Student Slain in Robbery."* Again he began to weep openly. "He was all I had. When his mother passed, I made him my world. The night he was born, I knew right then that the Lord was loaning him to me. He wasn't mine to keep. I knew that. But sho' as he left the house that day, I was sho' he was coming back. I didn't even get a chance to say good-bye. I was so tired. Lord knows I was tired. I worked a double at the plant. Went in at eight A.M., didn't get off until three A.M. I heard 'im when he left, but I was too tired to get up. He didn't bother me, though. He knew I was tired. But he left me a note." Mr. Henry rose to his feet and removed his wallet from his back pocket. "'Daddy, gone to work. Be back at nine. See you tonight. I love you. Stanley.'" Mr. Henry fell back on the bed, sobbing heavily. D'Ray felt his heart pounding in his chest. He wanted to say something, but he didn't know what.

"He said he was coming back. That's what he said in the note. 'Be back at nine' . . . But he ain't coming back, is he?"

D'Ray felt his own leg trembling. He fought against the emotion that Mr. Henry was making him feel. He was making him know his son. Making him care about him. He didn't want to feel. He didn't want to think. He stared at the wall, but he no longer saw the plain cement blocks. He saw Stanley standing there, staring at him with sad, tearful eyes. He watched Stanley reach out to his father, pleading, begging to come home. D'Ray thought of his own father. He remembered the day that he was carted off to jail. He remembered that empty feeling. He remembered the loneliness, the fear, the pain, the vow: he would never love anything again with all of his heart. He would never allow a loss to cause him to ache, to wish for death, to feel numb, void, worthless. Now, Stanley was him and he was Stanley, racked with pain, filled with sorrow, overcome with remorse.

"Maybe it was my fault," he heard Mr. Henry say.

D'Ray wanted to reach over to him, tell him, No, it was nobody's fault. It was . . . He didn't know what it was. He hadn't stepped out of bed that morning with the intent to kill. Life had played a dirty trick on him. Life had made him take one life in order to save another.

"Maybe I became too prideful," he heard Mr. Henry say. "Maybe the Lord is just trying to humble me. Maybe it's a test. That's it. It's a test. He's just testing me the way he tested Job." He paused and looked at the ceiling. "Stanley with his mama now. They done finally got over." He lowered his eyes and looked at D'Ray. "You believe in heaven?"

D'Ray didn't answer. He pondered the question. He didn't know what he believed. Maybe there was a heaven and a hell and a God. But then again, maybe there wasn't. If God was real, why did he allow bad things to happen to those who believed in him and good things to happen to those who didn't? His mother believed, and where had it gotten her? His people believed, and where had it gotten them? Everything was backwards. Evil people prospered and decent people suffered. He didn't know what he believed. He didn't answer. He couldn't.

"No, you don't believe," Mr. Henry answered for him. "If you did you couldn't have killed my son, could you?"

D'Ray didn't answer.

"Why did you kill 'im?" D'Ray heard the question that he knew had been coming since the moment Mr. Henry had entered his cell. But what did he want him to say? What could he say?

"What's gotten into you kids? Don't y'all feel? Don't life mean anything to you? Is it that easy for y'all to point a gun at another human being and pull the trigger? I don't know. Maybe y'all just don't care. And if you don't, I guess I'm wasting my time. But I came down here because I want you to know the consequences of your action. I want you to know the pain that you have caused and the lives that you have destroyed. I was my mama's only boy, and Stanley was my only child. So when you killed Stanley, you killed my name. You killed my grandchildren. You killed my daughter-in-law. You killed my family. You killed everything that Stanley had worked so hard for and everything that he could have been. I just want to know why."

"I didn't mean to kill him," D'Ray heard himself reply.

Mr. Henry leaped to his feet and leaned over the contents he had piled on the floor. "He didn't mean to kill you, Stanley," Mr. Henry shouted. "Does that matter to you, son?" Mr. Henry paused, raised his head, and looked deep into D'Ray's eyes. "Stanley didn't answer." He fell to his knees and scooped up the papers in both hands, crying. "Stanley didn't answer," he repeated.

In the distance, D'Ray heard the sound of footsteps resonating off the hard concrete floor. He looked up. The guard pulled the door open and slammed it shut as his mother walked through. Stunned, he snapped to his feet. Mr. Henry also stood, nodded to her, and moved to the far corner. D'Ray stood perfectly still, staring at her. She appeared so tired, so feeble, so old.

"Where did I go wrong?" Her voice was low and lifeless.

"Nowhere, Mama." He longed for her to put her arms around him and pull him close to her bosom and tell him that everything was going to be alright. Your mama is here and everything is going to be alright.

"Didn't I try to provide for you?"

"Yes ma'am," he mumbled softly. She was a good mother. At least she had been before she became tired. Before her husband went to jail. Before she lost her job. Before people turned on her because they turned on the man she had married. That's when he decided to be a man. That's when he decided to be an outlaw.

"Didn't I try to love you?" she asked.

"Yes ma'am," he answered her. He wanted to explain that he also loved her. Not the way she wanted, but the only way he could. He wanted to make her understand that he had killed so that she could keep the only thing that motivated her to get up every morning and draw another breath.

"Didn't I try to teach you right from wrong?"

"Yes, Mama."

She looked at him questioningly.

"Then why you so evil?"

He didn't answer her.

"Your lawyer wants me to talk for you at the sentencing, but I won't. I'll be there but I won't talk for you. Whatever that judge decides to do is gone be up to him. I ain't gone try to influence him one way or the other. You understand me?"

D'Ray nodded his head but didn't speak.

"Son, I want you to understand something else. When the sentencing is over, it's over. I won't be coming back."

"Aw, Mama, don't say that."

"As far as I'm concerned, you dead."

"Mama, you don't mean that."

"I wish I didn't. God knows I wish I didn't. But, D'Ray, you ain't been nothing but trouble since the day you come into this world, and I 'spect that's all you gone be until you leave it."

"Mama!"

She turned her back on him and her eyes met Mr. Henry's.

"I'm sorry for your loss."

Mr. Henry's bottom lip began to quiver. He took her hand, raised it to his mouth, and kissed it gently. D'Ray moved close to her. He touched her shoulder. She snapped her head and twisted from underneath his touch. She took one step toward the door and hesitated. The guard pulled the door open, then slammed it shut as she hurried from the cell.

For a brief moment all was quiet, save for the sound of her shoes striking the bare concrete floor. As the two men stood listening to her fading footsteps, Mr. Henry leaned his head against the cell and clinched the cold steel bars with his large powerful hands. He sighed heavily and released his grip. He moved next to the door and signaled the guard. D'Ray heard the key in the lock. The door swung open and Mr. Henry walked through. He stood for a moment with his back to the steel door. He turned and looked back at D'Ray. His eyes were cold, icy. He swallowed and composed himself. Then he whispered in a voice laced with a bone-chilling calmness: "Everything you took from me, you gonna give it back."

# CHAPTER THIRTEEN

As she HAD PROMISED, ON THE DAY THAT HE WAS SENTENCED, HIS MOTHER WAS PRESENT. SHE SAT IN THE SAME SEAT she had occupied during the trial. Sonny was with her. He sat close to her, and though only the upper portions of their bodies were visible from where D'Ray sat, it was clear to him that Sonny was holding her hand.

Several times during the proceedings, D'Ray turned and looked at her, but not once did she acknowledge his stare. Not once did she move. Not once did she speak. She was a tree, tall, firmly rooted, emotionless, immovable. Mr. Henry broke down on the stand, openly sobbing the loss of his only son and defiantly cursing the evil nature of hers. But even then she did not move or flinch. She was there, but she wasn't there. She heard, but she didn't hear. Just like everyone else in the courtroom, she knew what the sentence would be. All that came before and all that came after was merely a formality. She had simply to wait and bear it. No need to hope. No need to dream. No need to care.

"Mr. Reid, do you have anything to say?"

D'Ray heard the judge's question but he didn't answer. He turned and looked at his mother. Again her eyes revealed no sign of recognition. They remained fixed in one direction, looking only God knows where, seeing only God knows what. Dejected, D'Ray slowly turned back in his seat, lowered his eyes, and shook his head.

"Stand and face the court."

His order was clear. His tone was void of emotion. D'Ray stood and clasped his hands low in front of his crotch. The judge began to talk, but D'Ray did not listen.

"Having been tried and convicted of murder in the first degree, I hereby remand you to the Louisiana Youth Authority, where you will remain until your twenty-first birthday."

A tap of the gavel and instantly D'Ray felt the power of a single hand gripping his arm, forcing it behind his back. He felt the all-too-familiar sensation of the cold, hard steel digging into his small, aching wrists. He felt a pull. He heard a command: "Let's go!"

He stumbled, leaned against the corner of the table, and began looking about. Again he looked in his mother's direction. Sonny returned his stare, but not her. Somehow now he knew that she had meant what she said. He was dead. He was alone. There was a shuffling of feet. He felt the officer grab his arm. He felt the officer's fingers press hard against his relaxed biceps. The room was clearing; he watched the small crowd of people slowly moving out into the hallway. But neither Sonny nor his mother moved. He wanted to go to her and make her understand what he had done, make her understand why he had done it. But he did not move. So much had gone unsaid for so long, until now, there were no words to explain what he knew to her was unexplainable. Suddenly her face was that of a stranger, and he was a motherless child.

"Let's go home," the officer chided him.

D'Ray flinched. The word "home" touched something deep inside him. Something that he had intentionally tucked away. Something that he had tried to kill. In his mind he quickly did the math. Six years. The thought came to him suddenly. That's how much time he had been given. How would he make it? How would he survive? His knees began to shake. His palms became moist; his heart began to pound.

"Can't you hear, boy?" The officer was becoming impatient. "I said, let's go!"

D'Ray tried to lift his foot to walk, but it seemed heavy; he seemed weak. A second officer approached. D'Ray felt an open hand push hard against the center of his back.

"Go on! Walk."

D'Ray edged forward, his lungs not taking in or letting out air. He turned his head slightly.

"Mama," he called to her, but she did not respond.

The officer relaxed his grip.

"What you say, boy?"

D'Ray didn't answer.

"You want your mama?" The officer's voice was low, mocking.

D'Ray glanced at him, then averted his eyes.

"Mama can't help you now."

The satisfaction in the officer's voice snapped D'Ray back to reality. He looked at one officer, then the other. Yes, they wanted to see fear. They wanted to see him squirm. They wanted to see him cry or tremble or give them some sign that he, the tormentor, was now the tormented. No, he wouldn't do that. What was done was done. No need to look back. No need to look ahead. No need to feel. He followed the officers through the side door, down the stairs, and out of the building. A third policeman was sitting behind the wheel of the car that he had pulled next to the building. He lowered the window and poked his head through.

"It's over?" he asked.

"Yep, it's over," his partner said.

"Y.A.?" He asked a second question.

"You know it," his partner replied.

D'Ray heard the car door creak open before him and close behind him. One of the officers who had escorted him out returned to the building while the other climbed inside the car up front on the passenger side. He heard the soft, steady purr of the engine. He felt the car ease into the street, then accelerate. Then all was quiet, save for the sound of the four rubber tires moving across the hot asphalt. Through the window he saw a hawk perched high upon a limb extending over the still blue lake. He watched it leap from its perch, expand its wings, and soar effortlessly through the air, riding the invisible wind currents, rising higher and higher until it disappeared into the clear blue sky. He closed his eyes, imagining the feel of freedom. He felt his mind drifting back to happier times. Beggar Man was there. So was Crust. So was Pepper. They were in his mother's backyard, sitting in the cool night air, playing cards on an old makeshift table. And yes, there was ice cold beer. And there was music. And there was laughter. And they were footloose and fancy-free.

Suddenly the car slowed to negotiate a turn. D'Ray's body compensated. He pulled against the gravity pulling against him. The car sailed through an intersection. D'Ray turned and looked at the traffic light. It all came rushing back to him. He tried not to think about it, but how could he not think about the single event that had altered his life forever? It seemed like only yesterday that he was on this same road, sitting behind the wheel of a stolen truck, fleeing one scene, rushing to another. He saw the sign through the window. *Brownsville 10 miles.*

Little Man. Why hadn't she brought Little Man? How was he doing? Was he angry? Was he scared? Was he blaming himself? It wasn't his fault. It was nobody's fault. He lived; someone else died. That's it.

He looked out the window. In less than a few minutes, they would pass through Brownsville. Maybe one of the fellows would be walking along the road or sitting out on the stoop in front of the barbershop. He turned in his seat and looked through the back window. Soon Sonny and his mother would be traveling this same road. Would they discuss him, or would they ride in silence, pretending that he no longer existed? Why hadn't she acknowledged him? Why?

They passed the sign: *Brownsville Corp.* He sat up straight and leaned forward, excited. He was home. He saw the small liquor store on the opposite side of the street. He looked at the cars parked out front but did not recognize any of them. They crossed the small bridge just outside of town, passed underneath a yellow caution light, and sped past the radio station. He read the call letters painted on the side of the tiny red building, *KWCL Country Radio.* The car stopped, and without looking he knew they were at the traffic light across from the car wash. Parallel to the car wash was the road that he had traveled that night in the stolen truck. He looked at the road, then at the car wash. A solitary white man whom he had never seen before was busy washing a heavy coat of mud from a small pickup truck. For a brief moment he allowed himself to wonder about the man. He was either a farmer or a hunter. How else could he have gotten his truck so muddy on such a clear, dry day?

The light changed and the car eased forward. When they were even with the barbershop, he leaned against the window, looking. Someone was sitting in the barber's chair closest to the window, and several people were milling about outside on the stoop. He saw others, but not Beggar Man, not Pepper, not Crust.

The car continued forward, and reality set in. He became frantic.

He looked from one side of the street to the other, trying to memorize every building, every store, every tree, every landmark. They passed the school, then the slaughterhouse, then the last gas station. A car whizzed by. He turned and watched it disappear into the town that he could no longer see.

Inside his head things were moving too fast. He wanted to slow everything down. He wanted to savor the sunshine, the cool breeze, his freedom. They passed a pasture filled with cows grazing tranquilly on what looked like a never-ending sea of plush green grass. He looked at the long barbed-wire fence, four strands holding them in, restricting their movement. An image flashed in his mind of a collection of small tattered buildings, clumped behind a huge hurricane fence topped off with several strands of wire. Barbed, menacing, razor sharp.

What did Y.A. look like? Why didn't he know? Why hadn't he heard? Why?

They had long passed through Goodwill and were now approaching the small village of Mer Rouge. At the intersection, they did not keep straight as he assumed they would. Instead, they crossed the railroad tracks, turned left at the traffic light, and headed south toward Collinston. Some people traveled this route because it was a little shorter. Others refused, at least at night, for fear of taking the long, dark, windy road through the densely wooded swamps. Why were they going this way? What was the hurry?

He stared out the window watching the trees sail by until the car jutted out of the wilderness and pulled to a stop at an intersection. He turned and looked back over his shoulder. Had they made it through the swamps already? He wanted to relax, but he couldn't. They were going too fast. Soon he would be back in a cage. He would still be in the world, but not of it. Life would go on without his knowledge. Old people would die. Babies would be born. And Little Man would plug along without him. Or would he? Suddenly he retreated deep within himself. Was Little Man ready? Did he know enough to survive in the projects? In an instant, D'Ray's mind was filled with a thought that he could not shake. Papa World had left him, and now he had left Little Man.

The car rolled forward. The officers talked between themselves, but he wasn't listening to them. He had so retreated within himself that he was unaware when they passed through the little hamlet of

Swartz. Or when they entered the city limits of Monroe. Or when they turned onto the freeway. The noise of a semi truck roaring by in the passing lane roused him from his stupor. His eyes widened. He looked about, realizing they were only a short distance from the facility. Anxiety again gripped him. His heart began to pound. A tiny bead of sweat appeared on his brow and slowly rolled to a stop at the tip of his nose. Slightly irritated, he turned his head and tried to wipe his nose on the corner of his shoulder. He couldn't reach it. His cuffed hands had rendered him armless. Why had they cuffed his hands behind him? Why not in front? He saw the officer's face in the rearview mirror looking at him, smiling.

"Them cuffs too tight, boy?"

D'Ray shook his head but did not speak. He averted his eyes, watching the cars speeding past, hurrying to get to some predetermined destination. How strange it felt not to have any place to be or anyone to see, or anything to do. How strange it was trying to imagine being confined to the same small space, adhering to the same regimented schedule, day after day, night after night, for the next six years.

His mother was home by now. Was she in her bedroom behind a locked door, crying the way she cried the night Papa World was sentenced? The thought made him relive that night. It caused him to remember his innocent question: "Mama, when Papa coming home?" It caused him to remember her answer: "Papa ain't coming home. He ain't never coming home."

The car turned off the large busy freeway onto a small highway before turning onto an even smaller road. They passed a hospital. The levee came into view. A small boy was high upon the bank, riding a bicycle. The seat was missing and he was standing on the pedals, leaning over the handlebars. He had removed his shirt and tied the sleeves about his neck. Now it was no longer a shirt but a cape. And he was no longer a little boy but Superman or Batman or some other superhero, patrolling the river, ridding it of evil, making it safe for mankind.

They pulled to the guard station and stopped. Behind the station was a fence. Above the fence was the large, menacing sign: *Louisiana Youth Authority.* He read the sign and took a deep breath. Relax, he told himself. Don't let 'em scare you.

A guard emerged from inside the station, carrying a clipboard. As he approached the car, D'Ray studied him. He was a big, burly man, well over six feet tall. He could have been in his early fifties or a little older. He didn't wear a uniform. Instead, he wore a white shirt, dark pants, and a tie. His pants appeared to be black, but they could just as easily have been dark blue. His head was bald on top and his hair was beginning to gray around the temples. He had a large potbelly that fell over his belt and hung down in front of him. He didn't wear a badge, but he did have a gun strapped about his waist.

"How you boys making out today?" he asked, leaning against the window on the driver's side and spitting out a long, brown stream of tobacco juice.

"Aw, just another day in the jungle," one of the officers replied matter-of-factly.

"I know that's right." D'Ray felt the man's eyes on him, searing, intimidating. "What you got there?"

"Fifteen-year-old black male."

"What's the name?"

"D'Ray Reid."

The man looked at the pad.

"R-e-i-d," he spelled the last name.

"That's him," D'Ray heard the officer say.

"Good enough," the man said, disappearing inside the station. The gate swung open and they drove through. As they followed the long, narrow gravel road past one building after the other, D'Ray examined the place. It didn't look at all the way he had imagined. The buildings were old, but not drab. Some of them were made of wood, but most were tiny redbrick buildings surrounded by huge oak trees. Underneath each tree was a flower bed, each bed encircled with painted stones—all of which was set off by a neatly manicured lawn. There was a basketball court, a football field, and a track. Save for the fences and the razor wire, the place more closely resembled a school than a prison.

When they finally rolled to a stop in front of one of the buildings, the officer opened the door and told him to get out.

As soon as he was out, he saw them. He watched them round the corner and walk straight toward him. There were thirty of them, maybe forty. They were all dressed exactly alike. A pair of plain straight-leg blue jeans, a white T-shirt, and a pair of white sneakers. Their hair was cut close and their faces were clean shaven. They

walked single-file, flanked on either side by an adult. He felt the officer grab his arm.

"Hold on," he heard him say. "Let 'em pass."

As they filed passed, one of them looked at D'Ray and smiled but
didn't speak.

"You see that, boy?" one of the officers asked.

D'Ray didn't answer.

"Aw, he likes you."

D'Ray felt his heart pounding in his throat.

"Ain't out the car good and one of 'em already putting the moves
on you."

Suddenly D'Ray felt sick, nauseated.

"You think you like him too?"

The question was degrading.

"I ain't no punk," D'Ray yelled, feeling the need to assert his
manhood. "I ain't no punk, you hear?"

"You will be." The officer laughed. "You can bet on that."

They led him into the building, removed the cuffs, signed some
papers, and departed. He was taken into a large empty room, where
he was left alone. Soon two men entered. One was black, the other
was white. Both were in their thirties and neither was particularly
large. They wore no uniforms, only ID cards that hung about their
necks. Both were dressed in jeans, but they wore different-colored
shirts. The white one approached him first. He dropped a small bun-
dle of clothes on the floor and yelled: "Strip!"

D'Ray heard the command, but he didn't move. He couldn't. He
had expected him to tell him who they were or to explain the proce-
dure.

"You hard of hearing, boy?" The man was in D'Ray's face. His
nose was against D'Ray's nose. "I said strip!"

D'Ray could feel his hands trembling as he bent to loosen his
shoelaces. He looked up at the black man standing next to the door.
He didn't know why. Maybe he expected to find some answers in his
eyes. Maybe he hoped he would utter a comforting word. But the
man's eyes were cold, empty.

"Hurry up!" the white man shouted. He seemed annoyed that
D'Ray was taking so long.

D'Ray kicked his shoes off, stepped out of his pants, and pulled
his shirt over his head. Then he paused.

"All the way."

"Why?" D'Ray asked.

"Because I said so, that's why."

"But—."

He felt the butt of the nightstick crash hard against the back of his head. He fell to his knees, his hands clasped behind his head. His head ached; it throbbed. He looked up. The black man was standing over him with stick in hand.

"Ain't nobody playing with you, boy!" His voice was filled with anger. "Take off your drawers!"

D'Ray rose to his feet. He felt wobbly, disoriented, unstable. Using both hands, he pulled his underwear down over his genitals and let them fall to the floor. He had been publicly nude before, in the locker room and at the swimming hole when they went skinny-dipping, but this felt different. He felt violated, humiliated, degraded.

"Hold your hands up."

He lifted his arms shoulder level, bent them at the elbow and extended his hands in a ninety-degree angle.

"Not out, stupid. Up!"

He felt the stick crash against his elbow. He winced and threw his hands into the air.

"All the way up!" the white man screamed. "Reach for the sky! Reach for the sky!"

D'Ray reached his hands above his head and rose up on his toes, stretching as far as he could. His body reacted automatically to the command: "Open your hands ... Wiggle your fingers ... That's good."

D'Ray dropped his hands and glanced over his shoulder; the black man had moved closer to him.

"What you looking at me for?" The black man raised the stick, threatening to strike. D'Ray flinched and snapped back around. Suddenly he was stiff, tense, anticipating a blow.

"Open your mouth!" the white man ordered.

D'Ray's lips parted and his jaws dropped. He looked at the man with wide fearful eyes.

"Stop eyeballing me!"

D'Ray averted his eyes and lowered them submissively. At that moment he didn't know who he hated most, them or himself. He felt the white man's hand on the top of his head, pushing. Now his head was tilted back; his mouth was stretched open, and his eyes were staring at the dull gray ceiling. They felt moist. No, he wouldn't cry. He wouldn't. He wouldn't.

"Drop to your knees." D'Ray heard him but didn't move. He felt the sting of the stick across his back. He moaned; his eyes widened; he fell to his knees. He looked at the man pleadingly.

"Stop eyeballing me!" His voice was angry, enraged.

Again D'Ray averted his eyes.

"Open your mouth and tilt your head back."

D'Ray could feel his lips quivering; his mouth dropped open. His head fell back. The man removed a penlight from his shirt pocket and shined it in D'Ray's mouth. As he looked he barked out a series of instructions: "Pull back your top lip . . . Pull back your bottom lip . . . Lift up your tongue . . . Move it around . . . Close your mouth . . . Stand up!"

D'Ray pressed his hands against the cold concrete floor and pushed to his feet.

"Grab your rope!" the man shouted, shining the tiny light on D'Ray's groin. Without hesitation, D'Ray clutched his penis in his trembling right hand, wishing the entire ordeal was over.

"Lift it up . . . Stretch it . . . Skin it back . . . That's good."

D'Ray removed his hand and his penis fell back into place. He glanced at the man, then quickly lowered his eyes.

"Pull up your rocks."

D'Ray hesitated. He frowned, confused.

"Your rocks, stupid," the man shouted, shining the light on D'Ray's genitals. "Your balls."

D'Ray lifted his scrotum. It was warm and moist with sweat. He heard the man's voice again, stern, terse.

"Drop 'em . . . Run your hand through your hairs . . . Turn around and face the wall."

D'Ray turned. He was face-to-face with the black man. Their eyes met.

"Don't you look at me."

D'Ray dropped his eyes. He looked at the floor, then at the wall. He heard the commands from behind him.

"Bend over . . . Farther . . . Grab your butt . . . Pull your cheeks apart . . . Wider . . . Cough . . . Again . . . Stand up and turn around."

D'Ray turned and lowered his eyes.

"Lift up your foot . . . Wiggle your toes . . . That's good."

He pushed the pile of clothes to him with his foot.

"Pick up your drawers."

D'Ray looked at them. The crotch was stained.

"Mister, these things ain't clean."

He felt the nightstick on the back of his leg. His knees buckled.

"Put 'em on."

He pulled the underwear up about his waist, wondering who had worn them before him. Who had stained them? He felt dirty, filthy, unclean.

"Pick up your socks . . . Put 'em on . . . Pick up your shirt . . . Put it on . . . Pick up your pants . . . Put 'em on . . . Pick up your shoes . . . Put 'em on."

When he was fully dressed, he paused, looking.

"Let's go."

He followed them down a narrow hallway to a heavy steel door. The white man unlocked the door and moved aside. The black man shoved D'Ray inside. D'Ray stumbled, then regained his balance. He heard the white man's voice.

"Good night, sleep tight, don't let the bedbugs bite."

# CHAPTER FOURTEEN

They had PUT HIM IN THE NEWCOMERS' DORM. IT WAS A LARGE RECTANGULAR ROOM. THERE were no bars and no windows, only four gray cement walls and a thick, solid steel door. Both sides of the room were lined with bunk beds. The bathroom was in the back, five stalls, five urinals, and ten shower heads.

When he was shoved into the room, he had hoped to be alone, but to his dismay the room was occupied by four others. He glanced at their faces. He suspected that they had all come in around the same time. It appeared that they had formed some type of bond. Yet none of them seemed comfortable. They sat wide-eyed, huddled close together on the same side of the room. As he approached an empty bed, he heard them whispering amongst themselves. Their tone was low. Their words were short, terse, serious.

He tried to evaluate the situation without being obvious. He turned toward them as he spread the sheet over the foot of the lumpy mattress. When he raised the mattress to tuck the sheet, he stole a quick glance. None of them looked particularly large or seemed particularly tough. For a brief moment D'Ray wondered what they could have done. Were they murderers like himself, or were they shoplifters, or purse snatchers, or trespassers? Were they from the projects, or were they from some quaint little suburban neighborhood? Suddenly they looked silly to him. They were sissies. Already broken. All ready to be punked.

"What's your name?" one of them asked sheepishly.

D'Ray lowered the mattress and sat on the edge of the bed.

"D'Ray," he said. "D'Ray Reid."

"They call me Scooter," the boy said. He crossed the room and awkwardly extended his hand. D'Ray studied him for a moment, then took his hand. The boy was nervous. His hand was moist; it was shaking.

"That there is Willie, and Tony, and Pee Wee." He introduced the others.

D'Ray looked at them and nodded, but didn't speak.

"This your first time?" Scooter asked, a forced smile on his face.

"Yeah," D'Ray said, "first time." He looked past him to Pee Wee. He was so small. He was so frail. What could he have done? Why was he here?

"My second," Scooter said. He seemed proud. He began to relax. "Did a year the first time. Not here, though. Baton Rouge."

"Is that right?" D'Ray asked.

"Yeah, that's right." Scooter paused and looked at the others. "This here they first time too. I been showing them the ropes."

"I see," D'Ray said.

"You from 'round here?" Scooter asked the second question.

"Naw," D'Ray said. "Brownsville."

"That's north Louisiana, right?"

"Right," D'Ray said.

"I'm from down south, myself."

"You don't say."

"Yeah. New Orleans. Ninth Ward." He paused. "You ever heard of it?"

D'Ray sensed that he was feeling him out, trying to find out about him while letting him know who he was. He had done time. He was from New Orleans. He was from the Ward.

"Naw," D'Ray said, "can't say I have."

"Lot of niggers in here from the Ward, you know."

"Naw, I didn't know that," D'Ray said nonchalantly.

"Stay away from 'em if you can," Scooter warned. "Them niggers don't play. They'll take you out."

"Uh-huh." D'Ray played along. "I'll do that."

"Guess you met Murdock?"

"Who?" D'Ray asked.

"Murdock."

D'Ray stared at him, confused.

"You been strip-searched?" he asked.

D'Ray continued to stare, but now he no longer saw Scooter. Instead, he was remembering the indignities of the search, the pain of the nightstick, and the shame of allowing himself to be so treated. He had been afraid of them. He had trembled. He should have fought. He should have made them understand that he wouldn't be broken, he wouldn't be disrespected. He wouldn't be violated. Never again. Not by them. Not by anyone. He would die first. He would kill or be killed.

"Have you?" Scooter asked a second time.

"Have you?" D'Ray answered his question with a question. He stared deep into Scooter's eyes. Did he too share this dirty little secret? Had he been made to expose the most intimate parts of his body to another man in such a degrading fashion?

"Yeah." Scooter acted nonchalantly. "Don't mean nothing, though."

D'Ray looked at him strangely but did not respond.

"That's how they get off," Scooter explained, feigning indifference. "Bunch of fags." He paused. "You'll get use to it."

"Not me," D'Ray boldly asserted. "I'm a man. Just like him. I'm a man."

They looked at each other for a moment, then Scooter dropped his eyes.

"Fighting back just make it worse," he said. "That's what he want you to do."

"Who?" D'Ray asked.

"Murdock," Scooter said.

"Who is Murdock?"

"White man that—"

"Alright," D'Ray said, holding his hand up, stopping him. "I know who you talking about." In his mind flashed an image of his white tormentor's face. There was in him a hot ball of hatred. He felt the rage waxing deep inside of himself. "What's his nigger's name?" D'Ray asked.

"Who?" Scooter asked.

"His sidekick," D'Ray said through clenched teeth. "That Uncle Tom nigger with the billy club."

"Could have been anybody." Scooter paused and looked toward the door. "Ain't none of 'em your friend," he whispered. "They black, but they ain't your friend."

Friend. D'Ray thought the word strange. This was the jungle. No such monster existed. Here the game was the same as the one he had played his entire life. There were predators and prey. Survivors and victims. No, he would form no bonds. He would make no friends. He would show no fear. He would kill or be killed.

"They gone keep you in here a week," Scooter began again.

"Then what?" D'Ray was curious.

"They gone reassign you."

"Where?"

"Don't know exactly. Just know they gone put you in a dorm with the regulars."

"How long ya'll been in here?"

"Let's see," he said looking up at the ceiling. "Me and Willie been here five days, and Tony and Pee Wee been here four days. They gone ship us out any day now." He chuckled. "Ain't nothing but a thang, though. Ain't nothing but a thang."

"I guess," D'Ray said, not knowing what else to say.

"I know," Scooter bragged, pretending to be unconcerned. "I can do eighteen months in my sleep." He looked at D'Ray. "How much time you got?"

"Six years," D'Ray said. His tone was low and unemotional.

"Six years!" Scooter said, taking a quick step backward. His eyes narrowed. "Man, what you in for?"

"Murder," D'Ray said, calmly lying back on the cot and staring at the bottom of the bed directly above him. Suddenly, all was quiet.

# CHAPTER FIFTEEN

Toward NINE O'CLOCK ON HIS SEVENTH DAY, THE DOOR
SWUNG OPEN AND THE GUARD ENTERED THE ROOM.
He was a young black man in his early twenties whom D'Ray had never
seen before.

"D'Ray Reid." The man called his name. His voice was soft, not
hard like the others.

"Yessir," D'Ray said, rising to his feet. He had been lying on top
of the covers wearing nothing but his underwear.

"Roll up your bed and follow me."

D'Ray heard him but did not move. He had expected them to
come earlier in the day, not at night, an hour before lights out.

"Let's go, Reid," the man yelled. "Move it."

D'Ray stepped into his pants. Why had he hesitated? Suddenly
he was remembering Murdock's voice, seeing the look in his eyes,
feeling the sting of the nightstick against his back. He felt his body
tingle with rage. No, he was afraid of no man, no thing, no situation.

When he finished rolling the bed, D'Ray rose and faced the
guard. Their eyes met.

"Let's go," he said, grabbing D'Ray's arm. "Keep your eyes straight
ahead and don't try nothing, hear?"

"Yessir," D'Ray said on cue.

"Stick out your hands."

D'Ray extended his hands and the guard removed a pair of cuffs
from his back pocket and slapped them about D'Ray's wrists. Then,

with his bed linen cradled atop his outstretched arms, D'Ray followed the man out of the building and into the hot, humid night. Outside, the sky was filled with thousands of bright, twinkling stars. On clear nights like this, he and Little Man would climb atop the house on the flat part of the roof directly above the back porch and stargaze. They would lie for hours, staring into the heavens, wondering what was out there beyond the sky. If only they were white, the answer to the question would be within the realm of possibility. They would be astronauts, exploring the far corners of the universe. The stars, the moon, the planets—no place would be too far, no adventure too perilous.

Out of nowhere, a large passenger plane flew over. It was low, and D'Ray could tell that the plane had begun its descent into the airport that was located near the facility. Who were the people on board? Where were they coming from? Where were they going? Oh, to fly high in the sky, free as a bird, not a care in the world. He looked down at the steel cuffs girting his wrists and then up at his young black captor, guiding his steps. He was a bondsman, caught and chained, owned and controlled. How often had his African slave ancestors looked into the sky and wished that they could fly? How many nights had they longed, no, prayed for the moment when they would look into the heavens and see that lone sweet chariot, swinging low, coming for to carry them home?

Home . . . Where was home? The only home he had ever known had now been blotted out. It's existence no longer held significance for him. Strangers were welcome, but not him. Reverend Cobbs was welcome, but not him. Sonny was welcome, but not him. Now there was no permanent place upon the earth where he could hope to find refuge. When freedom finally came, what would it mean? Where would he go? What would he do? Who would care? His was now a life with no purpose or direction. He was a person with no destiny or destination. He was a ship without a sail.

"Turn left." D'Ray heard the order. He turned, and moments later he was standing before a building not much unlike the one in which he had spent the last week. The guard moved next to him and grabbed his arm with one hand and pounded the door with the other. Instantly the door opened. They entered the room and the heavy steel door slammed shut behind them.

"You Mr. Pete?" the young guard asked.

"Yep," the old man answered. "That's me."

"I'm Raymond."

"Glad to meet you, Raymond." Pete extended his hand and the two men shook.

"They told me to bring this inmate over here."

Pete looked at D'Ray.

"He a newcomer?"

"Yessir."

"He got a name?"

"Yessir," Raymond said. "Reid . . . D'Ray Reid."

"Well, welcome the hell home, D'Ray Reid," Pete said sarcastically. D'Ray looked at him but did not speak. "I got one rule in here," Pete said in a low, threatening tone. "You don't start nothing, won't be nothing. You understand?"

"Yessir," D'Ray replied.

Pete turned to Raymond. "Hold on a minute while I get my keys."

"Take your time," Raymond said, trying to act relaxed. "I ain't in no hurry."

Off to the side was a door that led into a tiny glass-enclosed office. Pete went inside, removed a key from one of the desk drawers, and returned.

"Ain't never seen you 'round here before," he said, talking to Raymond. "You new?"

"Yessir, Mr. Pete," Raymond said. "This my second day."

"Is that right?"

"Yessir."

"How you like it?"

"So far, so good. Mostly I just been watching. This here transfer is my first solo."

"Any trouble?"

"No sir," he smiled, proudly. "Not a bit."

"Well, don't go getting cocky," Pete warned. "Stay on your toes around here and let these inmates know who boss. Otherwise they'll try you. Don't let their age fool you. It's some rough customers in here and they'll do anything. And I mean anything."

"Yessir," Raymond said. "I understand."

"Good," Pete said, playfully slapping Raymond on the shoulder. "Come on and follow me."

They followed Pete past the office and around the corner to another solid steel door. He stopped and opened the small metal plate
covering a tiny window. Then rising to his tiptoes, he placed his face
against the glass and peeked inside.

"Clear the door," he yelled forcefully. Instantly D'Ray heard the
sound of shuffling feet. Pete pulled the door open, and they all
walked inside. The room was similar to that which he had just left,
only there were more beds and more boys—a lot more boys.

"Everybody on your bunks!" Pete shouted the command.

The boys scattered and D'Ray furrowed his brow, staring straight
ahead. He wanted to appear calm, mean, unconcerned.

"Walk all the way to the back." He felt Raymond's hand against
his back, pushing him.

As he walked to the back of the room, he could feel their eyes on
him. Mentally, he counted each bed as he passed. There were forty-
eight bunks in all, twenty-four on each side of the room: twelve bunk
beds, all but one bunk occupied.

On command, he halted before the last bed, near the doorway next
to the bathroom. The top bunk was empty. Raymond removed the
cuffs from about his wrists and D'Ray laid the linens on the empty
bunk. Wordlessly, Raymond turned and walked away. D'Ray heard the
door open, then slam shut. They were gone. A surge of adrenaline
swept his body. He felt tense, keyed up. He slowly unfolded the linen
and began making the bed. It was good that he had the top bunk. Now
no one could get to him without his seeing them first.

When he was done, he undressed, climbed atop his bunk, and
pulled the covers about his neck. He was tired, but sleep would not
come. He was too uneasy. They were still watching him. He could
feel their eyes. He could hear the low, dull murmur of the boys talking amongst themselves. Why were they mumbling? What were they
talking about? Were they plotting against him?

He lay still, pretending to be unaffected by them. His mind was
racing, trying to formulate a plan. There were so many of them. Oh,
if he only had a weapon. A strange noise behind him made him
flinch. He opened his eyes wide, concentrating on the sound. Again
he heard the noise. It was coming from the bathroom. He wanted to
ignore it, but feared he would not be able to rest without knowing
who or what was behind him.

Spurred on by curiosity, he quietly lowered himself to the floor and eased into the bathroom. Once inside he paused and listened. Again he heard the noise. It was coming from the shower. D'Ray eased forward. Was this a trap? Were they trying to lure him out of sight of the others and out of earshot of Mr. Pete? Predators and prey. He was a deer responding to a call, and they were the hunters, sitting behind a blind, drawing him closer and closer, preparing to strike. His mind cautioned him to stop, but that awful sound was like a magnet, drawing him near, pulling him close.

At the entrance of the shower, D'Ray stopped and slowly poked his head through. He saw a small naked boy lying against the far wall. The boy's back was turned and his body was curled in a fetal position. He was crying. Stunned, D'Ray stared at the trembling nude body. He saw a small stream of blood trickling from the boy's anus, running down his leg, and pooling on the floor just underneath him. Reality set in. He had been beaten; he had been raped. D'Ray could feel his heart pounding inside his chest. He looked over his shoulder. He was anxious. His chest began to rise and fall as he inhaled large quantities of air through his wide open mouth. What should he do? Should he help, or should he go to bed? He turned to leave, but the sound of the boy's shrill, painful moaning stopped him in his tracks. He was somebody's son. He was somebody's little brother. An image of Little Man flashed before his eyes. He was strapped to a chair. His hands were bound behind his back. He was crying; he was frightened; he was alone.

D'Ray turned back. He eased toward the boy slowly, quietly, cautiously. When he was close, he knelt and gently laid his hand on the boy's naked shoulder. Instantly, D'Ray felt him flinch; he heard his plea: "Please . . . Please . . . Please."

D'Ray snapped his hand back and stared at the boy's trembling back. He felt nervous, ill at ease. He glanced over his shoulder and then back at the boy. "I just want to help you," he said in a reassuring voice. He gently rolled the boy over and stared into his wide fearful eyes. It was Pee Wee.

"Who did this to you?" D'Ray asked, stunned. Suddenly he was stiff, immobile.

Pee Wee opened his mouth to speak, but no words came. Instead, his lips trembled and blood began to pour from the corners of his mouth. D'Ray slid his hand underneath Pee Wee's head and slowly helped him to his feet. When he was upright, D'Ray moved close to him and slid his shoulder underneath Pee Wee's arm.

"Can you walk?" D'Ray asked compassionately.

Pee Wee didn't answer. He grimaced and nodded, yes.

D'Ray inspected him more closely. His lip was split open and his face was beginning to swell just beneath his left eye. He had fought his attacker. What kind of person would single him out? He was so little, so small, so frail. There was a large white towel hanging on the wall just outside the shower. D'Ray draped the towel about Pee Wee's waist and guided him back into the crowded room. Once inside, he paused, looking. Where was his bunk?

"Pee Wee," he whispered, staring at the others who were silently staring at them. "Where you sleep?"

Pee Wee pointed and D'Ray lifted his head and looked. His was a bottom bunk, on the left side, near the middle of the room. D'Ray guided him through the onlookers and gently laid him on his bunk. He covered him with the bedspread and bent low over him.

"Who did this?" He asked a second time. Pee Wee slowly turned his head, raised his unsteady hand, and pointed. D'Ray rose, staring at the person that Pee Wee had singled out. He was a big boy. He was built strong with broad shoulders and thick muscular arms. Yes, he was a bully. D'Ray could tell by the way he stood, by the way he smiled. He was the one that all the others feared.

D'Ray forged forward, his feet guided by anger, his body propelled by a desire to do to the boy what he had done to Pee Wee. D'Ray's mouth was clamped tight and the fingers of his right hand were clinched into a fist. There were rules. You never hit a woman and you didn't go around terrorizing people smaller than you. Now the two of them stood face-to-face, neither one any bigger than the other.

"You want to try picking on somebody your own size?" D'Ray spoke through clinched teeth.

The boy was nonchalant. He smiled, hunched his shoulders, and opened his mouth to speak. But D'Ray's had been a rhetorical question. No answer needed, no answer expected. The sight of the boy's pearly white teeth signaled him to strike. With all the force he could muster, D'Ray rammed his knee into the boy's groin. He heard the boy scream; he felt the impact of his knee jamming the boy's genitals hard against his pelvic bone. He watched him fall to the floor. Then, without hesitation, D'Ray pulled his leg back and with the force of a placekicker, drove his bare toes deep into the boy's gaping mouth.

Blood spattered. Two teeth sailed into the air and skidded across the floor. The boy's head slammed hard against the concrete wall. He was unconscious. D'Ray grabbed the top of the bed for support. He drew his leg back and kicked the side of the boy's face. Now D'Ray was possessed. He raised his leg. He stomped the boy's face with the sole of his foot. The boy's nose was bleeding; his face was bruised; his eyes were beginning to swell. Now, this was a statement, and the boy was an example. "Dirty, low-down, good-for-nothing fag," D'Ray mumbled as he kicked, stomped, pounded the boy's head against the cement wall.

"Don't kill 'im." Pee Wee's tiny voice penetrated his consciousness. D'Ray paused and looked at the boy. Involuntarily, the boy's bloody body was jerking, twitching, quivering. D'Ray looked at Pee Wee and then at the others. He slowly crossed the room and leaned against his bunk. "If y'all don't know who I am," he said in a dry, threatening tone, "I suggest you ask somebody." He paused, took a deep breath, and looked over toward Pee Wee. "For the record, anybody who mess with Pee Wee mess with me."

Exhausted, D'Ray climbed atop the bed and rolled over on his back. He was breathing rapidly, deeply. A couple of the others lifted the battered boy from the floor and carried him to his bunk. The door swung open and Mr. Pete poked his head through.

"Lights out." His voice reverberated off the wall. Then the room was dark.

# CHAPTER SIXTEEN

Sunday MORNING. VISITING DAY. D'RAY LAY ON HIS COT WAITING FOR THE HORN TO SOUND. FOR THREE years everything had been exactly the same. Up at six. Lights out at ten. Mashed potatoes and gravy on Thursday. School in the morning, fieldwork in the evening, and Henry Earl on visiting day.

It was strange, but every second Sunday Mr. Henry walked into the dayroom, and every second Sunday D'Ray braced himself for the question that he had been asked following the trial: Why did you kill my son? He expected it and he prepared himself to hear it, but Mr. Henry never asked. He talked about a lot of things. His job, his hometown, his mother (her name was Beatrice, but everybody called her Mama Bea), his two sisters (Big Siss and Ida Mae), and Stanley. He always talked about Stanley. But even then, he never asked.

At first D'Ray listened to him just to get over the fence and walk among the free. But after a time the people and the places became real. They became etched into his consciousness. They became a part of his life. He thought about them. He dreamed about them. He tried to imagine what they looked like, what they sounded like. Hearing the details of their lives sustained his own. In many ways they became the family that he no longer had. They became tangible proof of the existence of a world to which he would someday return.

The horn finally sounded and D'Ray took a shower, got dressed, and made his bed. After head count, they formed a single-file line and proceeded to the cafeteria. They followed the officer down the hall and out of the building. The sun had only recently risen, but already people beyond the fence were busy living life. Old Man Grimes was feeding his hogs. D'Ray could hear the squeals. He could picture the large animals jostling for position around an old iron trough filled with the slop Mr. Grimes had gathered from around the neighborhood. Neither he nor his mates had ever seen the hog pen. But on certain days, when the sun was hot or the wind was blowing, its existence was unmistakable.

Somewhere across the street he could hear the sound of a lawn mower. Some child must have been mowing the yard. Perhaps he had risen early in an attempt to complete his weekend chores before the sun rose too high into the sky. Maybe his younger brother or a couple of friends were helping him. Maybe they were picking up sticks, or searching the yard for rocks or wire or any other objects that would damage the blade if gone undetected. It was the weekend. The sooner he was finished, the sooner they all would be able to begin their weekly game of touch football or baseball or whatever.

As they advanced across the hard concrete, D'Ray looked in the direction of home. It seemed so far away. He thought about Little Man. What was he doing at this very moment? Was he still in bed, sleeping? Was he sitting at the kitchen table with his mother, eating breakfast? How was he feeling? Did he cry a lot? Was he depressed? Was he lonely? Oh, if only he could be there through some small miracle just long enough to see him, to talk to him, to make sure that he was all right.

Did Mr. Henry have similar thoughts? Did he kneel down and pray for one more opportunity to see Stanley? Did he sit in his favorite chair and stare out into a world that was now empty and void? Did he walk the floors at night talking to a son whose voice he could no longer hear? Did he still cry, or had he cried so much that he could cry no more?

Why didn't Mr. Henry ask the question? Could he have peace with himself without knowing why his son had died? Could he make peace with D'Ray without knowing why he had killed?

And why did he come? Why did he bring him things? Why the boxes of candy or the chocolate cakes or the sweet potato pies or the books? And not just any books, Stanley's books. All written by black people. All written about black people.

D'Ray wished Mr. Henry would ask. He was no longer a stone. He was no longer void of feelings. He was no longer void of emotion.

Stanley was real now. So was Mr. Henry and Mama Bea and Miss Big
Siss and Mrs. Ida.

No, he didn't want to tell. He simply wanted to sit and listen like
he had done for the past three years. But now he couldn't; he had to
tell. He had to ease Mr. Henry's mind. He had to ease his own. And,
no, he still was not sorry for doing what he had been forced to do.
But now he was sorry for their loss and for their pain.

When they made it to the cafeteria, he filled his tray and sat at
the end of one of the long rectangular tables. Normally the tables
were bare, but every second Sunday, everything changed. Each table
was draped with its own cloth. Music was played over the intercom
and pancakes were served instead of the usual powdered eggs, bacon,
grits, and biscuits. They all knew that none of it was done for them
but for their relatives, who were free to tour the facility and eat in the
cafeteria. Nevertheless, it was a much-anticipated treat in an existence that offered very few.

D'Ray looked at the clock hanging high on the back wall. It was a
quarter till seven. Had Mr. Henry left yet, or was he still getting
ready? Did he travel the short route through the swamps, or did he
drive to Wilmington and take the interstate the entire way? D'Ray
paused. Which route would he take when his day came? Would he be
in a hurry to get home, or would he go the long way, taking his time,
getting reacclimated to freedom?

Why was he thinking such thoughts? Why was he counting
days? Why was he looking back? Why was he looking ahead? Why?

He finished eating and went to the chapel for Sunday services. He
went because Mr. Henry asked him to go, not because he believed. He
didn't know if he believed. He tried to believe. He wanted to believe.
But he couldn't. God could deliver him. That's what he had been
told. God would deliver him. He only had to believe. His mother believed. Mr. Henry believed. And Stanley believed. Maybe that's why
Mr. Henry could come. Maybe that was why he could give all of himself to the person who had taken all that he had. And maybe that was
why he could tell him.

He left the chapel and went directly to the dayroom. When he
pushed through the door, he spotted Mr. Henry awaiting him at their
usual table. And as usual Mr. Henry wasn't empty-handed. A small
plastic container sat in the center of the table next to what appeared
to be an old oversized book. The book intrigued him. Of all the gifts

that Mr. Henry had given over the years, it was the books that D'Ray came to love most. Over time, they became his lifeline. They introduced him to people that made him feel and understand things in a way he hadn't before. They allowed him to travel. Now, for the first time in his life, no place was beyond his reach. No trip was beyond his means.

What journey had Mr. Henry chosen for him this time? Who was the navigator? Who was the pilot? Was it Wright, Walker, Ellison, Baldwin, Morrison? Who?

What new people would he meet? What new adventures would he encounter? He took a deep breath and bound forward. Mr. Henry was a good man. He was a kind man. And yes, he deserved to know. It was the right thing to do. He would sit down, look him straight in the eye, and tell him.

He approached the table, and Mr. Henry stood and extended his hand. His grip was strong and firm. His eyes were soft, warm, inviting.

"How you doing, son?" Mr. Henry greeted him.

"Fine, sir," D'Ray answered. His voice was low. He was tense. "And you?"

"Oh, I'm making out," he said.

"That's good," D'Ray said, smiling.

"Please, sit down," Mr. Henry said, pointing to the chair directly across from him. D'Ray lowered himself onto the seat and scooted close to the table. He would just tell him and get it over with. No need fooling around. He would just come straight out and say it. He opened his mouth to speak, but Mr. Henry spoke first.

"How's school?"

D'Ray closed his mouth and swallowed.

"It's fine," he said.

"Still preparing for your exam?"

"Yessir."

"They set a date yet?"

"Yessir. Two weeks from Monday."

"Good!" Mr. Henry said, excited. "Then you'll have your GED."

"Yessir," D'Ray mumbled. "If I pass."

"You'll pass," Mr. Henry said. His voice was tinged with certainty. "You'll get your GED and then you'll go to college." He paused, smiling. "Maybe not the University of Chicago, but you will go to college." For a moment he seemed to drift away. His voice softened. His eyes became glazed. "You'll graduate and I'll be there to see you walk across that stage. Yes sirree. Neither rain, nor snow, nor the wrath of God could keep me away on that day."

Suddenly there was in D'Ray's mind an image of Mr. Henry standing outside his cell, staring at him, mumbling: "Everything you took from me, you gonna give it back." Yes, he would go to college. He would earn a degree. He would replace the pain he had caused with joy, with pride. "Yessir," D'Ray said with conviction. "I will, sir. I sho' will."

"Big Siss baked you some cookies." Mr. Henry pushed the container closer to D'Ray. "They real good, too," he said, smiling. "I ate a couple on the way up here."

Yes, he was a kind man and they were kind people. He would tell him while he was still convinced it was the right thing to do. He removed the lid and looked inside.

"Tell Miss Big Siss I said thank you."

"I'll do that."

D'Ray lowered the lid and while he snapped it closed, he looked at Mr. Henry. He had reached over and retrieved the book.

"I brought you something else," he said, pushing the book to D'Ray. It was a photo album. The cover was worn and the spine was beginning to come apart. "It's just the family," Mr. Henry said, sliding his chair around next to D'Ray. "Go on. Open it."

D'Ray opened the album. There was a single picture covering the entire first page. It was three women sitting around a quilt.

"That's Mama, Big Siss, and Ida Mae." Mr. Henry pointed to each person as he called their name. "They been quilting for years."

D'Ray studied the picture. They didn't look at all like the images he had conjured in his mind. He turned the page.

"That's me; that's my wife, Vanessa; and that's Stanley cleaning a fish. He must've been about ten years old when that picture was made." Mr. Henry paused and smiled. "You fish?"

"No sir, I don't."

"My boy loved to fish. We used to fish together. Couldn't neither one of us swim, so we just fished the bank. Had a little old spot up around Gasoway right under a big Scaly-Bark tree. It was a good spot. The grass under that old tree was as soft as a seventy-five-dollar mattress. Seem like there was always a breeze and the air always smelled of fresh honeysuckle. Sometimes we'd drop our lines in the water and lay back for hours staring into the heavens, marveling at this beautiful world that the good Lord saw fit to make. Those were good times. Stanley was a good boy. Aw, I'm sorry," Mr. Henry said. "Sometimes I get to talking and don't know when to quit. You can turn the page if you want to."

D'Ray lifted the page then stopped.

"Mr. Henry, it's something I got to tell you."

"What is it?"

"It's Stanley."

"Stanley! What about Stanley?"

"I got to tell you why."

"Why?" he asked, confused. "I don't understand."

"Why I killed him," D'Ray explained.

Mr. Henry looked at him but did not speak. He leaned back in his chair. His hands were trembling.

"My little brother was in trouble." D'Ray spoke with downcast eyes. He could feel Mr. Henry's penetrating gaze. D'Ray fought to steady his voice. He tried to calm his nerves.

"When I got there, Kojak had tied him to a chair. He was holding a gun to his head. He said he was gone kill him . . ." A floodgate had been opened, and now it was all coming back. D'Ray struggled for self-control. He was in a trance. He began to ramble. "He gave me a hour . . . Where could I get a hundred dollars in a hour? He was gone kill 'im . . . I know he was . . . I just didn't know what to do."

"I don't understand," Mr. Henry said. His brown eyes were wide, intense. "I just don't understand. Who is Kojak? Why did he want to kill your brother? I don't understand. Why?"

D'Ray looked at Mr. Henry. How could he make him understand a world of which he knew nothing? How could he make him understand Death Row? How could he make him understand drugs and prostitutes and boys who had to be men and men who had to kill to live? D'Ray looked away, then closed his eyes. He felt the warm tears roll down his face and pass across his lips. He opened his mouth and began to talk.

"He's young, Mr. Henry. She tricked him. He didn't know no better. It was my fault. I thought he was ready, but he wasn't. She tricked him."

"Tricked who?"

"My little brother."

"Who tricked your little brother?"

"Kojak's sister."

"I don't understand," Mr. Henry said. "I just don't understand."

"She told him it was alright and he believed her. But it wasn't alright. It wasn't her stuff. It was Kojak's."

"Son, what are you talking about?"

"Crack! They smoked Kojak's crack."

"This was about crack!"

D'Ray knew what he must have been thinking. How could something so vile touch someone so pure? Stanley never smoked. Stanley never drank. Stanley never cursed. Stanley believed. How could the end of his life, then, be connected to a place he had never been or to a world in which he never lived? No sir, this was not about crack. This was about the rules.

"So, you're telling me that your brother is a dope addict?"

"No sir, Mr. Henry. He ain't no addict. He was only ten. She tricked him. But because he got tricked, he had to die unless someone else could pay for his right to live."

"That's why you robbed the store?"

"I didn't know what else to do." D'Ray sighed. "Wasn't nothing else to do."

"That's why you killed Stanley?"

"I didn't want to hurt 'im. I told 'im that. I didn't want to hurt 'im. I swear I didn't."

"You talked to him?"

" 'Just give me the money.' That's what I told 'im. 'I ain't gone hurt you,' I said. 'I ain't gone hurt nobody,' I said. 'I don't have much time,' I said. 'He gone kill my brother,' I said. 'I just need a hundred dollars,' I said. That's what I told him. 'I ain't gone hurt you. Just give me the money. I ain't gone hurt you.' "

"Then why did you kill 'im?"

"He opened the register and everything was fine. Then he reached for the gun. I don't know why he did that. I wasn't go'n hurt 'im. But he reached for the gun."

"So you shot him."

"I didn't want to . . . He went for the gun . . . I didn't want to hurt him. I didn't want to hurt nobody. I didn't want your son to die; I just wanted my brother to live. I ain't asking you to understand that. I ain't asking you to forgive me. And I ain't trying to make no excuses for what I done. I'm just telling you what happened 'cause you a good man and you got a right to know."

Mr. Henry rose from his seat and turned toward the door, then stopped. He laid his hand on the top of D'Ray's shoulder and turned away. D'Ray lifted his eyes expecting to see Mr. Henry's angry face. But his face was not angry.

"I got to go," Mr. Henry mumbled. His voice was pained. "I'll be back," he said in a voice barely audible. "But right now, I got to go."

"Mr. Henry," D'Ray said softly. He wanted to say he was sorry, but he couldn't. He didn't mean it. At least not the way it needed to be said. "I thank you for coming all these years when nobody else would. I know it ain't been easy. You a good man, Mr. Henry. I just wanted you to know."

There was silence. Mr. Henry seemed bewildered. His lips moved, but no words came. He lifted his hands and rubbed his moist eyes.

"Son, do you need anything?"

"No sir," D'Ray said, shaking his head. "I don't need nothing. I just needed to tell you. That's all."

"Well," Mr. Henry said softly, "I need something."

"Yessir," D'Ray said, eager to do or say something to help ease Mr. Henry's pain. "What do you need?"

"I need you to write your mother. I need you to tell her that you love her. I need you to tell her that you've changed."

# CHAPTER SEVENTEEN

It was ONE HOUR BEFORE LIGHTS-OUT. D'RAY WAS ON TOP OF HIS BUNK, LYING FLAT ON HIS STOMACH, READING. DIrectly below, most of the boys were sitting on the floor, along the lower bunks, on either side of the room, watching two of the others playing a game of paper football. It was a simple game, not much unlike pitching pennies. The game board could be anything, a table top, the surface of a book, or two single straight lines drawn parallel to each other. The "ball" was a plain white sheet of paper folded into a flat, two-inch, three-corner object.

"Go'n, Pop-eye!" one of the boys said impatiently. "Shoot!"

D'Ray glanced down. Pop-eye's lean muscular body lay prone behind the ball. His chin rested on the bare concrete floor, his left eye was closed, and his middle finger was pulled back underneath his thumb, ready to *pluck* the tiny paper ball in the direction of the line. He concentrated, measuring the distance to the other line.

"Come on, Pop-eye!" someone else yelled. "We ain't got all night."

"Nigger, don't rush me!" Pop-eye said defiantly. He struck the homemade ball near the bottom point and watched it spinning wildly toward the goal line. It slid to a stop and the tip of the top point extended across the line.

"Touchdown, nigger!" Pop-eye yelled, leaping to his feet. A loud knock on the door interrupted his celebration.

"Mail call." It was Pete, the guard.

D'Ray looked toward the door, then lowered his eyes. For two and a half years he had written his mother and for two and a half years his letters had gone unanswered. At first he wrote to convince her of his love, but he soon realized the futility of declaring his love to a person who believed him cruel, evil, and incapable of such an emotion. For her, loving him was a burden that she was no longer strong enough to bear. Her motive was clear; her rationale was sound. By purging herself of him, she would have no love or hope to give her pain.

Over the years, he scaled down his letters. Not the quantity, but the content. Now, instead of declarations of love, he spent countless hours every week sitting before blank sheets of paper searching for different ways to say, Mama, I've changed.

"D'Ray Reid," Pete bellowed.

D'Ray looked up, frowning. Pete was holding a small white envelope above his head. He jumped from his bunk and pushed his way through the mass of milling boys, wondering who in the world would be sending him mail. He had just seen Mr. Henry a few days ago. Besides, Mr. Henry never sent him mail. No one did.

"Here you go." Pete handed him the letter, and instantly he was besieged by a thousand different emotions; he was staring at his mother's handwriting. How strange it was, holding an envelope that only a few days ago she had handled, an envelope that had lain in the same house in which he had once lived. A vision replaced the letter and he saw the cluttered little nightstand next to his mother's bed from which the envelope no doubt had been taken. Had she penned the letter there in her bedroom, or had she sat at the kitchen table underneath the light of the single bulb hanging from the ceiling? What words had she chosen to write after all these years? Was she still angry, or had she finally reached a point where forgiveness was at least a possibility?

"Tyrone Butler." Pete read the name from the next piece of mail, and instantly D'Ray felt a surge of bodies moving forward behind him. He stepped aside, and when Tyrone had passed, he went back to his bunk. He didn't read the letter immediately. Instead, he laid the envelope on his pillow facedown and ran his finger across the flap that previously had been sealed with moisture from his mother's tongue. For a brief moment he felt close to her. It was if by touching the spot that she had touched, he was also touching her.

Maybe she could not believe that he loved her, but maybe she could believe that he had changed. Maybe she would use her God to believe that he had finally done what she never dreamed possible. Why not? Wasn't that the cornerstone of her faith? Hadn't Paul been a murderer? Didn't he change? So, why not him?

Pete handed out the last pieces of mail and once again disappeared behind the heavy steel door. Someone had received a batch of homemade cookies and against better judgment had unwisely opened the container in the presence of all the others. Soon they had all descended upon the culprit's bunk like scavengers around a dead carcass. While the rest of them laughed and ate cookies, D'Ray removed the paper from inside the envelope, quietly unfolded it, and stared in disbelief. There was no date, no address, no salutation, no signature. Only three lone words: TIME WILL TELL.

# CHAPTER EIGHTEEN

His last VISITING DAY FELL ON THE SUNDAY BEFORE HIS MONDAY RELEASE. AS USUAL MR. HENRY WAS there and as usual he did not come empty-handed. But this gift, unlike the others, was not some abstract object given to make life behind the fence more tenable. This was a going-home gift—a new pair of pants, a shirt, some socks, some underwear, and a pair of shiny black shoes.

As Mr. Henry watched, D'Ray examined each item, then carefully placed them back in the bag, which he set on the floor next to his chair. He thanked Mr. Henry, who acknowledged his gratitude with a smile but did not speak. They looked at each other for a moment, then D'Ray lowered his eyes. Someone named Torrence had scratched his name on the tabletop, permanently ensuring that his presence would be known. D'Ray stared at the name but he was not seeing it. He was wondering about Mr. Henry. Neither of them had ever spoken about his release. He didn't know how to act because he didn't know how Mr. Henry felt. What was he thinking? What was he feeling? Was he happy? Was he sad? Was he indifferent? Maybe six years wasn't long enough. Maybe it seemed unfair. He was going home, but death would forever keep Stanley in the ground.

"What are your plans?"

Mr. Henry asked the question, then again it was quiet. D'Ray looked up, then quickly lowered his eyes. He began to slowly trace the outline of the boy's name with his finger. Birds have nests, foxes have holes, but the Son of Man has nowhere to lay his head. The thought caused D'Ray to think of himself. It caused him to ponder his predicament.

"Just be free," he said dryly. "Just be free."

He raised his head and looked at Mr. Henry. His eyes gave no indication of his mood. They gave no clue to what he was feeling. He was nice, but still, he was only a man, subject to the same pain, the same rage, the same frustrations as anyone else. A lot had been taken from him. Had it been given back? He said that it would. Was six years long enough? If not, what now? What more could he do?

"Where will you go?" Mr. Henry asked, then waited.

D'Ray pondered the question, not knowing the answer. Where does a person go who has no place to be? He would walk through the gate and follow his feet. Maybe another bus trip was in his future. Maybe Texas or Mississippi or Oklahoma. Who knows?

He saw Mr. Henry's eyes searching him, waiting for an answer. The only answer was the truth.

"I have nowhere to go," D'Ray finally said.

"That's not true," Mr. Henry said without hesitation.

D'Ray sat back in the chair, confused.

"You have a place," Mr. Henry continued.

"Where?" D'Ray asked.

"Home," Mr. Henry said with such conviction that for a moment D'Ray thought it plausible. But only for a moment. Then reality took over.

"I don't have a home," he said.

"Yes, you do," Mr. Henry insisted.

"No, I don't," D'Ray said emphatically. "I ain't welcome at Mama's house. You were there, Mr. Henry. She don't want me."

"But I do," Mr. Henry said. "I want you."

D'Ray looked at him, stunned.

"Son, I want you home with me."

D'Ray pushed back from the table. He had an impulse to rise, but remained seated.

"Mr. Henry, you don't mean that."

"You don't have to come," Mr. Henry said, making his position clear. "And I can't make you come. Nobody can. But I do mean it. I want you to live with me."

There was silence.

"Don't get me wrong. My house ain't that big, and it ain't fancy.

But you would have your own room and a key to the front door and my good company." He smiled. "What you say, D'Ray? Will you come?"

D'Ray looked at him, then looked off. He thought about it, but his mind told him the idea was foolish.

"No sir," he said, softly, "I can't."

"Why not?"

"I killed your son."

"Stanley's dead," Mr. Henry said, reaching over and taking D'Ray's hand in his own. The touch of his big, powerful hands, now hard and callused from years of grueling manual labor, was surprisingly gentle. "Ain't nothing neither one of us can do about that now," he said softly. "All we can do is go on with life and try to turn this tragedy into triumph. Together, maybe we can rectify the situation that made you kill in the first place. I believe we can do that. You and me. We can. And you, well, you can make Stanley's dreams live again."

"Me!" D'Ray said. "What can I do, Mr. Henry? I ain't like Stanley. What can I do that he wasn't able to do himself?"

"Take up where he left off."

"I can't do it."

"I say you can."

"No sir, I can't."

"Come home with me," Mr. Henry said. "Go to college. Be a credit to your race."

"The next Thurgood Marshall," D'Ray mumbled contemplatively.

"Something like that."

That night, D'Ray couldn't sleep. His mood was strange. It was something akin to the joyous anticipation of an anxious child the night before Christmas, but only, for him there was no Santa or reindeer or sleigh filled with toys. There was no thought of the birth or the crucifixion of the resurrected Christ. His was a peaceful joy brought about by the promise of his personal liberation from the living tomb that had been his home for the past six years.

At exactly five-thirty in the morning, he walked through the gate and back into the free world. Mr. Henry had parked his green Ford pickup truck on the opposite side of the street directly across from the facility. He must have been watching the gate, because as soon as

D'Ray walked through, the door on the driver's side flew open and Mr. Henry bounded forward, smiling. They shook hands and embraced, but their greeting was interrupted by the sound of the transport cart approaching from the other side of the gate. D'Ray turned and looked. Mr. Pete was behind the wheel and one of the inmates was sitting on the seat next to him. They were bringing his personal belongings.

"You picking up Reid?" Mr. Pete asked.

"Yes I am," Mr. Henry said.

"Where you park?"

Mr. Henry led them to the truck and stepped aside as Mr. Pete and the inmate lifted the heavy box, of mostly books, onto the tailgate and pushed them up toward the cab. After the box was loaded, Mr. Henry and D'Ray climbed inside the truck. Mr. Pete drove the cart along the passenger's side and stopped.

"So long, Reid," he said.

"Good-bye, Mr. Pete."

"You stay out of trouble now, you hear."

"Yessir, I will."

Mr. Pete stepped on the accelerator and the tiny cart skirted across the street and disappeared behind the gate. D'Ray heard the motor rev and he watched the two tiny red lights disappear into the still-dark morning.

"What's the first thing you want to do?" Mr. Henry asked.

"I don't know," D'Ray said, pondering the question. "Take a bath . . . lie on a sofa . . . sit out on the front porch . . . I don't know."

For a long time neither of them spoke. Subconsciously, Mr. Henry was giving him time to be alone with his thoughts. D'Ray, on the other hand, was staring at the sunrise, thinking how good it was to be free. He had survived the nightmare. He had done his time. Now, with each passing mile, he felt himself becoming more deeply metamorphosed. For six years he had been in a deep freeze, but now he was beginning to thaw. Slowly he was awakening from the deepest, darkest sleep that he had ever known, to once again participate in a world that he had never fully appreciated. He looked at Mr. Henry out of the corner of his eye. He was a man unlike any he had ever known. He was strong, kind, caring, loving, forgiving. He was the father he had always desired.

As they drove through the small town of Bastrop, D'Ray noticed the large clock mounted high upon the steeple of the tower next to the courthouse. He saw the time and instantly thought back to the detention center. It was six o'clock. The horn was sounding and everyone inside the dorm was scrambling to begin another day, just like the day that had ended the day before. For him the nightmare was over, but for someone else it had just begun. He closed his eyes and tried to purge himself of such thoughts, realizing that his body was free but his mind was still doing time.

It was exactly six-thirty when Mr. Henry turned off the road in front of his house. There was no driveway, only the outline of two tire tracks cutting across the yard and disappearing around the corner of the house.

As they neared the house, D'Ray began to wonder if he had made the correct decision. Could he actually live in a town in which he would surely be a pariah? And what about Mr. Henry's family? How would it be, meeting them? And how would it be, living amongst Stanley's friends? This whole thing was crazy. It was foolish. It was a mistake. Why had he agreed to this? Why?

Mr. Henry drove up even with the house and stopped.

"Well son, this is it. Home sweet home."

D'Ray looked at him but did not speak. He tried to think of a response but couldn't.

"Get out and let me show you around," Mr. Henry said.

D'Ray opened the door and got out, but didn't go anywhere. He was waiting for Mr. Henry to lead the way.

"See that house over there across the street?" Mr. Henry said, walking to the rear of the truck.

"Yessir," D'Ray said. "I see it."

"That's where Mama live."

D'Ray looked at the house. It was similar to those that he had seen in other black neighborhoods. It was a small white wood-frame house with a rather large screen-enclosed porch. There was a huge pecan tree out front just left of the porch. An old metal swing sat close to the road on the opposite side of the yard. Next to the swing was a car shed. The shed had a roof, but no sides. It was evident that someone over there fished. The tip of several bamboo poles that had been stored in the crawl space of the shed could be seen jutting from just underneath the roof. Kids played in her yard too. He could tell by the lack of grass underneath the swing and next to the carport.

"She live by herself?" D'Ray asked.

"Not anymore," Mr. Henry said. "Ida Mae and her husband moved in a few years ago after their home burned down."

"That's too bad," D'Ray sympathized.

"Aw, they fine," Mr. Henry said. "Mama loves the company." He stopped abruptly as though besieged by a sudden thought. "Any of your folks do any gardening?"

"Not that I know of," D'Ray said.

"Come on 'round back," Mr. Henry said, leading the way. "I want to show you something."

D'Ray followed him around the side of the house, past a fig tree, and into the backyard. A large black dog crawled from underneath the back porch, rose to his hind legs, and laid his big dirty paws against Mr. Henry's clean white shirt.

"Get down, boy!" Mr. Henry demanded, playfully pulling the dog down by the ears. "Bad dog," he said, lightly chastising the animal. "Look what you did to my shirt." Instantly the dog's tongue fell from his mouth, his body began to rock, and his tail began to wag.

As Mr. Henry bent low to pat the dog's head, D'Ray looked around the yard. It was a huge yard, probably one acre, maybe two. There was an old homemade basketball goal at the far end of the property that undoubtedly had belonged to Stanley. High up in one of the trees were the remains of a tree house. A picnic bench sat just off the dirt court between two large oak trees. On the west side of the yard there was a small wooden shed sitting in the middle of a moderate-sized garden. The shed seemed out of place. There was nothing else out there except for several rows of beans and okra and yellow squash on one side, a stand of corn on the other, and three short rows of greens that stopped only a few feet from the door.

He did not see Mr. Henry walk next to him, nor did he sense that he was there until he felt his hand on his shoulder.

"Come on," Mr. Henry said. "This way."

D'Ray followed him behind the shed to a watermelon patch.

"Ever seen anything like that?" Mr. Henry asked proudly.

"No sir," D'Ray said. "Never."

Mr. Henry squatted and plucked one of the largest melons with his finger.

"You know the secret to growing 'em this big?"

"No sir," D'Ray said. "What?"

"Fertilizer," Mr. Henry said. "It's all in the fertilizer."

"Is that right?" D'Ray said, pretending to be interested when in actuality his mind was wandering. He needed to find some way to still the anxiety racking his body and exciting his nerves. He needed to know that this decision was right. He needed to feel that this arrangement could work.

"White fellow up to Chickersaw taught me how to mix it," Mr. Henry continued.

"Look like he taught you good," D'Ray said, trying to figure out a way to turn the conversation back to Mr. Henry and himself.

"You better believe it," Mr. Henry said.

"Folks don't bother your melons when you gone?" D'Ray asked.

"Clayton keep a eye on things when I ain't here."

"Who?" D'Ray asked, confused.

"Clayton," Mr. Henry said. "My neighbor. He live right over yonder."

D'Ray looked over at the house, then back at Mr. Henry.

"He kin?" D'Ray asked.

"Naw, he ain't no kin," Mr. Henry said, smiling. "Just a close family friend, that's all."

"Speaking of kin," D'Ray said, using Mr. Henry's comment as a segue. "Where Ms. Big Siss live?"

"Up the road a piece," Mr. Henry told him. "Just this side of town."

"She come around much?" D'Ray asked.

"All the time," Mr. Henry said. "Why?"

"Just wondering how they feel about this."

"About what?" Mr. Henry asked.

"Me coming here."

"Well, I ain't gone lie," Mr. Henry began. "At first they didn't understand. They all thought the whole thing was crazy. Big Siss and Mama came around, though. Guess I talked about you so much that after a while they took to looking at you like family. Albeit a prodigal son." He paused. "Now Ida, she a different story."

"She don't like me, huh?"

"Like you! Son, she don't know you. All she know is you killed her nephew." He pursed his lips to say something else, but seemed to think better of it. "Aw, don't you worry 'bout Ida Mae," he said. "She'll come around. Everything gone be fine. I promise you that. Now, come on, let's go'n in the house."

They entered the house through the back door and passed through both the kitchen and living room before finally stopping in the bedroom that until that very moment had belonged to Stanley. Although D'Ray had never seen the room before, he sensed that not much in it had been changed. The furniture was probably the same. A full-size bed, a nightstand, a dresser, a desk, and a bookshelf filled with books. The posters on the wall were probably the same. Magic Johnson on one wall, Tony Dorsett on the other. His plaques and certificates still seemed to be where Stanley had placed them. Only, now, the diploma that Mr. Henry had once carried in a brown paper bag had been framed and hung on the wall over the bed.

"Let me show you something," Mr. Henry said, leading D'Ray to the small desk on the opposite side of the room. He pointed to a document on the wall above the desk. D'Ray stared at it for a moment before he realized that it was the diploma he had received from Y.A.

"You know what this wall is missing?" Mr. Henry asked after a brief silence.

"No sir. What?"

"This," Mr. Henry said, pointing to an empty frame mounted next to the one containing D'Ray's GED. "You know what this is?"

"Yessir," D'Ray said. "A frame."

"You know what it's for?" Mr. Henry asked.

"No sir," D'Ray said, slowly shaking his head.

"Your diploma," he said. "Your college diploma."

There was silence. Mr. Henry looked at the frame, then at D'Ray, with eyes made intense by the depth of his conviction. He smiled, and in an instant the moment was gone.

"You hungry, son?"

"Yessir. A little bit."

"Make yourself at home while I throw something together."

"I'll help you," D'Ray volunteered.

"That's okay," Mr. Henry said.

"But I want to," D'Ray insisted.

"Tell you what," Mr. Henry chided. "You let me do the cooking, and I'll let you do the cleaning. Deal?"

"Deal," D'Ray said.

Mr. Henry turned to leave, then stopped.

"By the way," he said. *"Happy birthday!"*

# CHAPTER NINETEEN

Sunday NIGHT, A FEW MINUTES BEFORE MIDNIGHT. D'RAY SAT AT HIS DESK STUDYING FOR HIS STATISTICS exam. For nearly an hour, he stared at a series of mathematical equations that his mind refused to grasp. The equations seemed simple enough, even sensible, yet as soon as he closed the book or diverted his eyes, his brain betrayed him by either shutting down completely or flashing only part of the equation before refusing to yield the rest.

Frustrated, he leaned back in his chair and locked his hands behind his head. His body was tired; he felt drained. Why was the last exam of the year always the most difficult? And why had he put stats off for so long? Why hadn't he taken it freshman year or sophomore year? Why?

He looked at his bed. Maybe he could concentrate better if he took a nap. He pushed back from the table, but before he could stand, the door creaked opened and Mr. Henry walked through carrying a cup of coffee and a slice of sweet potato pie.

"I brought you something to eat," he said, gently setting both the cup of coffee and the saucer containing the slice of pie on the corner of D'Ray's desk.

D'Ray looked at the pie, and in an instant he was no longer a junior majoring in history at North Louisiana State University. Instead he was once again a fifteen-year-old inmate beginning a long murder sentence at the Louisiana Youth Authority. This was visiting day, and the slice of pie was the first of many kind gestures from the man whose son he had killed. It was tangible evidence of the existence of a world to which he would someday return. Now, his low spirits were buoyed; his sad heart was still. If this man whom he had so victimized could go on, then so could he.

"How you coming?" Mr. Henry's voice snapped him back to reality.

"Fighting a losing battle," D'Ray said nonchalantly.

"Don't sell yourself short," Mr. Henry counseled. "The last load always seem the heaviest."

"Heavy," D'Ray said. "Try immovable."

"You'll move it," Mr. Henry said. "And you'll come through this semester like pure gold."

"I hope so," D'Ray said.

"I know so," Mr. Henry responded.

"You seem so sure," D'Ray said.

"I am sure," Mr. Henry told him.

"How can you be?" D'Ray asked.

"Because I know you," Mr. Henry answered. "You're a force."

"A force." D'Ray chuckled.

"That's right," Mr. Henry said. "A irresistible force. And a irresistible force can't be stopped."

"And an immovable object can't be moved," D'Ray added.

"That's true, too," Mr. Henry said.

"No sir, that's stats."

There was silence.

"What you reckon happens when the two meet?"

"Sir?"

"When a immovable object meets a irresistible force."

"Stalemate," D'Ray said.

"Ain't possible," Mr. Henry responded. "If a immovable object can't be moved and a irresistible force can't be stopped, when they meet, something got to give. But what?"

D'Ray looked at him, puzzled.

"I don't know," he said. "What?"

"The force finds a way around the object," Mr Henry told him. "Just like you always have."

"I'm an irresistible force!" D'Ray said, leaping to his feet and playfully pounding his chest.

"There you go."

"Sufficiently motivated," D'Ray exclaimed.

"And firmly determined," Mr. Henry chimed.

"How'd you know?" D'Ray asked facetiously.

"'Cause I know you," Mr. Henry said.

The two men laughed. Then Mr. Henry looked at the empty frame hanging on the wall above the desk and suddenly became serious again.

"Son, I'm so proud of you," he whispered in a voice that seemed to come from some faraway place.

"Me!" D'Ray exclaimed, startled.

"You didn't have to do it," Mr. Henry said, continuing to stare at the empty frame but not appearing to be seeing it.

"Do what?" D'Ray asked, sitting back on the chair.

"I tacked that frame on the wall, but you didn't have to fill it." Mr. Henry began to ramble. "You could have walked away. You could've done your time and walked away. But you didn't."

"No, Mr. Henry, I—"

"You've worked so hard," Mr. Henry said softly, then paused and began again. "Riding that bus to Monroe every day. Studying all night. Helping out 'round here. You didn't have to do that. You didn't have to care about me."

"No, Mr. Henry, you got it all wrong. You the one stood by me. After all I took from you, you stood by me. I ain't done nothing. You the one, Mr. Henry. You stood by me."

"This time next year, you'll be a college graduate," Mr. Henry said, lowering his eyes and looking directly at D'Ray. "Do you know what that means to me?"

"Mr. Henry—"

"I been thinking."

"Mr. Henry—"

"I want you to live on campus next year."

"On campus!"

"Don't get me wrong," Mr. Henry said tenderly. "I love having you here every day. You make this house live. You make me feel whole. You make everything seem right. But this ain't about me. It's about you."

"We can't afford it," D'Ray said, being practical.

"We'll find a way."

"No sir. I can't let you do that."

"A fellow ought to enjoy his senior year," Mr. Henry said with the conviction of a person who had already made up his mind. "He ought to be able to hang out with his friends and shoot pool in the union and go to the ball games and do a little courting." He paused. "It's more to college than classes and studying. And it's more to this thing than me. Now, ain't it?"

"I'm all right, Mr. Henry," D'Ray said. "Really I am."

Mr. Henry looked at the frame. His mind seemed to drift and D'Ray could tell that he was not listening to him.

"One more year and the dream is a reality. Right?"

"Yessir," D'Ray said. "But—"

"I love you, son," Mr. Henry said, then turned to leave.

"I love you too, Mr. Henry," D'Ray said, looking at the frame. "I won't let you down. I promise."

# CHAPTER TWENTY

Somewhere BETWEEN MONDAY MORNING WHEN HE LEFT HOME AND Monday evening after his last class, the unexpected happened; Mr. Henry became ill. No one had said it was serious, but he knew by the tone of the simple note that his roommate had left on his desk in his dormitory room. "Go home! Mr. Henry's in the hospital."

He threw a few things in an overnight bag and rushed out to catch the commuter bus to Lake Providence. He hated that bus. Not only was it old and slow and uncomfortable, but it departed from Lake Providence too early in the morning and it departed from campus too late in the evening.

The bus was on the opposite end of campus in the parking lot behind the football stadium. He walked out of his dorm, followed the long paved walkway down the hill and through a small stand of trees, ever aware of the familiar sounds of twigs snapping beneath the hard soles of his brogans. Out of the corner of his eye he detected a slight movement in the hedges. A squirrel, with its eyes ablaze and its long bushy tail arched high above its back, scampered across the lawn, leaped atop the large cement tomb in which lay the final remains of the university's first and most revered president. D'Ray stared wide-eyed as the tiny rodent snapped upright, balancing its small furry body on its powerful hind legs. D'Ray paused. He looked at the squirrel, then at the grave. A thought fought its way to the fore of his brain. Maybe Mr. Henry was dead. Suddenly, he was running. He raced past the small inverted fountain sitting in the center of campus, ran across the engineering quad, and headed down the sidewalk in the direction of the parking lot. With each step he became increasingly aware of the pull of the heavy shoes against the muscles in his tiring legs, the weight of the books shifting in the small bag strapped across his back, and that tug of the small piece of luggage against his stiff aching arm. As the side of the bus came into view, he slowed to a walk and shifted the overnight bag to his left hand.

As he boarded the bus, the driver looked up at him from behind the wheel.

"How you, Mr. Willis?" D'Ray spoke first.

"You run all the way over here?"

"Yessir," D'Ray said, breathing heavily. He paused to wipe the sweat from his forehead.

"What you do a crazy thing like that for?" Mr. Willis asked, bewildered. "You know I don't leave here until after five." Mr. Willis glanced at his watch. "It ain't even four-thirty yet."

"Just felt like running," D'Ray said, climbing aboard the bus and dropping his things on an empty seat.

"With all that stuff?"

"Yessir," D'Ray said, collapsing next to his luggage.

"Well," Mr. Willis said calmly, "I guess you know your own mind."

When the bus finally pulled off, D'Ray laid his head against the window and closed his eyes, hoping to lose track of time. But even with his eyes closed, his alert mind, made even more active by his eagerness to reach Lake Providence and unlock the mysteries of his roommate's note, measured every stop, every bump, and every turn along the all-too-familiar route. The vibration of the bus crossing the first set of railroad tracks told him they had just left the city limits and were entering the swamp. The foul scent, seeping through the ventilation and circulating throughout the bus amidst the moans and groans of his schoolmates, told him they had reached the paper mill. The slow, steady pull of the bus up the small incline and over the overpass told him they were only twenty-five miles from home.

For an hour, he lay very still, listening to the dull roar of the engine, trying to relax until the bus finally pulled into Lake Providence and stopped alongside the courthouse. Anxious, he quickly collected his bags and exited the bus. No sooner had his feet touched the ground than the sound of a car horn caused him to pause and look.

Mr. Clayton's old blue Chevy was parked across the street underneath a tree. As he stood staring, Mr. Clayton blew the horn a second time. Convinced that the horn was intended for him, D'Ray crossed the street and slowly approached the car. When he was in earshot, Mr. Clayton leaned through the window.

"Come on 'round and git in." His voice was soft but urgent. "Mrs. Bea asked me to pick you up and take you to the hospital."

Without speaking, D'Ray hurried around the car, pulled the door open, and climbed in next to Mr. Clayton.

"How's Mr. Henry?" he asked, focusing all of his attention on Mr. Clayton's face.

"I don't know," Mr. Clayton said, pulling the car into reverse and backing into the street. "Mrs. Bea didn't say."

An enormous feeling of dread swept D'Ray's body. He buried his face in his hand and leaned forward against the dashboard. "It's bad, Mr. Clayton. It's real bad."

"Now, you don't know that!" Mr. Clayton said sternly.

D'Ray sighed and leaned back against the seat. He wanted to be positive, but there was rising in him a sense of dread. "I can feel it," he mumbled softly as he stared through the windshield watching the highway unfold before him. "I can feel it."

"You just scared." Mr. Clayton's voice was steady and calm. "That ain't nothing but fear talking."

D'Ray's roused senses were not stilled by Mr. Clayton's explanation. Reason made him challenge his words.

"Why they call me, Mr. Clayton? Why?"

"I don't know," Mr. Clayton said after a brief silence. "You just gone have to wait and see."

When they made it to the hospital, Mr. Clayton didn't park in the parking lot. Instead, he pulled up close to the building and stopped alongside the curb.

"Leave your bags in the car. I'll take 'em home for you."

"Yessir."

Mr. Clayton turned and removed a small bag from the backseat.

"Give this to Miss Big Siss," he said, handing the bag to D'Ray. "Mrs. Ida sent it."

"Yessir."

"Tell her if she need anything else to call me."

"Yessir, I will."

"And don't you worry about Henry," he said, attempting to be re-assuring. "He tough as nails."

"Yessir," D'Ray mumbled, hoping that he was right but fearing that he was wrong.

"Let 'im know that he in my prayers."

"Yessir, I'll tell 'im."

D'Ray grabbed the door handle, then hesitated.

"Mr. Clayton."

"Yeah, son, what is it?"

"Thank you."

"Aw, don't mention it," Mr. Clayton said, gently placing his hand on D'Ray's shoulder. "Now gone. They waiting on you."

D'Ray exited the car, stepped onto the curb, and hurried toward the large glass door. Feeling anxious, he paused and drew a deep breath before pulling the door open. Directly through the door loomed the waiting area, and at the far end of the waiting room was the receptionist's station. A middle-aged white woman in loose-fitting hospital scrubs was sitting behind the desk. She looked up and her bluish gray eyes settled on D'Ray.

"Can I help you?" she asked in a businesslike tone.

"I come to see Mr. Earl."

He watched as she ran her fingers across the keyboard of the computer sitting on her desk.

"Henry?" she asked.

"Yes ma'am."

"Room 129."

D'Ray turned to leave, then paused.

"Which way is that?"

"To your left and down the corridor."

He turned the corner and walked down the long narrow corridor, fighting a mounting impulse to run. He stared at an old man walking toward him slowly, pushing an IV pole. The sight made him anxious. Instinctively he increased his pace. A woman was standing in the hall next to Mr. Henry's room. As he got closer, he recognized her.

"Miss Big Siss," he called to her.

The sound of his voice startled her. She looked up and he could tell she had been crying. She extended her arms and he fell into her tender embrace.

"How's Mr. Henry?" D'Ray asked, gently pushing away and looking deeply into her eyes. He could see traces of tears that she had tried to wipe away.

"Not so good." Her voice was soft and weak.

"What happened?"

She raised her hands to her eyes. They were trembling.

"He had a stroke."

"A stroke!" D'Ray's voice was louder than he had intended.

Her bottom lip began to quiver.

"Honey," she said, her voice breaking, "he paralyzed."

D'Ray felt his knees buckle. He fell back against the wall. His eyes were wide. His mouth hung open.

Miss Big Siss looked at him sadly.

"Baby, I'm afraid there's more."

D'Ray looked at her but did not speak.

"He can't talk."

D'Ray felt his head spin.

"He gone be alright, ain't he?"

There was silence.

"Doctor say we gone have to wait and see."

"I want to see him."

"He looks pretty bad."

"I don't care. I want to see him."

Miss Big Siss pulled the door open and D'Ray followed her inside. A lone nurse was standing next to the bed, changing an IV bag. The room was quiet. There was a television, but it wasn't on. The only sound was the soft steady bubbling noise coming from the small oxygen humidifier hanging directly above the bed. D'Ray stepped aside as Miss Big Siss approached the nurse.

"Any changes?" she asked.

"His pressure's down a little."

"It's so hard seeing him like this."

"Yes ma'am, I know," the nurse said compassionately. "We're doing everything we can."

The nurse moved and D'Ray caught his first glimpse of Mr. Henry. He was lying under a plain white spread and his head was turned away, but D'Ray could see the tiny plastic tube passing underneath his nose and the two tiny nodules jutting into his nostrils. He watched the nurse collect her things and walk toward the door. She grabbed the door handle, then paused.

"If ya'll need anything, just press the buzzer."

"Yes ma'am," Miss Big Siss responded. "We will."

Miss Big Siss extended her hand to D'Ray. He placed his hand in hers and she gently pulled him next to her.

"Henry, look who here to see you."

"Hi, Mr. Henry." D'Ray forced himself to smile.

Mr. Henry slowly turned toward him. His body didn't turn, just his head. He looked at D'Ray. Instantly his eyes widened and his lips began to quiver. D'Ray watched him struggle to gain control of the muscles in his badly twisted mouth. The words were inside of him but he had lost the ability to release them. Miss Big Siss took some tissue from the desk next to his bed and began to gently wipe the drool that had begun to seep from the corner of his mouth. Mr. Henry didn't look at her, only at D'Ray. He was trying to communicate with his eyes. Confused, D'Ray furrowed his brow and stared back at him. What was he trying to say? What did he want? Maybe he should say something. D'Ray looked at Miss Big Siss. She took the small handbag from him, placed it on the bed, and opened it.

"Doctor say you gone be here for a few days," Miss Big Siss said, "so Ida sent you some things from the house."

Mr. Henry looked at D'Ray, then turned his head away and closed his eyes. D'Ray glanced at the small handbag, then felt his eyes straying magnetically toward Mr. Henry's face. The stroke had caused the muscles to relax. Now he looked like an old man who was dying. His entire face had drooped. His skin was pale and wrinkled.

"She sent your robe, your razor, your hairbrush, and your Bible," Miss Big Siss said, removing each item from the bag and placing it on the bed next to him.

D'Ray watched her, thinking that this all seemed too familiar. But why? He looked at her, then at the bag.

"And she sent you this."

Miss Big Siss removed a portrait from the small handbag and placed it on the stand next to Mr. Henry's bed. It was the picture of Vanessa and Stanley that Mr. Henry kept next to his bed at home. D'Ray moved to the far corner of the room and fell back against the wall. He felt like crying but he knew he wouldn't. He had once heard Mr. Henry say that that picture was the first thing he looked at when he got up in the morning and the last thing he looked at before he went to bed at night. Why did she send that picture? How would that help him? D'Ray looked at the picture. Suddenly, he remembered. "The jail cell," he mumbled softly to himself. He closed his eyes, seeing a sad, sullen Mr. Henry standing before him holding a brown paper bag. "Hi, I'm Henry Earl and this is my son, Stanley."

"We figured you'd want your family here with you," Miss Big Siss said. "They always seem to make you feel better."

D'Ray stared at the picture. Why was this happening? What had Mr. Henry ever done to anybody?

"Mama really worried about you," Miss Big Siss said, lifting the picture from the nightstand. She looked at it again, then dusted it with the hem of her dress. "I just don't know what she would do without you. I don't know what none of us would do."

Maybe God was testing him, D'Ray thought. Maybe Mr. Henry had been right. Maybe God was doing him like he did Job. Didn't Job lose everything he had? Didn't he lose his wife? Didn't he lose his children? Didn't he get sick?

"Don't you worry 'bout that house neither," Miss Big Siss rattled on. "We gone see after it till you git better."

God didn't kill Stanley, you did, a voice screamed inside D'Ray's head.

"And you will git better," she said. "I promise you that."

Naw, he won't, the voice taunted D'Ray.

"You'll be up and around before you know it."

Naw, he won't. The voice was clear, certain.

"Might even make it to the graduation."

"I'm not going back," D'Ray said. "What's the point?"

Suddenly Mr. Henry's eyes opened and he looked at D'Ray. Still he didn't speak, but now his eyes seemed calm and the message they communicated seemed clear. You remember, don't you? Everything you took from me, you gonna give it back. D'Ray looked at him. Are you going to deny me twice? His eyes seemed to be asking. The next Thurgood Marshall. That's what Stanley wanted to be. A credit to his race. D'Ray averted his eyes. Look at me. He knew what Mr. Henry's eyes were saying. D'Ray wouldn't look; he couldn't. What could he tell him, anyway? Look at me. D'Ray could feel his eyes on him, penetrating deep into his soul. D'Ray looked up. Their eyes met. My life has to mean something, he felt Mr. Henry say. D'Ray looked away. He had to leave. He stepped out into the hall and leaned into the wall face first. His misty eyes fought back impending tears. Why had he allowed himself to care? Why? He felt a hand on his shoulder.

"He needs you," he heard Miss Big Siss mutter.

He looked at her through teary eyes.

"I'm not coming back." His voice was trembling.

"You have to."

"I can't sit here and watch him die."

"He won't die. Not if you're here."

"I'm not coming back. I can't."

"You have to."

"I can't."

"You owe him."

D'Ray looked at her.

"I know that!"

"Then pay him."

"I can't."

"Why not?"

"There ain't no time."

"You don't know that."

"I know death when I see it."

"He won't close his eyes before he see you walk across that stage. He wouldn't do that to you."

"What!"

"He got to let you pay him before you can be free."

D'Ray closed his eyes and let out a deep sigh.

"Honey, if you can give him a reason to keep his eyes open for the next three weeks, they just might stay open for the next fifty years."

"Don't do this to me," D'Ray pleaded.

"You got to be there for him."

"I got to go."

"When you coming back?"

He didn't answer. He headed down the hall, hearing Miss Big Siss's final order: "Stand by him like he stood by you." Her words touched something inside of him that he did not want to face. He gave in to the mounting desire to run . . . down the hall, around the corner, through the lobby. When he reached the front of the building he pushed through the door and stepped out into the fresh night air. It was a clear night. Bright shining stars. A full radiant moon. Across the street, from somewhere deep inside Old Man Thurman's pasture, he could hear the call of a lone bullfrog drifting on the still night air. As he passed through the parking lot and approached the long, narrow asphalt street he had no plan or destination in mind. He moved to the shoulder and walked along the bank of the shallow drainage ditch, trying to come to terms with what had happened. An empty beer can was lying on the edge of the ditch. He pulled his leg back and kicked the can with all his might. It sailed through the air, finally spinning to a stop in the center of the highway. Absentmindedly, he stepped out into the highway and walked toward the can. He had just drawn his leg back to kick the can a second time when the sound of screeching tires made him turn and look. Two bright headlights were bearing down on him; he watched paralyzed until the car was only a few feet from him. He whirled, dove off the road, and rolled into the ditch. He stared wide-eyed as the car swerved to a stop. The door flew open; a man leaped out and raced back to him.

"You all right?" He was hysterical.

D'Ray paused, looking at the white man who was standing and gazing at him.

"Yessir."

"What's the matter with you?"

D'Ray looked but didn't answer.

"Why you standing in the middle of the highway like that?"

"Just going home."

"I almost ran over you."

"Yessir. I know."

"For goodness' sake, stay out the highway before you git yourself killed."

A terse stare, a moment of awkward silence, and the man was gone. Relieved, D'Ray closed his eyes and swallowed. Then he rose to his feet and dusted the dirt from the seat of his pants. He turned and looked back in the direction of the hospital. Maybe he should go home and rest. He needed to try to relax. Maybe even go to sleep. Spurred on by a new plan, he quickened his pace. He crossed the street and passed over the tracks. Near the house, he cut through the neighbor's yard and followed the long narrow trail through the vacant lot and onto Mr. Henry's property. He passed around the right side of the house and started to climb onto the front porch, but he hesitated. He looked across at Mama Bea's house. There were several cars parked out front and although the window shades were drawn, he could tell that the living room lights were on. He had a strong desire to be alone, but he couldn't go home without looking in on her first.

The screen door leading onto her porch was open, but the large wooden door leading into her house was not. He paused, then knocked. He stood perfectly still as the curtain covering the small window in the center of the door moved and Mrs. Ida's familiar face appeared. The lock clicked and the door swung open.

"How you doing, Mrs. Ida?"

"Fine, baby. Come on in."

He stepped into the hall, then hesitated.

"Where Mama Bea?"

"She lying down."

He followed Mrs. Ida down the narrow hall, aware of the sound of muddled voices coming from the tiny living room. He stopped in the doorway and looked. A few of the neighbors had come to visit. He spoke to them, then walked across the hall to Mama Bea's bedroom. Although the room was dark, he still recognized her large form lying underneath a sheet that someone had spread across her legs.

"How you feeling, Mama Bea?" he asked, bending low and allowing her to kiss his forehead.

"Oh, I doing fairly," she said. Her voice was sad and feeble. "You been by the hospital?"

"Yes ma'am."

"You seen Henry?"

"Yes ma'am. I saw him."

She patted the bed with her hand and he sat next to her.

"How he look?"

D'Ray didn't answer.

"I know seeing you made him feel better."

"Yes ma'am," D'Ray replied.

"Ida went by earlier, but she come on back to be with me."

"Yes ma'am."

"I always thought that I would outlive my children."

"Don't talk like that, Mama Bea. Mr. Henry gone be alright."

"It partly my fault."

"No ma'am. It ain't nobody's fault."

"He got out there and got too hot."

"It ain't your fault, Mama Bea."

"Out there hoeing weeds during the hot part of the day."

"What weeds?"

"I hollered 'cross there and told him to wait till it cool off, but he wouldn't listen. He just kept on hoeing. He know his pressure too high to be carrying on like that. My mind led me to go over there. If I had—"

"It ain't your fault."

"Next thang I know he done fell out." She paused and sighed heavily. "Siss the one called the ambulance. She found him laying out in that garden. Tell me his body was all twisted up and his tongue was hanging out his mouth. I know they blaming me."

"No, they ain't."

"They ain't come out and said it, but that's how they feel."

"No ma'am. They ain't blaming you."

"They figure I should've put my foot down. Made him wait till it cooled off."

"No ma'am, they don't think that."

"Maybe I should've. But look to me like the only thing that give him comfort since he lost his family is working in that garden. That's why I didn't bother him." She looked at D'Ray with pleading eyes. "Do that make sense?"

"Yes ma'am. It do."

The bedsprings creaked as she readjusted her body.

"Ida and Siss thank I'm scared of Henry," she said in a low, steady voice. "I ain't scared of Henry. I had him; he ain't had me. I just don't want to hurt his feelings. He tenderhearted. Been that way every since he was little." She paused, reflecting. "You know he the baby?"

"Yes ma'am. I know."

The corners of her mouth turned up, forming a smile.

"He the only one of my children that didn't like to go outdoors and play. He was just as content knocking 'round in the house all day. I couldn't move, 'thout him holding on to my skirt tail. Even after he got up some size, he still liked to piddle 'round in the house." She paused and laughed. "Know what broke him from that?"

"No ma'am."

"Vanessa."

"His wife?"

"That's right. He turned me loose soon as he married. But even then he didn't go no farther than cross the street. I used to sat out on the garret and watch 'em knocking 'round over there in the yard. Not too long after Stanley came, Henry rigged up a little ole rope swing in that pecan tree next to the house. The three of them would play on that swing the biggest part of the day, Vanessa sitting down, Stanley sitting in her lap, and Henry just a-pushing. The higher they went, the louder that child laughed. And the mo' he laughed, the higher Henry pushed. And Vanessa, Lord, she'd just be a-hollering and begging for Henry to stop. Look like he'd just keep a-pushing out of pure devilment."

The thought seemed to amuse her. She threw her head back and began to laugh. Her eyes began to water. Her shoulders began to shake. She began to cough, softly at first, then uncontrollably.

D'Ray reached over and began to gently pat her on the back.

"You alright, Mama Bea?" he asked softly.

"Hand me my cup off the chifforobe."

He handed her the cup. She rose to her elbow, tilted her head back, and took several sips of water. It seemed to calm her. She thanked him, handed him the cup, and laid her head back on the pillow. She took a couple of deep breaths, then resumed.

"Boy, them children naturally tickled me." She paused, and the expression on her face suddenly became serious. "I should've made 'im git out of that sun."

"Mama Bea, everything gone be fine. Just fine."

"I'm scared he gone give up."

"No ma'am. He won't."

"He done been through so much . . ."

"He strong, Mama Bea. Real strong."

"I don't know what I'd do if he—"

"Mama Bea, he gone be alright."

"Promise me you won't let 'im give up."

"I won't."

"You promise?"

"Yes ma'am."

"I ain't able to go see after him, but you—"

"I'll see after him. I promise I will."

Reassured, she laid her head on the pillow.

"He crazy about you."

"Yes ma'am. I know."

"Guess you remind him of Stanley."

D'Ray stiffened. The sound of Stanley's name startled him. He stared into the quiet darkness, recalling the night of the murder, hearing the sound of the gun and seeing Stanley lying on the floor in a pool of blood. She reached over and took his hand.

"The Lord works in mysterious ways, don't he?"

"Yes ma'am," he mumbled. "He sho' do."

"Who would of thought you and Henry would have gotten to be so close? Who?"

"If I could change the past, I would."

"Baby, I didn't mean it that way."

"It's alright."

"No, it ain't," she said. "Sometimes I talk too much."

There was silence.

"You ate?" she asked, changing the subject.

"I ain't hungry," he lied.

"It ought to be something to eat in there on the stove."

"No ma'am." D'Ray rejected her offer a second time. "I don't want nothing." He looked at his watch. "I'm fixin' to go anyway."

"You ain't gone stay over there by yourself, are you?"

"Yes ma'am. I don't mind."

"You welcome to stay over here."

"No ma'am, I'm gone stay at home."

"You want a few pecans to take with you?"

"Yes ma'am," he said, knowing he had to accept something before she would allow him to leave. "I'll take a few."

"Look under the bed and hand me that bag."

D'Ray slid off the bed and dropped to his knees. Underneath the bed, near the foot, crammed amidst an array of small boxes and an assortment of whatnots, were several brown paper bags. Which was it? He poked about, groping one bag, then another.

"You see it?" he heard her ask.

The side of the bag caved in and he heard the soft clacking sound of the hard shells rubbing together.

"Yes ma'am. I see it."

"Be careful," she coached him. "Don't waste 'em."

He pulled the bag to him, slid his hand underneath it, and lifted it to the bed.

"I 'spect they still some count if them old rats ain't got in 'em," she said as she opened the bag and looked inside. "How many you want?"

"Uh . . ." He hesitated.

"Aw, take all of 'em," she said, handing him the bag. "Ain't but a few left nohow."

"Yes ma'am."

"You want a piece of sweet bread?"

"No ma'am, this is fine."

"It's plenty in there. You know you welcome to it."

"No ma'am. This is fine. I'm gone go on to the house."

"It ought to still be warm. Ida Mae ain't been too long took it out the oven."

"Maybe some other time," he said, turning to leave.

"Ain't you forgetting something?"

"Ma'am?" He turned, and she gently touched the center of her forehead with her finger.

On cue, he leaned over and she kissed him.

"Remember Henry in your prayers," she advised.

"Yes ma'am. I will."

She took his hand in her own.

"You be good, hear."

"Yes ma'am."

On his way out he stopped by the living room to bid everyone a good night. Mrs. Ida walked him to the door. As he exited the yard and walked into the narrow street, he could feel her eyes on his back, guiding him across the street, through the yard, up the steps, and onto the small wooden porch. He turned and waved. Instantly the porch light clicked off and he heard the heavy thud of the large interior door slamming shut. He reached deep into his pocket and removed his key. Then, by the light of the moon, he guided the key into the lock and twisted the door open. As he had promised, Mr. Clayton had left his bags next to the door. D'Ray moved everything inside, clicked on the light, and paused. The house was quiet. Too quiet. A half-empty coffee cup was sitting on the table in front of the sofa. D'Ray took it in the kitchen and placed it in the sink with the other breakfast dishes. The dishes were stacked in the sink but they had not been washed. But why should they have been? That had always been his job. "I do the cooking and you do the cleaning." That was the deal.

He moved to the sink, removed the small bottle of dishwashing liquid from the bottom cabinet, and squirted it into the sink. Then he turned on the faucet. As he held his hand underneath the tiny stream of water, checking the temperature, he pulled back the thin plain window curtain. Through the small kitchen window loomed the backyard. It was dark and he couldn't see out. Instinctively he clicked on the outside light and it cast a dim, ominous glow over the tiny vegetable garden. The short straight rows were clean, save for the tiny patch of grass near the end of the last row. His eyes fell on the hoe lying in the center of the row. "He was almost finished," he mumbled softly to himself. Absentmindedly, he walked out into the tiny garden, lifted the hoe, and examined it. Soon all was quiet save for the sound of the sharp blade scraping across the surface of the hard, dry soil.

# CHAPTER TWENTY-ONE

Time crept PAST UNTIL THE DAY FINALLY ARRIVED. IT WAS A MOMENTOUS day filled with pomp and circumstance. There were smiles and hugs and kisses and speeches. There were so many speeches. So many words carefully constructed to form sentences and paragraphs designed to celebrate what for many had been a glorious sojourn, and to anticipate what they hoped would be an even more promising future. The future, once simply a hollow field of dreams, was now a bountiful harvest of unlimited opportunity, carefully and skillfully cultivated by four long, difficult years of sacrifice, hard work, and sheer determination. The future, once some faraway, abstract concept, was now.

D'Ray closed his eyes, leaned back, and slid forward until his butt was barely resting on the edge of the smooth aluminum chair. He heard the voice of the tall, distinguished gentleman standing on the platform behind the microphone begin to fade. "Today, people"—the man paused for effect—"is the first day of the rest of your life."

D'Ray listened as the words reverberated off the walls of the coliseum. He heard the applause of the crowd, the cheers of his classmates, and the wild piercing scream of a single exuberant voice rising above it all and dissipating into the rafters.

Who cared about his day? D'Ray thought as he sat perfectly still, silently listening to the cheerful crowd of strangers, ever aware that not a single person in the congregation had made the trek from home to this place on his behalf.

"Enjoy!" The man ended his speech with a single word.

D'Ray opened his eyes and slid back in his seat. How could he enjoy his life? How could he be happy living in a world surrounded by so many people whose happiness he had destroyed? Could a piece of paper change what he had done? Could it change who he was? No, he didn't belong here. He was a fraud, a hypocrite, a misfit. This wasn't his day, nor was it his life. But what if it was? In his mind appeared an image of his mother. She was adorned in an elegant dress. A beautiful wide-brim hat sat atop her freshly styled hair, and her carefully painted lips were pressed into a wide prideful smile. Her back was straight and her head was held high. She sat nestled in amongst a sea of strangers, clinging to Little Man's hand, staring straight ahead. Her eyes, her beautiful brown eyes, were riveted on D'Ray. For the first time that he could remember she was happy for him, not sad because of him.

The sound of D'Ray's name brought him back to reality. He rose from his seat and moved toward the podium. As he walked, he was besieged by a strange feeling. He was in Stanley's place and Stanley was in his. How many times had he cheated death? How many people had he deprived of the simple joys of life? He felt Stanley's eyes on him, staring at him from some other reality. He felt Stanley's anger, sensed his outrage.

*It should have been me.* The voice was loud and clear. The speaker, though only a figment of his imagination, was unmistakable: Stanley.

He ascended the stairs, and with a firm handshake and the presentation of his diploma, reality flashed before his eyes; dream denied, promise fulfilled.

Mr. Henry would have been there if he could have been there. His own life had been a series of long, hard days and short, restless nights, sustained and fueled by an unfaltering love of family and an unshakable belief in honesty, integrity, and the sanctity of keeping one's word. He had said that he would be there to see the whole thing. D'Ray had to walk so that Stanley could walk. Stanley had to walk because no one else in the family ever had. Not Mr. Henry. Not Miss Big Siss. Not Mrs. Ida. No one.

He, Mr. Henry, had given him life. He had fed him and nurtured him. He had chastised, guided, and encouraged him. He had toiled and sacrificed for him, encouraged only by the belief that one day his legs would be sturdy enough to stand and his body and mind developed enough to walk. Neither rain, nor sleet, nor the wrath of God would keep him away. That's what he said. That's what he swore. But he had been kept away—or had he? D'Ray walked back to his seat, ran his hand deep into his pocket, and removed a watch. The watch was old and it was in poor condition. In fact, it didn't even keep time. It hadn't kept time for a long time. Nevertheless, Mr. Henry had carried it every day of his life for as long as it had been in his possession, until a few hours ago, when Miss Big Siss removed it from underneath his hospital pillow and gave it to D'Ray. D'Ray had seen the watch before. A thousand times he had seen Mr. Henry take it out of his pocket, click it open, and examine it. Sometimes he opened it at work. Sometimes he opened it while sitting in the living room watching television. Not a day passed when he didn't look at that old watch. Most times it was only a glance. But he always opened it and he always looked.

Sometimes he would sit out behind the house, under the shade of the old apricot tree, gently cleaning the watch casing with an old cotton cloth. He would sit for hours, patiently cleaning one side, then the other. And D'Ray would watch him. Sometimes he watched from his bedroom window. Other times he watched from the back door. But during the times that he had watched him, he never knew that the watch didn't even keep time. He had no idea that it served no purpose save to allow Mr. Henry to hold on to a part of himself. He never knew until this morning when Miss Big Siss told him the story behind the watch.

Mr. Henry's daddy had died while Mr. Henry was still young. In fact, he was too young to even remember him. And when he was old enough to ask questions, there were answers. But when he asked to see his daddy, there wasn't a picture or an image to be found. There was nothing, except for the old pocket watch that had been his daddy's most cherished possession. From that day on, Mr. Henry carried his daddy with him by carrying that old watch that didn't even keep time.

D'Ray reached down, took the hem of his gown, and gently rubbed it across the watch casing. Then he clicked it open and glanced at it. Overcome with emotions, he closed his eyes and clutched the watch in his hands.

"Class of nineteen ninety-seven, please rise." The command was strong, clear, forceful.

D'Ray opened his eyes and snapped to his feet.

"Tassel." The second command was given.

In perfect synchronization with his classmates, he moved the long gold and blue tassel from the left side of his cap to the right.

"Congratulations, graduates!"

A thousand caps sailed into the air. Cheers and applause drifted down from the stands. D'Ray raised the old watch to eye level. Suddenly he had a burning desire to see Mr. Henry. The music began to blare over the public address system. D'Ray pulled the diploma close to his chest and readied himself to march. He longed to look into Mr. Henry's eyes. He needed him to know that there was now another piece to the puzzle. He had walked. Stanley had walked. He stepped into the aisle and took his place in the procession. As he marched, he watched the people watching them. A smile, a nod, a flash, and a moment frozen in time. This was their reward—not simply knowing that this day had finally come, but actually watching the moment, participating in it. As he passed out of the auditorium and into the crowded lobby, he did not stop. He knew he was supposed to stop. Their instructions were clear. Do not leave the building without turning in your cap and gown. But he kept going anyway, through the lobby, out the door, down the steps, across the parking lot, and to the car. He pulled the door open and slid behind the wheel. He put the key in the ignition, then paused.

Mr. Henry would see him march. Yes, he would see him garbed in his gown, carrying his diploma, on his—no, their—graduation day. He turned the key and instantly the engine began to roar. He pulled the car into gear, wondering if he was too late. For three straight weeks he had hoped against hope that the situation would improve. Mama Bea believed in miracles, and Miss Big Siss believed in him. That had not always been so. But over time Miss Big Siss had come to realize that he was good for Mr. Henry just as Mr. Henry was good for him. Maybe late over into the night, while they were all sleeping, an angel would descend from heaven and touch Mr. Henry with one of the very fingers that had touched the hand of God. And maybe that touch would once again make him whole. It was that hope that enabled him to go back to that hospital every day when every fiber of his being told him that he couldn't. He was filled with that hope when he walked into Mr. Henry's room early this morning. But this morning, more than any other, Mr. Henry seemed closer to death than to life. Any minute, it seemed, he would close his eyes, never to open them again. D'Ray didn't want to leave, but Miss Big Siss forced him. She just handed him the keys to her old car and told him to go walk. Go walk for Henry.

A space of time passed in which he was void of recollection. The large sign next to the highway, which read, *Welcome to Lake Providence,* jarred him back to reality. He focused his eyes on the highway feeling even more anxious now that he was close. Several red lights, a short journey down a narrow street, a pass through the park, and he was there. He stepped out of the car, slid the watch back into his pocket, slipped his diploma underneath his arm, and positioned the cap atop his head.

Then he walked. With his head held high and his every step true, he walked. Into the building, through the waiting area, down the corridor, around the bend, and past the elevator. As he walked, he looked at no one, spoke to no one. He was in Mr. Henry's world now. He sensed that he knew he was coming. He could feel him watching him. Stand up straight. Chest out. Head high. Step. No, he wouldn't close his eyes until he had seen what he had stayed alive to see. The boy who had taken his boy was giving him back the joy of knowing that his life had produced a man. Strong, law abiding, dedicated, educated, a credit to his race.

D'Ray pushed through the door and paused. They were all there. Miss Big Siss, Mrs. Ida, and Mama Bea. D'Ray looked toward the bed. Mr. Henry was weak. He looked tired. But his eyes were wide, taking in D'Ray. Their eyes met.

"Walk," he heard the dying man's eyes say. D'Ray collected himself. He pulled his shoulders back, and he stepped. The space was short and the moment was brief. D'Ray crossed the room and gently placed the diploma on Mr. Henry's chest. No, he couldn't open it, or touch it, or handle it, or feel it. Nor could he verbally acknowledge it. But he knew it was there. Again they looked at each other. Mr. Henry's eyes became glassy. D'Ray watched a tear roll down his cheek and disappear underneath his chin. As the two men stared deep into each other's soul, Mr. Henry's eyes began to close, suddenly, slowly, gently.

D'Ray turned from him. He refused to look at that which he could not bear to see.

"Henry!" he heard Miss Big Siss scream.

As she hurried to Mr. Henry's side, D'Ray wandered out into the hall and leaned into the wall. He closed his eyes, listening.

"Get the doctor!" he heard Miss Big Siss yell.

The door pushed open and Mrs. Ida raced past him. Inside, he heard Mama Bea began to sing. Her voice was soft, steady.

"Precious Lord, take my hand, lead me on, let me stand . . ."

D'Ray unzipped his robe and allowed it to fall to the floor. Then he slowly lifted his hand and gently pushed the hat off the back of his head. Several times he looked to the door as though he were about to go back, but he stood still. His eyes were wet. Everything became hazy. He groped for the wall like a blind man. He found it and braced himself steady. His legs were wobbly; his head was light. Keeping contact with the wall, he ambled down the corridor, out of the building and into the streets. Inside, his heart pained; his mind was confused. Again he saw Mr. Henry's eyes closing suddenly, slowly, gently. He had seen death before, but now he knew he had never known her. He had never known her wrath. He had never felt her pain. He quickened his pace. He needed to put distance between himself and this place. As he walked, his mind told him that Mr. Henry was better off. He was whole again. He was free. D'Ray stayed close to the edge of the road. He walked with no firm destination in mind. There was no place that he needed to be or wanted to be except away from the pain and horror of this place.

When he came to the intersection, he crossed the highway, climbed atop the overpass, and turned down the railroad tracks. Soon he was moving between the two steel rails with his body swaying in perfect time to the soft steady rhythm of his feet as they struck first a cross tie, then the loose coal, then another cross tie. When he again became aware of himself, he was on the opposite side of town, standing across from the small brick church that had been so much a part of Mr. Henry's life. For a brief moment, he stared at the church. He had always wanted to believe, but something always got in the way. He descended the tracks and stopped at the edge of the ditch bank. It had rained recently, and the ditches on either side of the highway were filled with water. He leapt across the ditch onto the highway and started toward the driveway. There was no parking lot at the church. People simply parked on the grass under the trees or next to the building or over against the long barbed-wire fence that separated the church grounds from Mr. Gildoe's farm.

D'Ray walked past the church without stopping. He crossed a small wooden footbridge and passed through a short stand of trees. Behind the trees was a cemetery. He cautiously walked into the cemetery, passing one grave then another until he saw the tombstone bearing Stanley's name. He lowered himself to a squat and slowly ran his hand across the hard, cold granite. He thought of Mr. Henry. A chill passed through his body. He dropped to his knees, gently placed his hands on the center of the grave, and whispered ever so softly.

"I'm sorry."

# ABOUT THE AUTHOR

**ERNEST HILL** was born in Oak Grove, Louisiana. He received his bachelor's degree from the University of California, Berkeley, and his master's degree from Cornell University. He divides his time between Baton Rouge, where he is writer in residence at Southern University, and Los Angeles, where he is a Dorothy Danforth Compton doctoral fellow in history at UCLA. He is the author of *Satisfied with Nothin'* and is currently at work on his third novel.

Printed in the United States
By Bookmasters